The Keeper of Portals

The Keeper of Portals

Portals

V S Nelson

Matador
9 Priory Business Park,
Wistow Road, Kibworth Beauchamp,
Leicestershire. LE8 0RX
Tel: 0116 279 2299
Email: books@troubador.co.uk
Web: www.troubador.co.uk/matador
Twitter: @matadorbooks

ISBN 978 1785898 327

British Library Cataloguing in Publication Data.
A catalogue record for this book is available from the British Library.

Printed and bound by CPI Group (UK) Ltd, Croydon, CR0 4YY
Typeset in 11pt Adobe Garamond Pro by Troubador Publishing Ltd, Leicester, UK

Matador is an imprint of Troubador Publishing Ltd

MIX
Paper from
responsible sources
FSC® C013604

For my other, and often better, half. Thanks for your patience and support.

CHAPTER
ONE

The floor collapsed beneath Martin without warning. He ran for the nearest open door and jumped, just managing to grab the bottom of the frame. His feet swung into the wall and dented the ancient plaster. Martin climbed into a new room, dusted himself off and turned around to survey the carnage below.

The floor had flattened everything beneath it, scraping the walls clean as it went. A massive wooden desk had fallen too and now lay in a splintered heap. The yellowed papers that had been on it were scattered in every direction.

Martin returned to the corridor and kicked down the next door to find a room filled with musical instruments. He'd been in his new home only a few hours and had already found two other rooms just like this one. Martin ran his finger along the top of an old piano and the thick dust built up like a bow wave. He took out his mum's phone and photographed the instruments before scrolling back and deleting the pictures from the room that collapsed.

Outside the music room there was another corridor. Paintings of people long dead hung on the walls, staring at Martin with disapproval. He had no idea who any of them were. Didn't really care either, until he saw her, hanging above what must have been the house's grandest staircase.

The painting was large, enclosed in an ornate wooden frame and displayed an old lady standing in front of Martin's house. She had thick, grey hair flowing down her back and a smile on her face. Not an open smile, with teeth showing, but a smile that told of a secret. There was something about the woman in the painting which reached out to Martin. He leaned over the banister, mindful that it may decide to disintegrate like the floor, and tried to find out who she was.

Her given name was missing, only her family name remained. *Lockford*. His name. It wasn't a surprise, the house had been in Martin's family for centuries and was probably full of dead Lockfords. Though none of them were quite like her. Martin left the old lady with her knowing smile and walked along the corridor in search of more old junk.

Lockford Manor was more of a palace than just a house, 125 metres long (at least at the moment) and over 300 rooms. It used to belong to one of Martin's great uncles, but he died over twenty years ago and the house had been empty since. There was once talk of selling it, but no one foolish enough to part with their money could be found. This was to be expected, the house would be gone in a few years.

It was too near the cliffs. Or better put, the cliffs were too near it. When the house had been built they'd kept a respectable distance, but recently the cliffs had stormed ahead, sneaking up on the house and its aged inhabitant like a game of *What's the Time Mr Wolf?*

The house was at right angles to the cliffs and a chunk of it had already been lost to the sea. Forty years ago a vicious storm had battered the rock holding up the far corner and all three floors had vanished in the night. In the time since, the sea had worked hard, eroding more of the cliffs beneath the house to leave a massive three storey section that overhung by an entire room's length.

Despite the house's imminent death, Martin and his mum had no choice but to live there. With his dad gone they couldn't afford to stay where they were and had started to spiral into debt. So they'd packed up, sold off what was left of the house they still owned and moved to Lockford Manor until they found some money or the house fell into the sea. No one was sure which would come first.

Martin rolled onto his back. 'Well this is dull,' he said to the empty room.

He was ready to take a nap when a voice replied, 'Isn't it just?'

Martin jumped out of the bed.

'What the hell!' he shouted, his eyes wide with fear. 'Who said that?'

'I did, obviously.'

Martin looked around the room, but there was definitely no one there. It was only supposed to be him and his mum, but even though the house was miles away from anywhere, that didn't mean there weren't a few squatters knocking about.

3

'And who are you?' said Martin.

'Who am *I*? More like who are *you*?'

'The guy whose bedroom this is,' said Martin. He started to walk around. The room was large, probably four times the size of his old room, and the ceiling was at least three times his height, but despite this, it didn't look grand, just tatty like the rest of the house. It was as if the whole place had resigned itself to falling into the sea and breathed a huge sigh of relief before letting all of its ugliness out.

There was still no sign of anyone else in the room. Martin felt his heartbeat start to slow, but he could still hear it pounding away in his ears. The voice had made him jump, but as it continued speaking, Martin realised the voice sounded a little confused.

'So, are you going to tell me who you are?' asked Martin.

'You mean you don't know?' said the voice in amazement.

'Should I know?'

'Well, no, probably not. But it is nice to be recognised from time to time.'

'I hope I didn't disappoint you,' said Martin as he swiped at a pair of curtains to see if the mysterious voice was hiding behind them. It wasn't.

'Don't worry, I'm sure I'll get over it,' said the voice. 'Tell me, how old are you?'

'Fifteen. Why?' said Martin, beginning to feel uneasy for different reasons.

'Oh nothing, nothing. But are you absolutely sure you're just fifteen?'

Martin picked up a cardboard box hoping to find a

Stanley knife, but it was empty so he threw it by the door. 'Yeah, pretty sure.'

'Interesting, I thought maybe we'd spoken before, but if you're only fifteen then we can't have.'

'Why not?'

'Well, for a start, I've not spoken to a human for nearly four hundred years.'

'Four hundred years? Great, so not only is there some tramp hiding in my house, he's also completely mental, or drunk. Seriously, where are you? I'll call the police. Are you in the wardrobe?'

'I could be,' said the voice. 'I can be anywhere I want when I want.'

Martin opened a box of old Airfix models still hoping to find a knife. 'Can I suggest somewhere else, right now.'

'But I thought you were bored. Doesn't boredom love company?'

'That's misery. Boredom enjoys its solitude.'

'Interesting. You're bored and dislike it, yet you would rather stay bored than talk with me. Though I am confused. I can't have met you before but we have a connection, you and me. Do you feel it too?'

'No. I feel scared you're going to force me into a dress and make me your wife.'

Martin picked up an old Spitfire model he had made with his dad, one of many, but this one was his favourite. It was the only one they'd painted together. He put it on the bedside table.

'You are a funny one. You know, I think I *will* hang around for a bit.'

5

'You're going to hang around for a bit? Great!' said Martin, sitting down on his bed. He may as well humour the wacko. Probably safest. 'So if you're planning on staying, can you at least tell me where you are?'

'In your bedroom,' said the voice.

'Really? Why can't I see you?'

'Oh that's simple.'

'It is?'

'You're not looking at me,' said the voice.

Martin let out an angry breath. 'Well are you going to tell me who you are? Or am I going to have a conversation with some voice that's probably in my head? I bet all that dust I've inhaled has made me mad. I knew something like this would happen.'

'You're not mad, just privileged.'

'*Of course* I am.'

'Indeed you are! Because you're talking to the Keeper of Portals.'

'The Keeper of Portals? More like the Lord of Nutters.'

'No, the Keeper of Nuts is something else. A tough one to crack, at least that's what he likes to say. I am the Keeper of Portals.'

'So is that your name?'

'My name? Hmm, no. It is just what I am.'

'Great,' said Martin. 'Good to see I was right about the insane part. And what exactly are you doing here? It's not like there's anywhere interesting in about twenty miles of this place.'

'I can get to wherever I want from here. Interesting and boring. Though I don't tend to go to the boring places too

6

much, they are a little, well, boring. And I told you my job. I am the Keeper of Portals.'

'The Keeper of Portals? What does that even mean?'

'Hmm,' said the voice, 'It's probably best I show you, it's the only way you'll understand.'

'If you have to.'

'Walk over to your bedroom door and open it, then tell me everything you see.'

Martin walked to his bedroom door and swung it wide open.

'I see the landing. It's long and dark because most of the lights don't work. The stairs are right at the end, but I can't see them very well. There's a load of doors to other rooms along both sides. The floor is scuffed and stained and the ceiling is flaking.'

'Good, good,' said the voice. 'Now close the door, open it again and tell me what you see.'

Martin rolled his eyes as he swung the door back towards the frame. The latch clicked and he immediately turned the handle and opened it.

'I see the landing. It's long and dark and… what!'

A freezing blast of air slammed into Martin, firing a mixture of snow and ice clusters at his face and body. He looked back into his room, then through the open doorway before stepping out.

His bare feet sank into the snow. In front of him were mountains. Not the kind of mountains you find in England, all grassy or covered in slate, these were mountains designed by a five year old girl, tall and pointed and completely white.

He took a few more steps forward, then ran. Martin turned around. Behind him was a mountain chalet. He could even see people in the windows, looking out in confusion at the teenage boy standing in the snow with no shoes on.

And there it was, the other side of the front door, his bedroom, still as dark and old looking as ever. He ran back inside, kicking snow over the scratched wooden floor.

'What just happened? Was I in Switzerland?'

'Close the door.'

Martin did so just as another flurry of snow charged at him, dusting his bedroom floor like flour. He opened the door again but was greeted by the dark corridor of a dying house. He shut the door.

'What exactly the hell are you?'

'I told you, I'm the Keeper of Portals. I monitor all passages, gateways, doors, entrances and exits on the planet to make sure they are in order. That is my role as a Keeper.'

Martin walked back to his bed. His head was spinning. He was in his bedroom, then he had walked through his door only to find himself in the Alps or somewhere. Stuff like that just wasn't possible.

'That's it, I've gone insane.'

'You're not insane… well, actually you may be. I don't know what constitutes insane these days. But you did just walk through the door of your bedroom and out the front door of a mountain chalet. And yes, you were in Switzerland. Well done you for guessing correctly! My job is to make sure things like that don't happen. On a normal day you don't want to walk through one door and come out another, do you? That's why I need to look after them.'

'What? Whoever heard of going through one door and coming out another?'

'No one,' said the voice proudly, 'because I do such a good job.'

'Why would that even happen in the first place?'

'Well, let's just say things in this universe have a tendency of being a little unpredictable. The universe contains lots of things and so for every thing there is a Keeper. I am the Keeper of Portals, so I make sure that both sides of a doorway or opening always match up. And of course, I can swap them over, you know, if I'm feeling whimsical.'

There were books on Martin's bookcase, a games console and a TV in the corner and a few boxes of random stuff against one wall. It was everything he'd ever need. This may not be an ordinary room in an ordinary house, but that didn't mean weird stuff had to happen.

'I don't believe you.'

'What?'

'I don't believe you. That you're some god of gates or whatever, that doors just suddenly lead to other places. Everything you've said, it's nonsense.'

'But you just walked through your bedroom door into Switzerland. You experienced it. You know there's a word for people who don't believe something despite seeing the evidence.'

'What?'

'Moron,' said the Keeper of Portals.

'I just think it's all in my head. I think I've spent hours walking around this house, breathed in way too much dust and chemicals and stuff that's probably been banned for years because it sends people crazy, and now I'm sitting in my room, talking to myself and imagining I can walk through my bedroom door and go to Switzerland.'

'That's what you really think?'

'Yep.'

Martin's door blew outwards. He saw it fly off into the sky before being lost. A force pushed him from behind and he sped towards the open doorframe. He braced himself against it with his hands and feet and his muscles became as hard as rocks beneath his clothing.

His bedroom depressurised almost instantly. It was large for a room, but nothing when compared to the vastness of the sky. The force from the air outside burst the three leaded windows along the far wall simultaneously, sending showers of glass, lead and wood through the room and out of the door as a steady stream of air started to escape.

All Martin could see was the sky and the clouds. It was hard to breathe and the air was colder than anything he'd ever experienced, but they were the least of his worries. His arms would give up long before he ran out of oxygen or froze.

There were more noises behind him. Objects were flying around his room like cows trapped in a tornado, but they were irrelevant compared to the roaring drone of an engine coming from the other side of the door.

His arms bent slightly, he could feel his muscles weakening. His head edged past the doorframe for a moment before he managed to pull it back.

'You're just imagining that your door has come out the side of a Boeing 747 that's approximately 35,000 feet in the air,' shouted the Keeper of Portals. 'You're also imagining that your books are smacking you in the back of your head before flying out over the Atlantic Ocean.'

Martin's grip finally deserted him and he shot through the open doorway. He closed his eyes tight, but jerked them open again when he hit something solid with a thud.

He opened his eyes to find himself lying face-down on the landing. He stood up, aching all over, and walked back into his room which had become a mess of broken glass, cracked window frames and scattered books. There was no sign of his door.

'It's a good job you're imagining all of this,' said the Keeper of Portals, 'because it wouldn't be much fun to clean up.'

'OK. OK. You've made your point,' said Martin as he rubbed the back of his head, 'but you could've killed me, you know!'

'I told you, I'm the Keeper of Portals. Controlling doors is what I do. You were never in any real danger. Plus, it's your fault for being stubborn.'

'Don't you mean a moron?'

'Your choice of word, not mine.'

Martin started to pick up the books, but his arms and legs were hurting too much and he ceremoniously dropped them back onto the floor.

'You know what, I'll just move rooms. This one doesn't have any windows and it's not like there aren't 37 million others in this house.'

'You can't leave this room,' came the voice of the Keeper of Portals, more forceful than it had been before.

'There's glass all over the floor and it's missing a door. Why would I stay?'

'Because this room is the most interesting room in the entire house!'

'Really?' said Martin, 'you mean it has something to offer other than a total lack of privacy?'

There was a pause. Martin wasn't sure if the Keeper of Portals was thinking or had just left completely.

'I have been in this house for four hundred years,' said the Keeper of Portals. 'I leave when I need to. If there is a door, or a gate, or a passageway that starts to fluctuate, I go there and fix it. I also explore new doors when they are created to discover where they lead. In that way, I find new places. But I always return here. To this house. To this room.'

'Why?' said Martin. 'What's so great about this room?'

The room started to shake, only slightly to begin with, but gradually it became more pronounced. Martin stood up. The vibrations were emanating from the wall at the far end. Martin walked towards it.

Plaster was starting to fall, small flakes at first, landing on the floor in almost unnoticeable quantities, but then the vibrations became fierce. Entire chunks of plaster were shaken lose, tearing the wallpaper as they fell to reveal a solid brick wall. The brick wall too began to fall, crashing to the floor in clouds of red dust. Behind the brick wall was a wall made of wooden panels. In the centre of the wooden panels, directly in front of where Martin was standing, there was a door. It was taller than him, at least nine feet high and six feet across, and was made entirely of wood that was so dark it appeared black.

Martin's breath caught in his throat. There was something standing next to the door, a creature Martin had never seen the likes of before. It was tall, though not as tall as the door. It was also white, with smooth skin like rubber, and hips and shoulders that jutted out like blades. Its arms were long and thin, like the rest of its body, and reached all the way down to its knees where ten fingers were arranged in a circle. Long electric blue feathers grew down its back and curled around themselves in a tangle that reached the floor. The creature's face was avian in appearance, though not exactly like a bird's. It didn't have a beak, although at first it appeared to. Instead, its entire face tapered into a point with the sharp tip touching the creature's own chest. The eyes were slanted upwards in a feline manner and regarded Martin with a mischievous twinkle. Martin didn't need to ask who the creature in front of him was, he knew it was the voice that referred to itself as the Keeper of Portals.

'I know how to open every doorway, gate and entrance on the planet. All I have to do is think, walk through one and I come out another. There is nowhere I cannot get to, nor any lock that can deny my passage.'

The Keeper of Portals lifted a hand and stroked the ancient black wood of the door.

'I can do all that,' he said, 'and yet, after 400 years, I still cannot open this door.'

CHAPTER
TWO

'I can't believe I'm actually following you,' said Martin as the Keeper of Portals dragged him through countless rooms like a child holding a treasured balloon. They had been into the loft, the cellar and scores of forgotten bedrooms that had been abandoned at different periods in time. The Keeper had even shown Martin a room that used to belong to a little girl over a hundred years ago. Inside he'd managed to shrink himself and walk around the large doll house that took up nearly an entire wall. He explained that he would always change his size to fit the room on the other side of whichever door he passed through. Apparently this was a trick only he could do, so Martin couldn't tag along.

'I mean, I'm just supposed to believe you're some kind of god, is that it?' said Martin as he ducked under a wooden beam.

The Keeper of Portals stopped. 'There are currently 10,342 aeroplanes in the sky. I'll even let you pick.'

'No, you're OK,' said Martin.

'Are you sure? I could do it all day.'

Martin motioned for the Keeper to keep walking. 'I just don't get it,' he said.

'You don't get it?' echoed the Keeper. 'So it works like

14

this. I open a door, and that door can lead to any other door on the planet. Well, not any door, but we've already covered that. Anything something can pass through, I control.'

The Keeper of Portals stopped again and faced Martin. He made a circle with two of his fingers on one hand and poked a finger from his other hand through it. The Keeper's finger then came out of a crack in the wall and jabbed Martin sharply in the face.

'See?' said the Keeper.

'Ow! Do you mind?'

'Not in the slightest,' said the Keeper and poked him again.

Martin rubbed his cheek. 'It's not that I don't get *what* you do, I just don't get *why* you do it. I've never even heard of a Keeper before. Are there more of you?'

'More of us? Of course there are! More than you can count!'

'Well, where do you come from?'

The Keeper started walking again. He was smaller now, roughly the same height as Martin. Any taller and he wouldn't be able to fit down the tiny corridor they were currently exploring.

'We don't come from anywhere.'

'What do you mean you don't come from anywhere? How can you not come from somewhere?'

'Because we don't. We just poof! And then we're there. We weren't anywhere before, waiting to be born. We just appear, like an idea. One moment you don't have it, and then suddenly you do!'

'But you're made of stuff. Stuff doesn't just appear, it's

15

made from bits of other stuff. If stuff just appeared then that would break the law of the conservation of energy. That says matter and energy cannot be created, just changed from one form to another.'

'Oh, so you've met the Keeper of Conservation?' The Keeper of Portals asked with a smile.

'Err, no, I just learnt about it in school. Stuff can't just come from nowhere, it's a law of physics.'

'Yes, he's a law of physics. Trust me, I've heard. OK, so let me put it this way. There is a thing, either something physical or a concept. Now that thing needs to be maintained. When a new thing appears, so too does a new Keeper. The bigger the thing, the more important the Keeper. The big things are observed by the Major Keepers, like myself, and the small things are observed by the Minor Keepers. When the thing the Keeper was there to observe no longer exists, then the Keeper disappears. The universe no longer needs it, so gets rid of it. It likes things neat, you see. Some Keepers last years, some last only seconds and some will last all of time, such as the Keeper of Time and the other Fundamental Keepers.'

'So wait, there are three kinds of Keepers?'

'Yes. The Minor Keepers look after small problems that only exist for between a nanosecond and about a few thousand years. Any smaller than a nanosecond and the universe doesn't really care. The Major Keepers were created after the universe and will probably last for millions of years, though not all of us. Then you have the Fundamental Keepers. They were created at the start of the universe and will likely die at the end of it.'

'And you're sure all of this is necessary?'

The Keeper of Portals smiled, 'Oh yes, very necessary! You've got the Keeper of Chaos to thank for that. Because of her we're never sure what's going to happen next. Keeps us on our toes.'

'OK, I get you need to look after your *things*, but do there really have to be so many of you? Couldn't there just be one?'

'Ha!' spat the Keeper of Portals. 'Just one? For all the things? I mean, do you even understand how many things there are?'

'A lot?' said Martin as he scratched his head.

'A lot and then a whole heap more,' said the Keeper of Portals. 'There's probably a number, but it'll sound silly like septillion or quattuordecillion. I usually just say tons.'

'And just to check, this isn't something everyone else already knows and I'm only being told now?'

'No one else knows,' said the Keeper. 'Or at least very few. *I* certainly haven't spoken to any human about it because I haven't talked to one f—.'

'For four hundred years, I know. So what are you saying, that I'm special or something?'

The tiny horizontal slit that passed for the Keeper's mouth curled up into a smile.

'I wouldn't go that far,' he said, then paused thoughtfully. 'I feel compelled to show you a very special room, though I don't know why.'

The Keeper stopped suddenly and reached for a handle that stuck out from the darkness. The door opened and

17

Martin was met with more darkness, only this time it was total.

'This door has been blocked up,' said the Keeper of Portals. Martin could just about make him out. He emitted his own light, but it was very faint. More eerie than useful. 'At first I thought this door led to the one upstairs. I think they were sealed around the same time.'

Martin walked forward, hands out in front of him in case he tripped over something, but there was nothing there. He had no idea where in the house he was. This could have been the loft, the cellar or just a boarded up bedroom for all he knew.

Soon Martin couldn't see the Keeper anymore. The room mustn't be square, but more like a wide, crooked corridor. Without the Keeper of Portals standing next to him, all those parts of Martin's brain that had started to actually believe what he was saying began renouncing their convictions. Alone in the pitch black room, Martin nearly managed to convince himself he'd just woken up from sleepwalking: that would explain all those strange concepts about Keepers and why he was in this room. But no matter how hard he tried, he couldn't shake the knowledge that everything he'd experienced had been real. There was a word for people who didn't believe something they had experienced for themselves, or so Martin had been told.

Martin walked into something solid and immediately an intense blue light washed over him before fading to a cool glow. The source of the light was coming from the floor and

Martin bent down to see what it was. It was a crystal, the size of a mouse and shaped like a tear. Holding it up to his eye, Martin could see it had been cut and polished and its many faces painted a lazy blue light over the room. Next to where the crystal had fallen were a large book, some items of clothing and a handful of dried flower petals. He picked the clothes up but they felt brittle and broke apart in his hands.

Martin held the crystal up like a torch and used it to light his way. He could see the wooden walls on all four sides. The room was unlike any other in the house; the smell of dirt and damp wood was strong and there was nothing to suggest anyone had been in there for a very long time. Then Martin spotted something on the wall. As he got closer he realised it was writing scratched into the wood. He tried to read some of it, but soon grew uninterested. It appeared to be a diary. There were dates next to many of the entries, but the writing was hard to read because the spelling seemed strange and the letters were uneven. Why someone would scratch a diary into the walls of a room and seal it up was beyond him.

Martin slipped the crystal into his pocket. He wasn't sure why, but he didn't want the Keeper to know about it, not yet anyway. He had found it on his own, almost as if the crystal was somehow meant for him.

With the crystal in his pocket, the room became dark again. Martin reached out a hand and touched the wall, keeping in contact with it while he walked to make sure he didn't get lost. He felt the etched letters move underneath his fingertips. He could still feel them when he reached the Keeper of Portals who stood waiting by the door.

'There you are. I had to leave to fix a faulty toilet door in Japan. It kept trying to connect to the entrance of a school in China. Anyway, it's sorted now. Sorry for leaving you in here with no way out.'

The Keeper reached for the door and opened it into Martin's twilit bedroom.

'It's OK,' said Martin. 'I don't mind the dark.'

Martin stood in the middle of his bedroom, the bedroom that had been wrecked by air being sucked out into the freezing low-pressure sky at 35,000 feet. There was no helping it, he was going to have to clean.

The Keeper of Portals had replaced the windows and the door, claiming something as trivial as that was easy for him, but had quickly grown bored of Martin trying to rid the floor of glass and opened a door to an Arctic research station before jumping through.

Martin reached into his pocket and took out the glowing crystal and the walls gratefully reflected back its blue glow. He set it down on his bedside table and covered it with an upturned coffee cup. Everything became dark. But it was a different dark to the one Martin was used to, where the street lights managed to burst their way in and the noise from outside never completely ceased. This darkness felt hungry and Martin was struck by a sudden longing for his dad. He pushed that longing aside, just like he'd done hundreds of times before.

Martin felt cold hands push him across his bed and against the wall. He struggled, fighting the hands and flinging himself around. He was asleep, he knew that much, and his dream was starting to deteriorate as he ran through it, screaming and clawing at himself in an attempt to wake up. Eventually it happened, not with a jump or a shout, but with a gentle opening of the eyes. Martin could see his pillow and the wall next to the bed and he lay there for a moment, trying to work out why he was awake.

He thought about it for some time, deciding whether he needed the toilet or not and finally concluded that it could wait. He rolled over, ready to go back to sleep, but when he saw the state of his room, his eyes sprang open and his breathing stopped.

There was blood everywhere. Some of it ran in streaks across the floor and up the walls. More appeared to have fallen in a massive pool while the rest had been flung about with wild abandon. Martin quickly jumped out of bed. One foot landed in blood. It still felt warm. The other foot landed on something else. He stepped onto a clean area of floor as he fought down the rising feeling of dread. Bending down, he picked up a feather. It was as long as his arm and spiralled like a helix. Martin waited for his eyes to adjust, and as they did, more and more of the Keeper of Portals' feathers appeared like stars in the early night sky.

Martin was about to call for the Keeper when he noticed something at the far end of his bedroom. The door that had kept the Keeper of Portals intrigued for 400 years was open.

Martin walked towards it, feeling the feathers and warm patches of blood soft and sticky beneath his feet. There was a room on the other side of the door. His room.

The position of the windows and door, the ornate coving that ran along the top of the walls, even the wooden floor was identical. But where Martin's room was dilapidated, the room on the other side of the door was pristine. The wood on the floor was rich and shiny, the walls vibrant and the three grand candled chandeliers that hung from the ceiling mocked the single bare lightbulb in Martin's room.

The light was different too. Late morning sun broke through the curtains and illuminated the room brilliantly. Martin was just about to ask what the hell was going on when he noticed the woman lying on the floor.

He watched her for a moment. At first he thought she was sleeping, but then he noticed her cream coloured dress start to move. She rolled over and ran her hands down her brown apron before checking the scarf tied around her head. Martin could just make out chestnut coloured hair beneath it.

When she was finally standing, Martin realised she was younger than he first thought, much closer to his own age, but it was hard to tell when her body was hidden behind so many layers of clothing that, like her hands and face, were covered in blood.

Martin left his muggy bedroom and stepped into the crisp chill of the room behind the door. The girl was right at the far end and Martin began to jog towards her.

'What happened?' asked Martin, but the girl didn't reply. She just stood there, staring out of the window.

When she turned to look at Martin, he didn't see the face of a young girl in pain. She was glaring at him.

Her lips had curled into a sneer and she flashed her teeth menacingly. Martin stopped.

The girl charged, grabbing a bloodied fire poker from the floor as she ran. She held the poker at chest height. Martin took a step back, not sure whether to cry out or wake up. He raised his hands, knowing it probably wouldn't help.

Someone moved at the far end of the room. They were too fast for Martin to make out. Inhumanly fast. They sped towards the open window, jumped onto the desk and dived out of the room.

The end of the fire poker was nearly in Martin's chest when an incredible force smacked into him from the side. Martin flew through the air with only one thing left to stop him.

He was unconscious the moment his head struck the wall.

CHAPTER
THREE

Martin woke up in bed. He tried to sit but his head began to ache powerfully and he crashed back into the pillows. Moving slower this time, he eased himself onto his elbows and looked around his bedroom. It was clean. Something was trying to tell him that his room should be anything but clean, yet the evidence was right there, gleaming in the morning sun.

Leaning over to his bedside table, Martin lifted the upturned coffee cup to check on the crystal. He stared for a moment, then checked the floor, under his bed and inside his bedside table drawers. The crystal had been taken. Even after he closed his curtains and turned off the light, he was still unable to spot its tell-tale blue glow.

'Err, Keeper of Portals. Have you seen a crystal?'

There was no response from the Keeper of Portals. He must be fixing some broken toilet door somewhere. Martin laughed to himself. For all the grandeur of his title, he really was just a caretaker.

Stopping by the door, Martin thought that all might not be what it seemed. There was something immature about the Keeper. Opening this door could lead anywhere. He wouldn't be surprised to see the inside of a tiger's cage or

24

the hatch to a beehive. He opened the door slowly, but all he found on the other side was the long, derelict corridor. It was exactly where it was supposed to be, still dim despite the summer sun surrounding the house.

A strong smell of smoke greeted Martin as he entered the kitchen. He wafted the thick air in front of him and walked over to his mum who was standing by the wood-burning stove. Next to it was a basket of chopped logs and Martin watched as his mum simultaneously stirred a pot and placed a log in the fire.

'Morning, dear. How was your first night?'

'Quiet.'

Martin tried to find somewhere in the kitchen to sit. It was a long room with many old pots and pans hanging from the ceiling. He couldn't see any chairs or stools so jumped up onto the counter. The wood felt sticky after absorbing the fatty kitchen air for so many years and the pans above him threatened to drop snowdrifts of dust onto his head.

Martin's mum jumped back as the fire spat. 'That's what happens when you move out here. It's easy to forget how much noise a big town makes, even at night. I don't know about you, but I missed it.'

Martin shrugged. 'I didn't miss it. It was just different.'

'You look a bit off this morning,' said Martin's mum. She walked over and placed a hand on her son's forehead before pulling back and rubbing his arms. 'You've not got a temperature, though. Did you sleep OK?'

'I had some strange dreams. At least, I think I had

25

strange dreams. I can't really remember. My head hurts a bit though.'

'You must have knocked it in your sleep. Do you feel up for breakfast?'

'I dunno,' Martin slipped his mum's phone out of his pocket and handed it to her. 'Here.'

'Anything good?'

'Some of it. A lot of it's damaged though and other bits are just weird.'

Martin's mum flipped through the pictures on her phone and nearly dropped it when one image appeared on her screen. 'Why on earth did you take a picture of this?' she said, holding up her phone to show Martin the decomposing sheep on a bed.

'I thought it was contemporary art,' said Martin. 'That's probably the most expensive thing in the house, we could sell it to the Tate Modern for millions.'

'Sadly, I don't think you're completely wrong. I'll go to town and see if I can look this stuff up on the internet and find out what it's worth.'

'I haven't finished yet, so I'll need your phone back at some point.'

'No problem. Thanks for doing this. I'd help, but I've my hands full trying to sort out this room.' Martin's mum ran her fingers through her son's hair before going back to the fire and feeding it another log. 'That reminds me, did you hear a crash last night?'

'Crash? No, I don't think so.'

'Really? I could've sworn the overhang fell into the sea. You sure you didn't hear anything?'

Martin shook his head. 'Pretty sure.'

'You must've been dead to the world,' said Martin's mum. 'Though I suppose it was right at the other end of the house. How about we take a look in a bit? What do you say?'

'Checking to see how much of the house has fallen into the sea? Country living at its best!'

'Don't be glib! So, after breakfast?'

'Maybe, but I think I'm gonna skip breakfast and go back to bed for a bit.'

'All right, dear. I'll bring you something up in a few hours. Actually, that reminds me, were you in my room last night?'

'Your room?' said Martin.

'Yes, I could've sworn I saw you.'

'Not me, not unless I've started sleepwalking.'

'I must be going crazy. Maybe I dreamt it, that and the house falling apart.'

'Maybe,' said Martin. 'But we'll check it out later. Who knows, you may beat the odds and actually be sane.'

'Oi!'

Martin smiled and jumped down. His head hit one of the pans and it started to swing, knocking into the others like a Newton's cradle and showering dust over the kitchen.

Martin's mum watched with her arms folded. 'Maybe when we've checked outside you can come back in here and clear that lot up.'

'I guess I don't have much choice,' said Martin as he rubbed his head.

'You guess correct.'

Martin was just about to leave when he stopped himself. 'You didn't take a blue crystal from my room, did you?'

His mum smiled, 'No, Martin. I barely even remember where your room is. In fact, I don't know where anything is in this place. It's just… well, it's just so big.' She walked over and gave Martin a hug. 'I'm sorry I had to bring you here, but there was nowhere else for us.'

Martin put his arms around his mum. 'I know, mum.'

Bright sunlight beat down relentlessly on the grounds outside the house. They must have been impressive once. There were remnants of a topiary maze and Martin was able to make out a number of large ponds, one of which had completely drained while in the process of falling into the sea. All that was left was half an empty pool surrounded by a cluster of concerned looking statues.

The gardens were wild and unkempt. The grass had grown long and was a mixture of dirty greens and browns. The only thing that still projected an air of grandeur was the line of redwoods in the distance that marked the boundary of the estate. But really all they did was mark where the bizarreness ended and the real world began.

Martin shut his window.

'Keeper of Portals, I'm gonna sleep for a bit. Can you make it rain on the other side of my window, please? It helps.'

Martin waited a moment then opened his window. He still saw the garden.

Martin asked again and waited for a full minute before

opening the window to what he hoped was a monsoon style downpour, but there was nothing.

'Are you here or am I talking to myself?'

Silence.

'OK, so I am talking to myself.'

Martin realised saying that aloud made it worse.

He would have to fall asleep without the power of a mystical super-being. Martin settled himself in bed. He was just over the lip of consciousness when he heard a noise from the end of his room. He reached up and pulled his pillow over his head, but that wasn't enough. The noise persisted, groaning and creaking, becoming louder and louder. In a flurry of swear words, Martin threw back his bedding and got out of bed.

As he approached the end of his room, he realised that the noises were coming from the door. Martin stopped just in front of it. It stood a solid fifteen metres from his bed, protruding out of the wall like an afterthought. The Keeper had taken Martin into the room on the other side, but it was completely empty: no bed, or chest of drawers or even paintings on the wall, just a bare room with no sign of a second door.

Martin noticed a large crack extending from the door and across the wall. The room groaned again and the crack split into three. He stood watching the wall, waiting to see if another crack would emerge. It did, growing out from the door in a flash and fracturing like a bolt of lightning. Martin jumped back. He waited for a moment before stepping closer.

That was when he saw it, something that wasn't

noticeable from the other end of the room, but right up close, it was painfully obvious.

The door was open.

It was only ajar, really just the merest hint of being open, but that didn't change the fact that the door, which had been sealed shut for 400 years, was finally open. Grasping the handle, Martin pulled the door towards him. On the other side of it was an exact replica of his room, bathed in red-tinted sunlight.

He stood like that for a moment, his eyes darting around the room on the other side. The furniture was old. At least, it looked old, but it clearly wasn't. Polished wood gleamed brightly and the intricate rugs were nothing like the threadbare excuses in Martin's house. He breathed in; this room smelled fresh too, not decaying like his room. A memory of something similar flickered in Martin's mind, but when he tried to focus on it someone blew it out.

Martin shut the door.

He didn't care. Didn't care that what was on the other side of that door was impossible and didn't care that really he *should* care very much.

Martin walked back to his bed and flopped onto it face first. He reached up for a pillow and pulled it over his head. He figured he'd probably stay like that for a while and maybe decide what to do with the rest of the day later. He cleared his mind of thoughts and decided to just exist.

That was when it popped into his head: the answer to a question he never asked.

Yes. You want to see what else is behind that door.

Martin ignored it. He hadn't wanted to know what else

was behind the door or any other door for that matter. He pulled the pillow down harder.

No, Martin. I won't go away. You really want to step through that door.

The answer was there again, but he had never even asked the question. In the next instant Martin was off the bed. He knew the answer, which felt like it had been whispered directly into his brain, was true. He did want to know what was on the other side of that door. He *had* to know.

Martin tore across his room, threw the massive door at the end wide open and ran into the room on the other side.

The sunlight was glaring directly at him but the room felt cold. Wherever he was, it wasn't summer. Had he actually stepped through to Australia? Looking back, he could see his own hot bedroom.

The answer continued to burn inside his head, but as he stepped further into the new room, he felt it begin to fade. The desire to discover the truth of that answer diminished, being replaced by his own curiosity. Martin walked across the floor and out of the room. This time he actually wanted to explore.

Martin descended two flights of stairs until he was on the ground floor. He realised that if he was going to find anyone they'd probably be in one of the living rooms or maybe the kitchen.

Martin pushed open the heavy oak kitchen door and stepped inside. He was not alone.

Standing next to a brand new electric oven was a young

girl. She was facing away from him and as Martin watched her, strands of his memory started to pull away the hazy curtain that had shrouded the figure from his dream: a girl wearing a large dress with brown hair tucked away beneath a headscarf. The same girl that now stood in front of him.

Martin thought about leaving, remembering what he had seen in the dream, but quickly changed his mind. That had only been a dream and this girl didn't appear to be angry. At the very least, Martin couldn't spot any fire pokers.

'Er, hi there.'

The girl turned around. Her sleeves were rolled to her shoulders and she had blood up both of her arms. In one hand she held a rabbit pelt and in the other a peltless, headless rabbit. Behind her, other skinned animals had been hung up, four more rabbits, two pheasants and something that looked like a peacock.

Martin noticed the girl had a bruise across the right side of her face and there was a very large knife on the table. Her eyes widened as soon as she saw Martin.

'Who are you and why are you in the master's house?'

The girl put down the rabbit and its pelt and started to walk purposefully towards Martin.

'Well? Who are you?' the girl continued. 'And what *are* you wearing?'

Martin could have said the same thing; she was dressed like a living museum exhibit.

'I'm Martin. And I guess I'm just wandering around your house. Hope you don't mind.'

'Mind? Of course I mind! Now I suggest you leave before *he* gets here.'

'Who's he? And what were you doing with that rabbit? You're not actually going to eat it, are you?'

'Of course. It is meat. But that is irrelevant, you need to leave before the master of the house hears us.'

'The master of the house? You mean your dad?'

The girl ignored Martin and spun around swiftly, causing her many underskirts to throw themselves out. She marched back to the work surface and picked up the rabbit and the knife. The girl then cut a long slit down the middle of the rabbit before reaching in and pulling out its viscera while staring at Martin. Then, with the rabbit guts in her hand, she walked back to Martin and held them in front of his face.

'If the master finds me talking to some street urchin instead of doing my job then I shan't have a job very much longer. Now, you either leave and never come back, or I shove these rabbit innards into your mouth.'

'Jesus! Calm down. I'll go. I'll go,' said Martin, more confused that a girl was actually threatening him with rabbit guts than anything else.

Just as Martin was about to leave the kitchen, he heard loud footsteps on the other side of the door. He looked at the girl, whose face was horror-stuck. She pointed to a small outside door with her knife. Martin charged for the door, closing it shut behind him only moments before hearing voices in the kitchen. He ran from the house, careful to keep out of view of the kitchen windows, but was stopped by a large barn in front of him.

A flock of sheep were presently being herded past by a giant of a man, but as they approached the door, Martin realised the man was normal size and the sheep were tiny, no bigger than Border Collies.

Martin looked around, hoping to find someone who'd give him a lift home. But when he saw the house, he knew he'd need more than just a lift.

The house was the one he and his mum had just moved into. Everything was in the same place as his house, the four floors of red brick that made up the central section with the three storey wings either side were a perfect mirror to his house, so too were the sand-coloured stones around every window and the tall, red chimneys all along the roof. But there were differences. The grand four-columned entrance at the front of the house was missing and so too was the driveway which surrounded an enormous fountain. However, those differences were trivial when compared to the fact that no part of this house had fallen into the sea.

Martin looked to the right of the house, where the cliffs should have been, but saw only a field. Further beyond that, at least four hundred metres away, the garden stopped abruptly and the sea waited patiently beyond.

Martin heard something running towards him from behind. He swung his head around, ready to register the terror before fleeing, only to see a little girl of about five charging towards him with outstretched arms. She wore stiff, filthy rags that would soon fall apart and nothing on her feet. Her hair was blonde, or would be when cleaned, and she had a pretty little face which was covered by the happiest smile Martin had ever seen.

Without stopping, the girl threw her arms around Martin's legs and she squeezed him as tightly as she could.

'Er, can I help you?'

The girl didn't respond, she just kept on hugging him. When she finally did let go, Martin saw that she was missing her right hand; instead her arm just ended in a ragged stump.

The little girl looked up at Martin again, though not quite focusing on him, and smiled before she ran off towards a field and was lost in crops that towered above her.

Martin turned back to the house. There were no satellite dishes, no telephone cables, no cars and no electrical pylons in the distance. In fact, Martin couldn't see any sign of modern technology.

That was when Martin realised the answer was wrong. It wasn't *what* was on the other side of the door which was important, it was *when*.

CHAPTER
FOUR

Martin opened the small door into the kitchen. Inside stood a man facing away from him. He was tall, wearing a form-fitting, black three quarter length overcoat embroidered with gold around the cuffs and collar. The girl was there too, facing Martin but looking at her feet. The man brought his hand up and hit the girl across the face, knocking her to the floor.

'You know that room is not for you.'

The man pulled the girl up just to knock her down again, 'If I find that you have been in that room again I will be forced to hire a new girl to remove the body of the old one. Am I clear?'

The girl nodded.

'Now,' said the man, 'you will bring my food to the dining room and then you will tend to your appearance.'

Martin took a step away from the door. A huge part of him desperately wanted to leap in and help. That man had hit the girl hard. He wasn't just disciplining her: that was abuse. And what made it worse was that Martin knew she was in trouble because of him. He was the one who had gone into the man's study, not the girl. But if Martin burst into the kitchen now he would only make things worse.

Martin crept up to the door again and watched the girl arrange rabbit, pheasant, wild boar and a huge collection of vegetables on a large silver serving dish before carrying it out of the room. Once she had left, Martin snuck back in.

The kitchen was just like Martin's, only everything looked much older. Even the pots and pans were rough compared to their cobwebbed counterparts in his house. The one thing that didn't make sense was the electric oven. Martin walked over to it. The time flashed 17:00 between the dials. Five hours later than Martin's watch. He brushed a hand over the smooth surface of the electric hob. Maybe he wasn't in the past at all. Maybe he was just in a museum. But why would they have such a modern oven if they were trying to appear authentic?

The kitchen door opened and Martin ducked out of sight behind a large oak table. Cautiously, he peered round the table leg to see who'd come in.

The girl had only just managed to close the door behind her before she fell to the floor in tears. Martin tried to sneak away, but he banged his head on the table corner and cried out in pain. The girl's head shot up.

She looked horrified to have been caught crying and quickly wiped away her tears before standing up and beating the creases from her skirts with a little too much force.

'It was your fault. You went into his room and left the door open.'

'I'm sorry, I had no idea. Are you all right?'

'I can take a beating, if that is what concerns you. I have endured enough of them.'

37

Martin brushed some of the girl's hair away from her face.

She slapped his hand down hard. 'Do not touch me!'

'Sorry, I just wanted to see the bruises. Anyway, that guy just smacked you across the head and you're worried about me touching you?'

'Of course. I do not know you. 'Tis indecent to have you touch me.'

'No, indecent is a grown man smacking a kid. You should go to the police.'

'For one,' said the girl as she busied herself cleaning the kitchen, 'I am not a *goat*, I am a young woman of 16, and furthermore, he is my master, and therefore owns me. He can do with me what he wishes.'

'You're not sixteen, you're thirteen. Fourteen at best. And *can do what he wishes*? Apart from sounding *really* creepy, I just watched him beat you!'

The girl slammed a knife down onto the table, embedding the tip into the wood so it stood up by itself. 'When I gestured towards the door it was not an invitation for you to return through it.'

'That guy attacks you and you're worried about being in the same room as me?'

'Yes,' said the girl. 'And if you have not noticed, I am currently busy. Do you not have a home of your own to return to?'

'Actually,' said Martin. 'This is my home.'

The layout of the interior was slightly different, but the room itself was identical, even down to the beams that ran across the ceiling. Then his eyes dropped to the brand new oven, the one thing that didn't make sense in all of this, 'At least, I think it's my home.'

'I can assure you that this is not your house,' said the girl, 'and therefore will ask you to kindly leave,' she paused and pulled the large bloodied knife out of the table, 'before I make you leave.'

Martin wanted to leave. He wanted to walk up the two flights of stairs, go into the master's study, through the door at the end and into his own bedroom. He then wanted to close the door and never again think about what was on the other side. He had his books, he had his games consoles and he had his mum. He didn't need anything else in his life.

His feet didn't move. Martin realised his hand was outstretched and before he knew what was happening, his mouth was opening, ready to speak.

'I'm Martin,' he said, 'Martin Lockford.'

The girl's hand clenched around the handle of the knife before she put it down. She looked at Martin, and as she did, her face softened.

The girl pulled her hand away from the knife.

'Isabel,' she said.

'Isabel what?' asked Martin.

'I do not have a family name. I am just Isabel.'

'Well, Just Isabel, it's nice to meet you.'

Isabel smiled and cocked her head to the side. 'You do realise that I am not a man.'

'Of course. Why?'

Isabel motioned to Martin's outstretched hand. 'Because you choose to greet me as one.'

'Oh, sorry.'

Martin let his hand flop back down. Not sure of the correct way to greet a girl, he decided to just stand awkwardly.

'You believe this is your house,' said Isabel. 'Have you any kind of proof?'

It took a while for the smile to appear on Martin's face. Maybe he did need something else in his life.

'So is the master your dad?' said Martin as he led Isabel up the stairs.

'No, he is my master, hence the title. My parents are dead.'

'Sorry,' said Martin. He could relate to that, but decided to keep his mouth closed.

'I have a question for you,' said Isabel.

'Go for it,' said Martin as he opened a door for them.

'Why have you tied a cloth to cover my eyes?'

Because we're going into the master's study.

'Because it makes things more exciting.'

'I do not believe that to be true,' said Isabel.

Martin didn't reply, but the smile crept back onto his face. He opened the door to the master's study and led Isabel inside with her headscarf tied to cover her eyes.

Martin stopped them in front of the large wooden door. He reached for the handle and turned it before pulling the door inwards. His room awaited him on the other side. The heat engulfed them like a hot towel.

'Where are we? Why did it become warmer?'

Martin led Isabel through the open doorway without

saying a word before shutting it behind them. They were in his bedroom, but Martin decided he didn't want Isabel to take the blindfold off just yet. He had somewhere else in mind for that.

Martin could feel the sun boring through his clothes as soon as he stepped outside. He felt sorry for Isabel with her many skirts, but if she was uncomfortable she didn't show it. He led her away from the front door and further into the garden. He checked his watch; the time was 12:15.

'You can take the blindfold off,' said Martin.

Isabel reached up and undid the knot at the back of her head. She looked up, then fell to her knees.

'The house! What happened to the house?'

Martin and Isabel were in exactly the same place Martin had been when he first saw Isabel's house. It was the same house, but different. Many of the bricks had either fallen out or turned to dust and there was a hole in the roof with a good-sized tree growing out of it.

While most of the windows remained, a number of them were smashed and others had been boarded up. But the biggest difference between the two houses, apart from the enormous entrance on Martin's house, was the amount that was missing. The overhang that had been there yesterday had vanished, leaving a messy wound in the side of the house. Wooden floorboards and the odd wall now stuck out in a gravity-defying manner.

There was another difference between the two houses, something even Martin hadn't been expecting. A massive crack ran from the top of the wall all the way to the ground.

Martin started to count the windows just to make sure, but even without doing that, he was fairly certain where that crack started. His bedroom.

Isabel turned to Martin in horror, then spotted the cliffs that were only a few metres away. She fell over herself as she tried to escape inland.

'The sea! Who moved the house so close to the sea?'

Martin walked over to Isabel and sat down next to her. 'The house hasn't moved, the sea has. It's eroded the cliffs right up to the house. I think some of it actually fell in last night, we could check it out.'

'Fell into the sea?'

'Yeah,' said Martin, 'I was asleep, but my mum heard it.'

Isabel turned back to the house, flicking from one dilapidated feature to the next.

'How did you do this to the master's house so quickly? Such a thing is not possible.'

'I didn't do it. This isn't the master's house. This is my house where I live with my mum.'

'No. This is the master's house. Look over there: the hills are the same, you see. And right behind the house the land rises up to one of the cliffs so from this angle it looks like the house sits against a green sky. I have sat here and seen it many times. I know this is the master's house. And there are the barns and farm...'

Isabel turned around, staring at the barren remains of a once grand garden.

'Where are the barns and the farm?'

Martin moved to stand next to her. The gardens looked

like the skeleton of something that had survived a nuclear war.

'Isabel, I need to ask you something.'

Isabel nodded.

'What year is it?'

'1623.'

Isabel stood in Martin's room looking through the open door into the master's study.

'This is a different house?'

'Sort of. It's hard to say. Kind of yes and kind of no.'

'You are not making yourself overly clear,' said Isabel. 'Are you a dullard?'

'A what?' said Martin, before shaking his head. 'I guess they are *different* houses, just connected by that door.'

'If I went through this door and into the garden…'

'The house would look fine,' finished Martin. 'The pillars at the front would be gone, there'd be no holes in the roof and the end wouldn't have fallen into the sea.'

Isabel breathed a sigh of relief before shutting the door.

'So where is this house? It looks to be in exactly the same place as the master's, but that is not possible.'

Martin, who had been sitting on his bed, stood up and walked over to Isabel. 'This door,' he said, 'it doesn't go to a different place, like a normal door. It goes to a different time. I don't want to frighten you, but you're nearly four hundred years in the future.'

Isabel's eyes grew wide. 'Frightened? Why? Do you have dragons here?'

'No.'

'Warring nations? Are we about to be besieged?'

'Well, no.'

'Are there giant snakes hiding in the woods waiting to devour us?'

'No, no,' said Martin. 'There's nothing like that here.'

'Oh,' said Isabel, deflating slightly. 'Then what is it, exactly, that I am to be frightened of?'

'Ah.' Martin hadn't actually thought about that; he'd just assumed she'd be hysterical. 'I guess that means there's nothing to be worried about.'

Isabel walked away from the large wooden door, inspecting Martin's bedroom as she went.

'Are you positive I now stand four hundred years in the future?'

'Yeah, I think so.'

'Oh.'

'Oh?' said Martin.

''Tis nothing, I just did not expect the future to look so dilapidated. Four hundred years have passed; you could have cleaned.'

'We just moved in. No one's lived here for decades. Actually, I think the house has been condemned. Most places are much nicer than this: clean with lots of lights and technology and stuff. Look, let me show you something.'

Martin ran over to his TV and turned it on. Isabel jumped back at the sight of two men fighting on the screen. She even ducked to avoid a couple of punches before looking up to see Martin smiling at her.

'A trick of some kind? Very amusing.'

'This is a television. It's basically a mix between a book

that reads itself and moving pictures. We've invented other stuff as well. Look.'

Martin showed Isabel his iPad: he had a movie playing on it that he quickly un-paused to let her see. He then brought over his smartphone and flicked through the pictures he'd taken of the house before booting his laptop up and demonstrating a computer game. Isabel was less than impressed.

'I admit, when I first saw your moving picture trick, I was impressed, but is that really all you have achieved?'

'I didn't just show you a TV, I also showed you my iPad, smartphone and laptop.'

'Well I have never heard any of those words before, but the way I see it you showed me a large moving picture, then two small moving pictures followed by a moving picture that you can close. It appears that in the future you have invented a moving picture and then placed it everywhere whilst neglecting cleaning. You have had four hundred years, could you not have done better?'

'But, but,' Martin spluttered, 'you've come four hundred years into the future and seen things you never could've imagined. You should be pointing at them and screaming *it's witchcraft* before chanting bible verses!'

'I am not stupid! If I am to accept that this is four hundred years in the future then it would be prudent to believe that you have inventions we have yet to think of. The same is true for us. We are the future for people living in 1523. Granted, some people would call this witchcraft, but it behoves me to inform you that I am not one such dullard.'

Martin switched off his television. He really had

expected Isabel to completely freak out. That she didn't was, well, it was pretty cool. A girl who can make a meal from road kill and doesn't become hysterical when you take her 400 years into the future can't be found just anywhere.

'What I fail to understand,' said Isabel, 'is how familiar this all seems.'

'Familiar?'

''Tis like I have seen this room before, yet I know that cannot be true. I have been experiencing some peculiar dreams recently. I feel like I am not seeing everything for the first time, yet something is trying to convince me I am.' Isabel shook her head. 'Well, enough of this. You are correct, you do live in the master's house.'

'And?' said Martin.

'And now I must return to my work. The master will have finished eating and will expect me to clear up.'

'But he hit you!'

'I told you,' said Isabel, 'he is my master. He owns me, which means he can do what he likes with me. That includes hitting me.'

'Look, I get all that. In your time it's fine to hit young girls, hang people in public for stealing a loaf of bread and use a flower pot in the corner of the room as a toilet. But it's not like that here. You could be safe; all you have to do is close the door.'

'You wish me to stay with you?'

Martin shrugged. 'I don't know what I want these days. But you going back doesn't seem right.'

Isabel sighed. 'It is not that easy. I cannot simply leave him. I owe him too much.'

Isabel looked upset as she reached for the door handle. To Martin it seemed like she was trying to silence a very loud voice inside her head telling her to stay.

'The master told you to clean yourself up,' blurted Martin.

'And what of it?'

'Well, how'll you do that?'

'I will lift some water from the well, clean myself with it, then I will tend to my clothes and fix the places where they have torn.'

Martin nodded, 'Well fun as that sounds, you could get clean here.'

'Do you have a well?'

Martin shook his head. 'Sorry, no well. We do have a bath, though,' he said with a smile. 'A large bath that can be full of hot water in about five minutes. Not as good as a well…'

Isabel's face lit up. 'Hot water? I can bathe in *hot* water?'

'If you want to, that is.'

Isabel let go of the door handle and walked back towards Martin. 'It appears that after four hundred years you have finally managed to accomplish something.'

CHAPTER
FIVE

Isabel watched as the water splashed over her hand and into the bath.

'The water is hot!'

'Yeah, I'm surprised too,' said Martin. 'Nothing else in the house works.'

'The water is so hot it scalds me!'

'Then take your hand out and put some cold in.'

'No,' said Isabel with a smile. 'I like it!'

Martin had been given the task of hunting for a working bathroom as soon as they'd moved in. This one was on the first floor of the house on the side furthest away from the cliffs. Most of the bathrooms he'd found didn't even have running water and in many cases the toilet was just a hole in a wooden seat.

Martin walked over to a cardboard box in the corner of the room full of shampoos, bubble baths and shower gels. He picked out some bubble bath and poured it into the bath.

'What is that?' asked Isabel.

'Soap.'

'Really? Not any soap I have seen.'

'Trust me, it's soap. It makes bubbles. I think you'll like them, most girls do.'

The green snake of bubble bath slithered towards the turbulent water underneath the flowing tap. Isabel's eyes lit up as the two mixed and bubbles started to appear.

'And what do I do with the bubbles?'

'Nothing really, they're just kind of there. I used to stick them on my face and make a beard. I guess you could do that. Everyone has to make a bubble beard at least once in their life.'

Martin brought over some more bottles for Isabel, who was already playing with a handful of bubbles.

'This one is shampoo. You use it to wash your hair. This one is conditioner, you use that after the shampoo. I'm not sure why, really, but my mum swears by the stuff.'

'She swears by it?'

'She thinks it's really good. You'll want to use a lot of the shampoo. Your hair doesn't look like it's been washed in a while.'

'I only wash it when I need to. Washing too much is bad for a person.'

'Yeah, I heard people used to think like that. We don't any more; now we wash every day.'

'Every day? Is there really a need for such excessive washing?'

Clearly Isabel hadn't twigged why Martin never stood close to her. 'Trust me, there's a need. OK. Well I guess you're all set. I've left a couple of towels for you and an old dressing gown of my mum's. You'll be able to find my room again, won't you?'

'Of course.'

'Good. I'm not so sure I can though… Anyway.'

49

'Wait. Why are you leaving?'

'Because you're going to have a bath.'

'And?'

'Well,' said Martin, 'I'm giving you some privacy.'

'You wish to give *me* privacy?' said Isabel, shaking her head. 'You really do think some queer things in the future.'

It had been an hour since Martin had left Isabel in the bath. In that time he'd tried to sort out his bedroom. The cracks had grown faster than he could have imagined, reaching out from the door and along the walls like witch's fingers, and a huge chunk of ceiling had fallen and crashed to the floor. Martin had dragged in three large wardrobes from unused bedrooms and created a barrier halfway across his room. To get to the door you now had to walk through the middle one which he'd kicked the back out of. It would be like stepping into Narnia, but instead of fauns, talking beavers and white witches, you'd find a cruel master in a house with no flushing toilets.

Martin knocked on the bathroom door.

'You may come in.'

Bubbles billowed out from the bath and spilled over the floor, covering it with a thick, foamy carpet.

Isabel stuck her head out from the mountain of bubbles. 'The water started to go cold so I twisted the spinner again and more hot water came out!'

'Yeah, taps will surprise you like that.'

Martin kicked away the bubbles from the floor. He'd probably have to find another bathroom now as this one would need condemning. He picked up an empty shampoo bottle from the floor. At least she's clean.

'You may want to come out now. You're probably quite wrinkled.'

'Oh, of course.' Isabel stood up. She was covered head to toe in bubbles so Martin couldn't see anything beneath them. He felt guilty over the slight disappointment he felt. She had said she was sixteen, after all.

Martin turned on the pre-war shower and closed his eyes.

'Ah! Hot rain!' cried Isabel.

Martin hunted around blindly for the towels and dressing gown and held them out for Isabel. He heard her step out of the bath.

'Why do you close your eyes like that?'

'Because you're naked.'

'Do you have an issue with nudity?'

'Well, it's embarrassing.'

'It is? I am not embarrassed,' said Isabel.

'I am!'

After a few moments, where Martin could hear the sound of a towel being rubbed over a wet body, Isabel declared that she was ready and, as she put it, decent.

Martin opened his eyes. What a difference a bath makes.

Isabel wasn't just pretty, she was beautiful. Or, at least, she would be without the bruises and cuts still on her face, now actually more visible due to her skin finally being clean. Her hair was long and lighter than he first thought, though not actually blonde, and it reached all the way past her shoulders. Martin thought back on the girls he had known in school, but none of them compared to Isabel. And here she was, only wearing his mum's dressing gown.

'Right,' said Martin in a squeaky voice. 'I mean, right,' he corrected an octave lower, 'I guess you'll want some clothes.'

Turns out, girls from 400 years in the past weren't all that different to girls of today when it came to choosing clothes. Nothing seemed right to Isabel and she flat out refused to wear trousers and insisted on a floor length skirt. The best Martin could find were some old clothes of his mum's from the 70s. In the end she settled for a long, white, hippy-style skirt and a tie-dye T-shirt. Martin thought they looked particularly awful but Isabel was enthralled by clothes with such bright colours. The issue of underwear had been a delicate one, especially as Isabel had never even heard of a bra. The details of those awkward fifteen minutes were soon erased from Martin's mind with the knowledge that a solution, despite being a little unorthodox, had eventually been found.

There was a knock on Martin's door.

'Honey, are you in *here?*'

Martin cringed.

'Yeah, this one's mine.'

'Finally! Are you feeling any better?'

'A bit,' Martin called back.

'Can I come in?'

Martin looked at Isabel and then the door. 'I guess so.'

Martin's mum opened the door and nearly jumped back when she spotted Isabel.

'Oh! Hello! Martin, you never told me you'd made a friend.'

'We just met, really.'

'Well, I'm glad to see you've not just been playing computer games.' Martin's mum addressed Isabel. 'It's nice to meet you. I'm Jo.'

'A pleasure to meet you too. My name is Isabel.'

'Wow! What a well-spoken girl.'

Isabel just smiled and nodded. Something about what his mum said struck Martin as odd. Isabel was very well spoken. Why would a maid have such a posh voice?

'I haven't even seen any houses around,' said Jo, looking confused. 'In fact, I didn't think there was anything for miles. Where exactly are you from, Isabel?'

Isabel flashed a grin at Martin. 'Around.'

'Oh, well, OK then. If you need anything just let me know. I'd better get back to it. Whatever *it* is; finding my way around this house, I suppose. Martin, be nice to Isabel. You're not likely to find many other friends out here. Or people, for that matter.'

'Oh Martin has been very attentive to my needs,' said Isabel.

'I'm glad to hear it.'

'Yes, he led me here blindfolded then told me to bathe,' said Isabel, flashing a coy smile at Martin.

'He what?'

'He even handed me a towel when I had finished. He is a remarkable host.'

Jo stared at her son open-mouthed and left the room shaking her head. Martin imagined they would be having a *talk* later.

Martin gave Isabel her poorly folded clothes. 'The door, have you seen it before?'

Isabel nodded. 'There was no door when I first came to work for the master. Then one day it appeared. That was when he told me never to go into his study. However, I still do.'

Martin walked Isabel to the closed door. He passed an old desk he'd managed to drag in from another room. That was where he kept his laptop, the same laptop he'd shown Isabel. Martin didn't notice that his laptop was missing, replaced by a stack of thick parchment paper, a pot of ink, a wax seal and a large quill pen cut from a black feather.

'You go into his room?' asked Martin. 'But that's why he beats you.'

'It is only one of many reasons. And I know, yet I cannot help myself. I am fascinated with this door. It has always been locked. I had to find out what lay on the other side.'

Isabel opened the door slightly to make sure the master wasn't in. The room was empty, so she opened the door all the way and stepped through. She looked back at Martin. Her, standing in 1623 and him, almost 400 years in the future.

'Thank you, Martin. Today has been the most enjoyable day I can remember.'

'Really?' said Martin. 'You got beaten, I dragged you to my house, made you take a bath and you call that fun?'

'Yes, I do. I have never met anyone like you. And as you are 400 years in the future, I suppose I shan't ever again.'

Martin couldn't stop the blush that grew over his cheeks. This may not have been the best day of his life, but it had certainly been the best day he'd had in the last year. Looking at her in the master's study, Martin began to realise how much he'd missed the company of people his own age.

'Can I come too?' asked Martin.

'Here?'

'Yes. I'm looking for the person that opened this door. I think they're in your house.'

'And I presume you mean to ask for my help in finding them.'

'Kinda. You see, I don't think this door was supposed to open. Not to your time, anyway. But because it is, it's breaking my house. I think it's something to do with the time difference putting strain on it or something. I don't really know. But these cracks,' Martin pointed to one that had run all the way to his other bedroom door, 'they weren't here this morning. They're spreading. Listen.'

Martin and Isabel were silent. After a moment the sound of birthing cracks could be heard. Isabel jumped.

'I just saw one. It was not there a moment ago and then out of nowhere it appeared.'

'This place is all we have now,' said Martin. 'My mum and I can't go anywhere else. If this falls down then we'll have to live on the street, or I'll end up in care. I need to find him so he can shut the door properly. Maybe then the cracks will stop growing.'

Isabel smiled. 'Then I suppose you had better come and find the man who opened this door.'

Martin thought it best not to mention that this *man* was really the Keeper of Portals. Isabel had dealt with enough for one day. He left the warmth of his summer bedroom and stepped into the master's immaculate study, closing the door behind him.

There was a creaking noise along the landing.

'The master, he is returning.'

Isabel grabbed Martin's hand and dragged him to an imposing desk, pushing him under and then joining him to hide.

The master walked into the room only seconds later. From under the desk, Martin was able to get a good a view of him. It was the first time he'd seen his face.

Martin had envisioned a cruel man in his fifties with a heavily lined face and an ugly beard, but the real master was nothing like the image he had created. He was a tall man, even by Martin's time, about 25 years old, but with a dignity and refinement that could only come from someone much older. The master was also handsome, almost excessively so, and Martin couldn't help but think less of Isabel for wanting to stay with him despite the beatings she received. His hair was charcoal grey and tied behind his head in a simple ponytail and his face had been expertly shaved. It was hard to imagine this man could be the tyrant Martin had created in his mind, but he had witnessed Isabel's beating for himself, so knew it to be true. When the master paused and looked around the room for a brief moment, Martin caught his eyes. They explained everything. Despite the master's looks, he had impossibly cruel eyes. They were completely devoid of colour, a black dot residing in a dull-grey disk.

The master strode up to the door and drew a deep breath through his nose before exhaling out of his mouth.

Martin and Isabel watched as the master took hold of the door handle and started to open it.

'My mum's alone. I need to stop him.'

Martin jumped out from underneath the desk and ran at the door.

The door opened and the master threw his arms out wide before collapsing. Martin stopped and watched as the master cried out in pain, writhing around like a witch doused with holy water. The master continued to convulse wildly, scratching grooves into the floor and clawing at his face. He didn't seem to notice Martin right in front of him. His cruel eyes were unfocused, staring at a point in space only inches in front of his nose.

Ignoring the door, Martin took a tentative step closer to the master. As he drew nearer, Martin saw that the master's skin was turning grey and starting to flake, falling to the floor like ash.

Isabel ran past Martin and slammed the door shut. The master stopped moving and lay unconscious on the floor, his once immaculate face weathered and beaten. Isabel returned to the master and threw her arms around him. There were tears in her eyes.

CHAPTER
SIX

Martin stepped back as Isabel knelt beside the master and stroked his hair.

'Master? Master? Can you hear me?'

Isabel waited but the master didn't stir.

'He has taken ill. We must do something.'

'Like tie him up?' said Martin.

'No! We must help him. Can you not see he may die?'

'Yeah, and good bloody riddance.'

'You are not helping!' cried Isabel. 'I shall carry him to his room.'

Isabel picked up the frail master with no effort and carried him to his bedroom while Martin followed. Once inside, Isabel pulled back the blankets with one hand and slid the master into bed.

'Do you really think he's dying? All he did was open a door.'

'Martin, will you be quiet! *You* do not understand why this has happened, *I* do not understand why this has happened, so stop asking questions like answers will simply appear from the air!'

'Sorry,' said Martin, looking to the floor. He couldn't understand why the master had collapsed, but even more than that, he couldn't understand why Isabel cared.

Martin took a step towards the master as Isabel fetched more blankets. He had aged, but not by a few tens of years; he looked older than it should be possible for a human to be, at least 150 years old, if not 200. His skin was grey and the wrinkles across his face were delicate and numerous. Martin poked the master's cheek and left a hole. He brushed off the dust from his fingertip.

Isabel spread the blankets over the master and then ran to the fireplace to fill the bed warmer with hot coals. She stuck it in the far side of the bed, trying to warm it before moving the master over to that side.

After Isabel had finished, she addressed Martin like he was a misbehaving schoolboy.

'The door to your room is in the master's study.'

'I know,' said Martin, a little confused.

'Martin, this place is not for you. This is where I live with the master. You have a world of moving pictures and hot baths and your mother. You should not be somewhere like this. Prithee go, Martin.'

'Why?'

'I can see it in the way you look at me. You do not understand why I care for the man who beats me. It is a different time here. Just leave us to continue with our lives.'

Martin didn't want to leave Isabel with the master, no matter how old he looked.

'What about the person who opened the door? You said you'd help me find him.'

Isabel took the master's hand and began to stroke it. 'I

want to help you, Martin, but I cannot. Not whilst he is like this.'

'He's asleep. There's nothing you can do until he wakes, and even then…' Martin just shrugged. 'But you're right, I don't understand. I just thought I'd, oh, I don't know, made a friend or something lame like that. Look, my house is falling apart and I know it's because of that door. If I can get it closed then I'll have a home to go back to, but if I don't then all my mum and I will have is a pile of bricks.'

Isabel placed the master's hand on the blankets but continued to stroke it. 'If I do help, then you must promise to leave once we have found him.'

Martin looked down at the body of the master before catching sight of the tears that remained in Isabel's eyes. Even though he beat her, it was clear to see that Isabel loved her master.

Martin nodded.

The autumn twilight sprinkled gold over the fields and buildings surrounding the house. These were not the grandiose gardens that still remained as forgotten relics in Martin's time. This land was practical and maintained by people from the local village. The farm had been lived in before the master took over residency of the estate, but once that had taken effect, the occupants were forced to leave. Those who worked on the land did so as if the main house wasn't there. Not once did they stop to marvel at its splendour. To them, the area occupied by the house was nothing but a barren field.

'He is not in the house or I would have seen him.

There is no need for me to clean every single room as most of them are never used. But I check each one every day should the master have been in there.'

'But he could've snuck into one after you'd checked it.'

'Do you believe he simply hides in the house?'

Martin shook his head. This was the Keeper of Portals. He could be anywhere on the planet, so why would he be sitting in the room of a house he'd effectively been living in for the last 400 years? 'But if he's not hiding in the house then how are we going to find him?'

'I believe I know where he may be,' said Isabel as they continued to walk across the vast lands which surrounded the house. 'I have heard the master talk to someone in his study. I do not know whom, for I have never found anyone in there, but I often sit outside and listen. I believe he is trying to taunt someone, though that may not be the case. In truth, I worry he has lost his mind.'

'So if the master has captured him, then where is he?'

'The farmhouse.'

Martin stopped walking. There was something bright red hiding behind one of the barns. It was a tractor and sitting on it was the little girl with the blonde hair and missing right hand. Like the oven, this tractor didn't belong in 1623.

Martin was stood watching the little girl pretend to drive the tractor while singing to herself when Isabel ran back over to him and grabbed his sleeve before marching him away.

'Will you hurry up! You are the one that came seeking my help, remember.' She kicked open the door to the farmhouse

61

and pushed Martin through. It was an old building, perhaps even hundreds of years older than the house. The walls were thick and uneven and the ceiling was low. Inside there was little furniture, only a few marks where a table had once stood.

Isabel scratched her head as she searched for something she could have missed.

'Doesn't seem like he's here,' said Martin.

'No,' said Isabel, 'I am certain I heard the master speak of holding someone here.'

'You also said you thought he was going crazy. Maybe he was talking to himself.'

'*You* are not permitted to speak such things!'

Martin took a step back to avoid Isabel's sudden vehemence. 'Well, it's a two room farmhouse and we've looked in both rooms. To me that says he's not here. We should check the house. There must be some rooms in there even you don't know about.'

'I know that house,' said Isabel as she spun herself around the empty room, 'and he is not inside it.'

'And I know empty rooms,' said Martin as he swept his arms out.

'Are you saying you do not believe me?' Isabel stopped searching and squared up to Martin, the top of her head level with the bottom of his nose.

'No, I'm saying you won't admit you're wrong. Either that or you don't want me to find him.'

'Do not want you to find him?' said Isabel. 'And why would I not wish for that, pray tell?'

'You did seem very close to your master. Maybe you don't want to admit he's a kidnapper.'

Isabel slapped Martin across the face.

'No! I do wish to find him because once I do I shall be rid of you!'

'Fine, we'll keep looking in here!' said Martin as he rubbed his sore cheek. 'I mean, it's *completely empty*, but who knows, maybe he'll just magically appear! ...Wait a minute, what's with the little door?'

'Little door?'

Martin pointed to the waist height door next to the fire.

Isabel ran over to the door and stroked its black surface. 'This was not here before.'

'So it's new. It'll only lead outside.'

Martin and Isabel exchanged a look.

Martin ran outside and was back a moment later. 'There's no door on the other side. Open it! Open it!'

Isabel lifted the heavy bar that lay across the door. It was stiff at first, but after giving it a good tug she managed to shift it.

'Oh my!'

Martin followed Isabel into the room on his hands and knees. Inside, it took him almost a minute before he was able to say anything, and even when he did, it was nothing profound.

'Blimey.'

The room was the size of a large hall and though it was nearly dark outside, some light managed to enter, creating long rectangular patterns on the walls and ceiling.

''Tis all doors,' said Isabel. Martin could only nod in response.

The walls, ceiling and floor of the large hall were completely covered by doors of every different size, shape and colour slotted together perfectly to leave no gaps.

Standing in the middle of the room were two creatures. Martin began to approach them. One of them he recognised instantly as the Keeper of Portals, but there was something wrong about him. He *did* look the same: smooth white rubber-like skin with a pointed face, feline eyes and a row of blue feathers falling down his back and onto the floor; but while the individual pieces were the same, the completed picture was not what Martin remembered.

'Keeper, are you all right?'

The Keeper of Portals bent his head down and regarded Martin quizzically.

'A human boy. Hello, human boy.'

'Human boy? What? No. Well, yes, but it's me, Martin. Don't you remember?'

'Remember you? No I do not.'

'What *are* they?' said Isabel. She stood a few metres behind Martin, but didn't look scared, more cautious. Clearly they were far more unsettling than seeing an iPad for the first time.

'They're Keepers,' said Martin. 'Well, this one is; he's the Keeper of Portals. I'm not sure about the other one. He certainly doesn't look human, that's for sure.'

Martin turned to the other Keeper. It was taller than the Keeper of Portals, and slightly thicker, though by no means fat: they were both very thin when compared to a person. It didn't have skin, but was instead covered by larger silver scales like fragments of a broken mirror. Its face was smooth, perfectly silver and covered with crystals. But it wasn't how the Keeper looked that Martin found so strange, it was how it changed.

The Keeper stood still, but was constantly in motion. Martin watched as parts of its body grew old and fractured before his eyes. Once a body part had turned to dust, fresh growth would appear beneath the decay and the process would start again. At first it was the left arm, decaying and re-growing twice before stopping. Then it was his broken-mirrored chest, which fractured from a single mirror pane and crumbled until a new one grew. Next it shifted to the right side of his face. Martin watched it grow old and crumble as the left side remained untouched. The Keeper's body always aged and grew anew, it never went backwards.

'You're the Keeper of Time, aren't you?'

The Keeper nodded. 'I am.' His voice sounded like the most beautiful music ever created, a thousand harmonies played at once.

Martin couldn't stop himself from taking a step back. He was in the presence of a Fundamental Keeper.

'Keeper of Time? What is that?' asked Isabel, now standing next to Martin.

'He controls time. That's right, isn't it?'

The Keeper of Time nodded slowly.

Martin had come to find the Keeper of Portals and here he was just hanging around with another Keeper. He was expecting chains, shackles, mangles and a whole heap of torture devices, but instead they were in a room filled with hundreds of different exits.

'What are you doing here? I thought you'd been kidnapped,' said Martin, addressing the Keeper of Portals.

'Doing here?' said the Keeper of Portals.

'Yes. You managed to open the door you'd been obsessed with for so long but then you never came back. Isabel made it sound like you'd been kidnapped.'

'I remember no door.'

This was definitely the Keeper of Portals, but he looked different to how Martin remembered him. Then he realised this wasn't *his* Keeper of Portals, this was the Keeper of Portals from Isabel's time, a younger Keeper of Portals. That's why he didn't recognise Martin and that's why, when the Keeper of Portals had first met Martin, he thought there was something familiar about him. But that didn't help Martin now; he still didn't know where his Keeper was.

'Well, you might not be my Keeper of Portals, but you can still help me. You have the same powers, after all.'

Martin went to leave, but the two Keepers didn't move.

'Come on,' said Martin. 'We need to go.'

'Go?' said the two Keepers in unison. 'We do not understand *go*.'

'What? How can you not understand go? This isn't the time to be all mystical. My house is literally falling apart. Time to leave!'

'Leave?' the two Keepers spoke again. 'We do not understand *leave*.'

Martin marched back to the Keepers. 'Go. Leave. Exit. Vamoose. Scoot. Depart. All of those things, we need to do them now!'

'We do not understand the meanings behind the words you spoke,' said the Keeper of Time.

'What? How—?'

'He got to them,' spoke Isabel in wide-eyed fear.

'He got to them? What, the master?'

Isabel nodded. 'He can do things: make you think things, make you not think things.'

'Seriously?'

Isabel walked up to the Keeper of Time and touched his hand. 'He has confused them. They cannot leave.'

'You are correct,' said the Keeper of Time, 'confusion plagues us. We try to fight it, but it is too strong. Now we just wait for it to be lifted.'

The two Keepers towered over Martin like skyscrapers. Were these supernatural beings asking for their help?

The Keeper of Time reached up and pulled a crystal from his cheek. The remaining crystals rearranged themselves to fill the space. He held out the crystal to Isabel. She took it.

The Keeper of Portals reached behind his back and plucked a blue feather. He gave it to Martin.

'Eat them,' the two Keepers spoke in unison.

Martin and Isabel shared their confusion as they placed the offered items into their mouths.

Instead of feeling the feather in his mouth, Martin realised that it was dissolving as soon as it touched his tongue. Isabel's crystal had done the same, disappearing before she had to swallow it.

Martin felt something move on his crown, like a worm pushing its head out of the earth. He reached up and felt the feather growing around his fingers. The single feather curled around itself and finally stopped just above his shoulder blades. Something was changing in Isabel too. Cutting her forehead in half was a thin, tear shaped crystal that sparkled a turquoise green.

'Why did you do that?' said Martin. 'Why did you make us eat those?'

'You will help us lift our confusion, but not in here. These items will assist you,' said the Keeper of Portals. 'And when you need them most, they will protect you.'

There was an almighty bang from the door they had come through.

Martin watched the feathers on the Keeper of Portals' back shimmer as the door grew to full size. It opened and on the other side of it stood the master.

He was still old, though slightly younger than when Martin had last seen him. There was purpose to his stride, and while his body was withered, there was a surprising amount of power left coursing through it.

The master approached Isabel.

'Those clothes you wear are disgusting. They make you look a fool.'

Isabel cast her eyes down.

'Why are you in here?' the master asked Isabel.

'Martin wished to find the Keeper of Portals because he believes he can stop his house from falling apart. I told Martin I knew where they were being kept so I led him here.'

Martin gaped at Isabel. She hadn't even tried to lie.

The master looked at Martin. 'The boy has returned,'

he said as his withered face formed a cruel smile. 'It seems you are as dull-witted as you appear. I would remind you of the punishment your return has bestowed upon you, but I doubt one as obtuse as you will appreciate the gesture, if you can even understand the words I speak.'

The master grabbed hold of Martin's neck and squeezed it with a vice-like grip. Wanting to answer the master, Martin struggled for words, but he couldn't understand why the master thought he had seen him before. His back was turned when Martin spied him in the kitchen and surely he'd been in no state to issue threats while convulsing on the floor of his study.

The master approached the two Keepers.

'Something has happened to the door. It leads to a time that drains me. Return it to the beginning.'

The master, dragging Martin behind him, walked up to the Keeper of Time.

'There is something you are not telling me, Time. That door led to the future, that much I know. The future wasn't… conducive to my continued existence as I am. I plan to change that.'

'To change oneself is a fool's errand,' spoke the Keeper of Time.

'It is not myself I will change.'

The master pulled Martin from the room. Martin tried to struggle, but despite how old he appeared, the master was the stronger of the two. He looked back to see Isabel following on behind, refusing to meet his eyes. He wanted her to see the hatred he bore her. She had deceived him. He hated himself for it almost as much as he hated her.

CHAPTER
SEVEN

Martin sat on the floor and waited for his eyes to adjust to the darkness, but after five minutes he had given up. The room was completely black.

He stood up and walked until he reached a wall. Eventually his hand touched the cold wood and he started to follow it in the hope of finding a door. A feeling of déjà vu overcame him as he followed the contours of the room. The way it turned ninety degrees before heading straight on was naggingly familiar. And there was a smell to it that he'd only ever smelled once before, a combination of dirt and damp wood. Martin realised he may be in the room the Keeper of Portals had taken him to, the one with the writing scratched onto the walls.

Martin stroked his hand up and down as he walked, but the walls were perfectly smooth. Whoever was going to fill them with words clearly hadn't got around to it yet. In fact, they probably hadn't even been born.

The wall turned another ninety degrees and Martin felt his fingers move over the raised surface of a doorframe. He padded his hands up and down, trying to find a handle, but couldn't. Martin laughed to himself in the darkness. He'd been locked in that room for a reason; it would have been pointless if he could just turn a handle and walk out.

Martin took a step back and kicked the door. It didn't even rattle. He tried again, harder this time, but the same thing happened: a lot of noise and little else. Martin took a few paces back before running at the door and performing a jumping shoulder barge. He missed and felt his shoulder crunch against the protruding doorframe and his head bang into something solid.

Staggering backwards, Martin rubbed his aching shoulder and pounding head. He felt something that shouldn't be there. It was the feather the Keeper of Portals had made him swallow. What was the point of it? Did it do something? By having a feather from the Keeper of Portals sticking out of his head did Martin actually have some of the Keeper's abilities?

Ignoring the pain that ran down the left side of his body, Martin squared up to the door. He closed his eyes, though it made no difference to what he could actually see, and concentrated. With everything in him, he willed the door to open. He imagined the first crack of light appearing as the door shyly entered the room before throwing itself wide to reveal a completely different part of the house.

Martin opened his eyes in hungry anticipation only to find the room was as dark as ever. Even if he did have some of the power of the Keeper of Portals, he still wasn't able to open a door without a handle.

Martin collapsed to his knees. He was right the first time: he was going to have to smash the door open. He just hoped there was something in the room heavier than his shoulder.

Martin's hands had found a number of things as he crawled around the dirty floor. Most of those had been made of wood and upon being thrown at the door had either shattered or bounced back and smacked Martin in the chest. On the verge of giving up and awaiting the punishment the master would administer, Martin lay down on the floor. The darkness and his lack of patience did little to distract his brain and it wasn't long before his thoughts drifted to Isabel.

Martin knew he was angry with her, but the problem was he wasn't sure why. Did he really have the right to be angry? She worked for the master, so of course she wasn't going to lie to him. It was just the way she had done it. She hadn't hesitated or even shot Martin a quick glance to say *I'm sorry*. She'd just blurted everything out as soon as she was asked. Martin wasn't sure exactly what he had been expecting, but he had gone out of his way to help her. He had taken her home, allowed her to have a bath and given her clean clothes, which she'd even admitted to liking. Yet after all that she'd turned him in as if he'd held her hostage. Martin felt stupid. He actually thought he'd made a friend. So what if she was technically 400 years older than him, dressed funny and had no problem ripping the skin off a rabbit? He still liked her. Perhaps this was the problem with not speaking to anyone but your mum for over a year: when you try and make new friends, you pick the wrong ones.

After a full five minutes of waiting, Martin was able to stay still no longer and started to crawl around again in the hope of finding something to break open the door.

In the corner of the room, Martin found a large chest. At first he'd tried to pick it up, but it wouldn't move. The best he could manage was to push it, but he'd only scraped it along the floor a few centimetres before giving up.

Martin opened the chest, certain that there must be something inside to make the thing so heavy. He wasn't sure what he was looking for exactly, but something large and made of metal would be ideal. He was 400 years in the past, so surely a sword or a mace shouldn't be too much to ask for.

Martin quickly pulled his hand out of the chest when his fingers brushed against something that felt suspiciously like bones. He slammed the chest shut again and sat down on the floor with a thump. Martin let himself flop forward and hugged the closed chest.

'I'm never getting out of here.'

He sat up with a start. Again Martin closed his eyes and focused. He thought of the chest, thought of its lid and of opening it to a different place. Information flooded into him. It was too much and his brain struggled to understand it. Martin felt like he'd suddenly been granted thousands of extra limbs with no idea how to control them. Then it appeared. In the chaos of his mind Martin's brain had created a way of understanding the information it had received.

Martin now imagined himself standing in a room full of thick electrical cables. They hung just above his head and stretched up as far as he could see. The cables were many different colours and each one represented either a door, window or some other kind of gateway. All Martin had to do was reach up, grab two cables and connect them. The only problem was he had no idea which cable represented what gateway. Martin grabbed one. As soon as he had it in his hand he knew it felt about right. He attached it to the cable he already held in his hand, the one that represented the chest.

Martin's eyes shot open as he threw back the lid.

The room filled with light and Martin could see the unmarked wooden walls around him. Poking his head through the top of the chest, Martin found himself looking out along a corridor. To the left and right were rows of candles burning in lanterns along the wall. He pushed his head out further to try and work out where he was. Judging by the height, he must be coming out of a window on one of the landings. And though he couldn't be certain, Martin was sure he was still in the house. That made sense. When his brain had created the room full of cables, he hadn't been able to move his feet, so could only grab the cables nearest to him. If each cable was a portal near his actual body, then not being able to move meant that his range was limited.

Martin took his head out of the chest and tried to lower himself into the room. It was difficult because the window was at a right angle to the ground. So while his legs were going down into the chest, they were coming straight out of the wall.

Martin's hands slipped and he fell into the chest. The moment gravity changed from pulling him feet first to body first nearly made him vomit and he ended up in a heap on the landing floor.

Standing up, Martin leaned through the open window into the dark room that'd been his prison. He reached up and pulled the chest lid down, closing the connection.

He walked down the corridor a few paces before spotting a large mirror. Standing in front of it, Martin inspected the long blue feather that curled its way out of his floppy brown hair and fell down just shy of his back.

'I've met a god, travelled back in time and now I have door powers.' Martin ran a hand through his hair. 'At least I've not gone crazy.'

Martin skulked along the corridors of the house. He wasn't exactly sure where he was, but that wasn't a problem. All he needed to do was open a door at random, think about where he wanted to go and that's where the door would lead him, more or less. The only problem was, Martin didn't know where he wanted to go.

He could just walk into the master's study, go through the door and back to his house without worrying the master was going to follow him. But what good would that do? His house was falling apart because of that door; that was the whole reason he'd come back. Martin had to find the Keeper of Portals, *his* Keeper of Portals, not the young, stupid version that had been locked away.

Martin walked into an empty room and searched for something small enough to use as a gateway. He came across a chest of drawers. He closed his eyes and focused on the master's study. If anyone knew of another Keeper of Portals in the house, it would be him.

Martin opened one of the drawers slowly, so as to make

as little noise as possible. He heard something on the other side and poked his head through.

The drawer opened into the door of a wardrobe. Peering through the crack, Martin could see the master at the end of the room, sitting with his back to him at a desk in exactly the same place Martin had his bed. His long hair was thin and lank and his body appeared lost inside his dark doublet and breeches, which too appeared to have aged like the master.

On the far wall, wooden doors had been opened to reveal large shelves lined with glass jars like the kind you would have found in an old sweet shop. But it was not sweets that filled those jars; the things inside were alive. Some were listless and lay on the bottom while others flew around inside, bashing at the glass with their tiny fists. Martin wasn't sure what he'd call them. The first word that came to mind was 'faeries', but that wasn't right. They didn't all have wings and some of them were actually rather heavyset. They weren't animals, or in fact like anything Martin had seen before. The closest things they resembled were the Keepers, but they were much, much smaller. The largest one appeared to be the size of a cat and had been rather clumsily shoved into a glass jar while the smallest were the size of house flies and flew around in an angry cluster. Martin realised they must be Minor Keepers.

The master stood up and walked over to the shelves. His finger ran along the jars until he found one he liked and picked it up. Sitting down, the master placed the large glass jar on the desk. The Keeper inside was the size of Martin's hand and appeared to be part faerie and part mouse, with a series of fine wings that danced around it like hair trapped in a strong wind. Martin watched as the Keeper sank to the bottom of the jar and collapsed to its knees.

The master removed the thick cork stopper from the jar, reached inside, and lifted the Keeper out by his golden wings.

'And what are you the Keeper of?'

The Minor Keeper stared the master down defiantly. 'I am the Keeper of Buttons.'

'Buttons?' The master laughed. 'Is that all?'

The Keeper of Buttons didn't answer and continued to threaten the master with his gaze.

The other Minor Keepers in their jars started to bang as loudly as they could against their glass cells. Even the ones that only moments ago appeared catatonic were now hammering away and shouting something Martin couldn't hear.

The master released a sigh and shook his head. As his hair spun out it transformed into the thin grey feathers of a dying bird. His entire head changed, growing large and avian but with a short black beak. Feathers died and fell to the floor as they sprouted from the master's face and neck. Even as he was changing, he looked like he was decaying.

Martin watched in amazement. The master was a Keeper. By looking at him, he couldn't tell which one, but surely he must be a Major Keeper, if not a Fundamental Keeper. How else would he have been able to capture the Keeper of Portals and the Keeper of Time?

The change from the master to the Keeper only affected

his head and neck. The body of an old man remained sat at the desk. But after the change, Martin could still make out the cruel eyes of the master, now much larger, on the Keeper's face. Human or Keeper, those eyes would always remain.

The master held the Keeper of Buttons high over his head and opened his mouth wide. He extended his tongue, a set of writhing black tentacles that squirmed and curled around each other, as a thick viscous liquid like tar dripped off them and onto the master's clothes.

The tentacles extended past the master's head and Martin couldn't help the bile rise in his stomach as he watched them wrap around the Keeper of Buttons like boa constrictors.

The Keeper of Buttons was brought closer until his head was directly in front of the master's eyes.

'Such pride. Such passion,' spoke the master from somewhere that wasn't his mouth. 'Your death shall intrigue me.'

Martin watched as the tongue wrapped around the tiny body of the Keeper of Buttons tighter and tighter. The whole time the master regarded the little Keeper fixedly until finally the Keeper of Buttons' twisted spine gave out with a tiny snap.

The lifeless body of the Keeper of Buttons started to glow and was quickly consumed as the hideous tongue recoiled in an instant.

As the master chewed, something about him began to change. He wasn't younger, not like he was when Martin first saw him, but something appeared to flash over him, giving him strength. Some of the feathers that had been withered were now full and places where his once pristine clothing had been ripped were instantly fixed. The master was still an old man, with the head of a Keeper, but by devouring the Keeper of Buttons he had grown that little bit stronger.

The Minor Keepers pressed themselves to the back of their glass jars as the master stood up once more, ready to pick again.

CHAPTER
EIGHT

Martin closed the drawer, breaking the connection to the wardrobe in the master's study. He'd seen that Keeper die. The master had picked him out, killed him and eaten him. A large part of his brain was telling Martin that it didn't matter. The Keepers weren't human and eating each other was probably natural. But he spoke, the Keeper of Buttons. He was not just a dumb animal: he had a mind and he had a voice. He did not want to die, but he knew there was nothing he could do to stop the inevitable, so he faced it without fear.

The Keeper of Buttons reminded Martin of somebody. His dad.

Martin ran for the bedroom door which took him into the hallway. He slammed it shut and charged at the one in front of him, concentrating hard as he threw it open. He came out on the top landing and crashed into a door that dropped him further along the corridor. Martin ran across to the room on the opposite side. He dived through the door and fell into the landing right next to the master's study.

Martin ran up to the door and started to bang on it.

'I am not to be disturbed!' the master shouted.

Martin banged harder.

'I told you! I am not to be disturbed!'

Martin stopped. He could call out, that would probably get the master to leave. But if he did that the master would know he had escaped. He searched for something else that would grab the master's attention and spotted a massive chandelier hanging above one of the house's many staircases. Martin ran to it, stopping himself on the thick banister.

The chandelier was a mass of candles and wood the size of a small car. Anything that big crashing to the ground would be loud enough to wake the dead. While Martin had quickly worked out a way of getting the thing to fall, he hadn't managed to come up with a method that didn't also include a certain amount of dying on his part.

The trick to surviving would be Martin's newly gained abilities from the Keeper of Portals, he just wasn't sure exactly how they would help in this situation.

Martin stared at the study door, willing for it to open, but even he wouldn't interfere with the master's door and risk actually coming face to face with whatever terrifying Keeper he truly was.

Martin looked back to the stairwell. It was built against the outside wall. Part way down, on the same level as the floor below, was a large window. Martin stared at the window, pleading with his brain to come up with an idea that had better odds of survival. None came.

He almost didn't do it. He almost let himself believe that it wasn't his battle to fight, but he couldn't ignore the fear he'd seen in the eyes of the Minor Keepers, trapped in their glass jars, and more – the sound the Keeper of Buttons' spine made as it snapped in half. No one could ignore something like that and still call themselves human. Martin focused on that sight and sound and used it as adrenalin. Holding on to the side of the wall, he climbed on top of the banister.

Balancing with his arms, Martin made his way along the banister until he was right in front of the chandelier. He bent his legs and threw himself forward. The safety of the floor disappeared from beneath his feet and for a few moments he flew above a drop of over ten metres. His hands made contact with the chandelier and he grabbed desperately for something that wouldn't snap.

Once attached, Martin started to swing the chandelier back and forth while tugging at it violently. Slowly he felt it start to detach from the ceiling. Then it began to fall.

Throwing his body as hard as he could at the wall, Martin let go and the chandelier plummeted to the floor. He curled his body into a ball and smashed through a window.

A shower of glass and the body of a fifteen year old boy destroyed the calm of an unused bedroom in an instant. Picking himself off the floor, Martin could hear nothing but his racing heart.

His legs were shaking, and his first attempt at standing ended with him falling back onto the floor. He decided to stay there for a moment. That was the most reckless thing he had ever done. Martin knew he wanted to save the lives of the Minor Keepers, but never had he tried to accomplish something for others at such a great risk to himself. What had changed?

'Isabel!' The intensity of the master's shout was so great that Martin was certain he could feel the walls quiver. Martin raced to the door and pressed his ear against it. He heard footsteps running along the corridor.

Martin stepped out of the cupboard in the master's study and ran to the row of glass jars at the far end. He stopped at the desk. There was another empty jar next to the one that had held the Keeper of Buttons. He hadn't been fast enough. Another Minor Keeper had died.

Martin approached the Minor Keepers, captive in their glass jars. Some looked out with fear, some with curiosity and some with hope. The larger ones tried to speak to him, but what remained of their voices after travelling through the glass was too quiet for Martin to understand.

'I don't know if you can hear me,' said Martin, facing the row of imprisoned Keepers, 'but I'm here to get you out.'

Martin picked up the jar closest to him. Some of the Keepers, the ones who were scared and at least half of those who were confused, start banging against their jars in protest.

Martin tried to pull out the cork, but he couldn't work it loose. Holding the jar between his legs, he tried with both hands, but even that wasn't enough.

If he took so long opening each jar then he'd be lucky to have freed even two Minor Keepers by the time the master returned.

Martin set the jar down on the desk and searched for something heavy. He found a large metal paperweight on the corner of the desk. He grabbed it and lay the jar down on its side before raising the paperweight high above his head.

All of the Minor Keepers, even those who had looked upon Martin as some kind of saviour, were now banging furiously against their glass prisons. Martin looked down at the terrified creature. It was one of the largest Minor Keepers and resembled a cat with exceptionally long limbs and a neck that had been wound around its body. The head unfurled slightly and Martin could see the fear in the Keeper's eyes. The thing was actually shaking. Martin could understand why, there was no way he'd be able to smash the jar without injuring the Keeper. He might even kill it.

Martin could almost hear the collective sigh of relief from the Minor Keepers as he carefully placed the paperweight back onto the desk and started to search for something else.

Martin opened a desk drawer. Then he closed it again. Realising he was an idiot, Martin opened the drawer to the inside of the glass jar. The image below him was distorted around the edges as the round top of the jar was stretched to fit the rectangular drawer.

Careful not to frighten the thing, Martin reached down into the drawer, at the same time his hand appeared in the glass jar on the desk. Being as gentle as possible, he picked up the Keeper.

Martin placed the contorted knot of fluff on the desk and waited for it to untangle itself. Slowly it managed to produce a long, thin leg followed by another and another and another. Finally the neck uncoiled itself from the body and the Minor Keeper stood at its full height on the desk. Its head was the same level as Martin's.

'Greetings, I am the Keeper of Pleasantries,' spoke the Keeper, 'and from the bottom of my being I thank you for rescuing me from a fate I have witnessed more times than I can bear.'

'That's OK,' said Martin, 'I couldn't just leave after seeing what happened to your friend.'

'Then you are brave. Not so many would risk so much when pitted against *him*.'

'Brave or a fool,' said Martin as he tried to push the ominous words of the Keeper of Pleasantries out of his head. He was only just beginning to realise how dangerous the master truly was and, much to Martin's fear, it didn't appear to be a journey of discovery that would end any time soon.

Martin worked as fast as he could to free each of the Minor Keepers from their jars. Some had to be coaxed out gently and some even bit his hand with their tiny mouths, or, in one case, at least five tiny mouths. Other Keepers were much more relieved to be released and leapt out of the drawer with gusto or exploded in a swarm of microscopic bodies.

Some of the Keepers were able to speak, but the ability appeared to depend on their size. The larger Keepers, though classed as minor, spoke the best. They were the Keepers of the most important things like certain human emotions and small animals. The smallest of the Minor Keepers preserved things that only lasted for a short amount of time or living creatures that would soon go extinct. These could only manage to speak in broken sentences, if at all.

A short, fat creature with glossy purple fur and a face that moved over its body like a pond leaf on water rolled towards Martin.

'You know him not, do you?'

'Know who?' said Martin. 'The master?'

The creature smiled a smile which stretched along the length of its body.

'Yes. Name now, not always.' The voice was deep and each word spoken was measured and appeared to take a lot of effort to voice.

'He's a Keeper, isn't he? What's he the Keeper of?'

The creature ruminated. 'A Keeper, he once was. But now, possibly not. Dangerous. Greedy.'

'But a Keeper of what?' pleaded Martin. 'What is it he controls?'

'Scared,' said the creature. 'Growing stronger, but now threatened.'

The Keeper of Pleasantries, who had been making sure the other Minor Keepers were recovering from their prolonged imprisonment, walked over, his long limbs brushing lightly on the surface of the desk.

'The Keeper of Ennui is right. He is a dangerous Keeper. But it is not *what* he preserves that is important, for he has changed that beyond what it was before. It is what he can do with that which he preserves that you should fear. But what that is remains unknown to such a Minor Keeper as myself.'

The banister creaked loudly enough to be heard in the bedroom. The Minor Keepers and Martin froze. The master was returning.

Martin focused, trying to find the furthest connection he could make and ran for the nearest set of windows, opening them to the windows in the small farm building on the grounds of the estate.

'Quickly!'

Without another word, the Minor Keepers flew out of the window. All of them could fly. Even those seemingly without wings managed to unfurl them from some hidden place before escaping.

When the last Keeper had left, Martin shut the windows and ran for the door at the end of the master's study. There was nothing else to do now but go home. His Keeper of Portals probably wasn't even in this time and it was too dangerous to keep looking for him. For a split second Martin's thoughts fell to Isabel, and what would become of her when the master found the glass jars empty. But Martin remembered he didn't care about her. It was her fault he'd been locked up.

Martin reached for the handle and went to pull the door open. It didn't move. He tried again, gripping the handle with both hands and turning until he felt his arms were going to fall off. The door still didn't open.

Martin's only way home had been sealed shut and if the Keeper of Portals was right, it wouldn't be open again for 400 years.

The study door started to creak and Martin managed to rip his hands off the handle. Sprinting as fast as he could, Martin threw himself at the wardrobe. He felt it start to fall, with him on it. He quickly opened the door and thought of the first place that came to mind.

Martin landed in the kitchen. He could hear the crash made by the falling wardrobe followed by a cry from the master upstairs. When he looked up, he saw Isabel before him. She was crouched on the floor underneath the table, her head in her hands. She was crying, and she was bleeding.

Martin sat for a moment watching Isabel cry as the blood dripped from the cut by her temple. Her hair was a mess and hung over her face, partially concealing the delicate blue crystal that glowed in the centre of her forehead. The problem was he didn't know what to think about Isabel. He was certain of her loyalty to the master, even despite the beating. If it had all been an act, then she could have escaped with him.

They could have gone to his house, boarded up the door and left the 17th century behind completely. But she hadn't wanted to do that. She had defended the master, cared for the master and even forsaken Martin just to appease the master. But seeing her like this, as a mixture of tears and snot ran over her lips and dripped to the floor, Martin realised that maybe, just because she was loyal to her master, that didn't mean she was a bad person.

Martin picked himself off the floor and joined Isabel under the table.

'He beat you because of the broken chandelier, didn't he?'

Isabel nodded.

'I was ready to hate you, you know. I still kind of want to, if I'm honest. Every time I think you're actually all right, you go and do something to prove you're not. But that doesn't mean I can leave you here until he beats you to death. Just because I don't like you, doesn't mean I want you to die.'

Martin crawled out from underneath the table and held out a hand for Isabel. She refused to look at him as she took his hand and stood.

'The door won't open,' said Martin. 'I don't know what he's done, but it doesn't go anywhere now. I think he made the Keepers do something to it. We need to get them to put it back, so it goes to my room again, then close it forever. After that, you can do what you want. They'll probably put you in care, or maybe you'll get fostered. I don't know. All I'm going to do is get you out of this house. After that, you're on your own.'

The door to the kitchen flew off its hinges and sped across the stone floor before crashing into the wall on the other side. In the doorway stood the master. His hands were clenched into tight fists and his face was covered in deep lines from blinding rage.

Isabel turned to Martin and wiped her mess of a face with her sleeve. 'What have you done?'

'He was torturing Minor Keepers. I watched as he snapped their spines and ate them. I couldn't let him get away with that. So I freed them.'

Isabel's eyes grew wide. 'You should not have done that.'

The master entered the room but stopped as soon as he

was inside the doorway. He looked at Martin and raised an eyebrow on his wrinkled face before turning to Isabel.

'You freed the boy?' The master spoke with honest surprise. 'You bring this child into my house twice and you allow him to see the prisoners. Then, after I have locked him away, you free him?'

The master started to walk forward as Isabel stood there desperately trying to form a sentence. Without being aware of what he was doing, Martin moved to place himself between the two of them.

For a moment he just stood there before realising he had to say something. It wasn't so much that he wanted to protect Isabel, though despite everything she'd done he couldn't deny that a little part of him wished to be a hero, it was more that he didn't like the idea of her taking credit for what he'd accomplished.

'Actually, I got out myself. Though to be fair, you didn't do a very good job of locking me away. Oh, and the chandelier. That was me. And all those little creatures you had locked away in glass jars, that was me too.'

'Why are you telling him all this? Do you know?' said Isabel.

'Know what? I'm telling him this because... well I don't really know what to do anymore. Unless the Keepers of Time and Portals help me, I'm going to be trapped in 1623 for the rest of my life, and judging by how angry the master is, I'm guessing that's not really going to be long enough to make a significant contribution to society.'

The master grabbed the iron poker embedded in the embers of the fire. As he took it out, Martin saw the end glow red from the intense heat. Once the master had it firmly in his hand, he threw it at Martin's head like a javelin.

Martin wished he had a little more time to ruminate on his life in the few moments before his head was pierced by red hot death. The only thing his mind did manage to process was that there were times when honesty was not always the best policy.

'Martin!' cried Isabel as she lunged for him. Her hands were around his arm and she was pulling him out of the line of fire, but there was no way she'd be able to save him. She just wasn't quick enough. Without meaning to, Martin closed his eyes.

CHAPTER
NINE

'Huh?'

Martin's hands flew up to his head – there was no hole in it. He opened his eyes and there it was, level with his eyes and less than a metre away.

The poker moved ponderously as if travelling through treacle. The master too was almost motionless. A fire burned in the hearth and Martin watched the flames dancing languidly with each other.

Suddenly, everything moved again. The poker flew through the air and embedded half its length into the wall. The master turned to Martin and Isabel, a mixture of confusion and anger on his face. Martin looked at Isabel, who still held his arm, then at the crystal that shone from her forehead. Much as he hated it, he knew he was going to have to trust her with his life.

'Do you think you can do that again?'

Isabel let go of Martin's arm and grabbed his hand. 'I believe so.'

The master was almost touching them when time slowed like a car braking sharply. Outside the birds in flight appeared to hang in the sky and the churned water of a nearby stream froze in seconds, turning it into an elaborate sculpture.

Martin and Isabel ran from the statue-like master and through the grounds of the house that time had neglected.

Martin pushed the door shut before following Isabel into the barn.

'I thought what I could do was cool, but that's incredible. You can actually stop time!'

Isabel sat down on a mound of hay and stroked the crystal on her forehead. 'I cannot stop time,' she said, shaking her head, 'I can only slow it down. And 'tis not their time I change, it is ours. If I speed our time up it makes everyone else appear to slow down. But in reality, we are the only ones that experience a change.'

'Even your explanation's impressive. I mean, I'm not trying to take the piss, but you're a girl from 400 years in the past, it's not like you've watched a Brian Cox documentary.'

'You should not be too impressed. 'Tis the crystal's comprehension, not my own.'

Martin stood in front of Isabel. He still had reservations about sitting down next to her. They weren't friends.

'Still, it feels peculiar. I find even myself disbelieving of what happened. That was me, was it not?' said Isabel.

'Well I certainly didn't do it,' said Martin. 'But it makes sense when you think about it. I can go through one door and come out another and you can control time.'

'You can really do that? Go through one door and come out from another?'

Martin nodded. 'Watch.'

Martin ran to the glassless window on the right side of

the barn and vaulted through it. At the same moment, he came in through the window on the left side of the barn, right in front of where Isabel sat. Fear spread across her face.

'But? You? How were you able to do that?'

'Oh don't look at me like I'm the devil, you're the one who slowed down time.'

'Sped up our time,' Isabel corrected.

'Whatever, same thing.'

Isabel tried to fix her appearance. Her hair was still a tangled mess and the blood and snot had dried on her face. She was barely recognisable as the girl Martin had seen standing in his bathroom wearing only his mum's dressing gown.

Martin stood up and walked to the end of the barn.

'Where are you going?' said Isabel.

'To get something.'

Martin came back a moment later with a pail of water and set it down by Isabel's feet.

'You should probably wash.'

Isabel reached into the water and started to wash her face.

'I know you hate me,' said Isabel. 'For that, I cannot blame you. But you must understand. When I told the master we were with those two creatures at your insistence, it was to protect you.'

'Protect me?' said Martin. 'You sold me out so you wouldn't get in trouble. At least admit it.'

'He is different, the master. He is not like anyone else. I have told you this before, that he has this intensity to

94

him. Only, 'tis more than that. There are certain things he cannot abide. You cannot lie to the master. That is a rule. If he asks you a question then you must answer immediately and it has to be the truth. If you do not, it angers him.'

'Angers him? How angry are we talking here?'

'Do you not think it strange that such a large house has only a single maid?'

'Yeah, I guess,' said Martin.

Isabel lowered her head. 'There were others.'

'What happened to them?' asked Martin.

'The master asked something of them and they lied. The master got angry and now they are no longer here.'

Martin was about to speak but Isabel quickly cut him off.

'And they did not leave for work elsewhere.'

Martin nodded to himself. 'Well, he did throw a red hot poker at my head, so I guess his version of angry is probably a little more extreme than mine. Sorry. And, err, thanks, I guess.'

'I accept, and I am sorry for not warning you.'

Isabel had finished cleaning her face. Martin picked up the bucket and emptied it by the far door before returning. There was something he needed to tell Isabel.

'The master—.'

'You needn't tell me how much you loath him, I am aware. I also know you think me a lunatic for staying with him.'

'No, it's not that,' said Martin. 'It's something else.'

'What?'

'The master, he's one of them.'

'One of what?'

'The creatures we saw in the room full of doors, the ones the master keeps as prisoners. They're Keepers. The master's one too.'

Isabel's face betrayed the feelings she refused to voice as the realisation struck her. 'Do you imply he is not human?'

Martin nodded. 'I wanted to find out if the master had my Keeper of Portals locked up too, so I spied on him. I saw him change, well, part of him. His head became big and grey and just like a bird's. And those little creatures in the jars, the Minor Keepers, he was eating them.'

Isabel's hands shot up to her mouth. 'Eating them?'

'Yeah, but it was more than that. I saw him kill one before he ate it. The way he did it, I don't know, it was odd, like death was some kind of science experiment. In a way, it wasn't even cruel.'

'Death?' said Isabel, but she didn't say any more.

'He also got power from eating them. Not a lot, but a bit. Him being a Keeper, I think it explains how he can get into people's heads. I guess that's why he hates it when you lie to him.'

'So you think he is one of these Keepers? The Keeper of Lies, perhaps?'

'Or Truth,' said Martin. 'Something like that. But I wouldn't have thought the Keeper of Truth would be bad. It just seems wrong.'

Isabel stood up and beat the wrinkles from her clothes.

'Keeper or not, I do not think he wishes me in his service anymore. Furthermore, he tried to kill me.' Isabel looked down. 'He did not turn out to be the man I thought he was, or at least, the man I hoped he would be. I suppose that means I am to be stuck with you.'

She smiled a little.

'Feeling's mutual.' Martin couldn't help but let out a little laugh. 'So, what're we going to do?'

'We shall have to find those other Keepers and ask them to return the door to your time.'

Martin nodded. 'But what if they can't? Or won't? Then what?'

Martin stood up and walked over to the window, looking out at the dark landscape in a time he knew nearly nothing about. He didn't even know who was king.

'You could just stay,' said Isabel, suddenly appearing next to Martin.

'Stay? Here?'

'Here, but also *now*.'

'You mean stay here in the past with you?'

Isabel nodded. 'I know where there are some horses. We could steal them and ride to a town far from here.'

'But the house and my mum…I can't just leave her.'

'None of that has happened yet. Your mum will not even be born for another 350 years.'

Even though Isabel was right, that didn't make Martin feel any better. His mum was still there in the house, just behind the door in the master's study. If they could get that open again then the 400 years that separated them would mean nothing. Martin had already lost one parent without saying goodbye; he didn't want to lose another.

'I can't stay,' said Martin. 'Not forever, anyway. It wouldn't be right. Plus, what if I did something that stopped me from being born. You don't realise, but travelling through time and messing with the past isn't a good idea. I've seen it in movies. You go back in time, step on a bug, assassinate the pope, then you don't get born, or the Nazis win or you end up starting a nuclear war.'

'I do not know what Nazis or nuclear wars are,' said Isabel as she touched Martin's arm. 'But I know you are here.'

'What do you mean?'

'If you stay, then you cannot do something that stops you from being born, because you are here.'

It seemed that Isabel had managed to grasp the concept of time travel faster than he had. It must have been because of the crystal. At least, Martin hoped so.

'Well what if I stay, have a family that then becomes my family and I end up my own great, great, great granddad or something.'

'That would be interesting,' said Isabel with a smile.

Martin let out a sigh. He would get that door open again, no matter what it took. But if for any reason he couldn't and he became trapped in the past, he would leave something for his mum, a message, so that even if he never saw her again, she would know how much she meant to him and how proud he was of her for dealing with everything after his dad died.

The door to the barn swung open with an almighty bang. Martin and Isabel both jumped. They turned around, expecting to see the master, but instead an old man with a pitchfork in his right hand and a bale of hay under his left arm stood there.

'Why are there children in the barn?'

All expression left the old man like the final flame of a dying fire. His eyes closed before screwing up tightly. He then began to mutter to himself. At first what he spoke were barely even words, just a jumble of noises forced together, but soon a pattern started to emerge.

'The children are dangerous and must be destroyed. The children are dangerous and must be destroyed. The children are dangerous and must be destroyed.'

The old man's eyes snapped open and his confusion was replaced by anger. His voice was now strong and clear and reached to fill the barn.

'The children are dangerous and must be destroyed.'

The old man dropped the bale of hay and charged at Martin and Isabel. The pitchfork extended out from his body like a jousting pole.

Isabel grabbed Martin's arm and pulled him to the side. The old man tripped and stumbled into a pile of hay.

Isabel stared at the man. 'Oh no.'

'Oh no? Why "oh no"?'

'I have seen this before.'

Martin and Isabel ran out of the barn as the old man tried to pick himself up.

Outside, a ring of villagers had gathered around the entrance, blocking off any escape. Each of them held something that could be used as a weapon, even if that wasn't the object's original purpose. One woman in a long hessian dress was wielding a wooden post, a young man, only a year or two older than Martin but already with missing teeth, clutched a small dagger and started to slice the air with it.

Martin and Isabel took an instinctive backwards step towards the barn.

'Produce your dagger,' said Isabel. 'Show them we can fight.'

'I don't carry a dagger!'

'Why not? You are a young man. Or are you merely a coward?'

'It's got nothing to do with being a coward. I don't carry a knife around because I don't want to go to prison,' said Martin, taking another step back.

'Oh quite right,' said Isabel, 'much better to be dead!'

The villagers were mumbling something under their breaths. At first it was inaudible, but with each progressive step their voices became louder as they chanted in unison.

'The children are dangerous and must be destroyed.'

The old man had managed to stand and was once more levelling the pitchfork. This time it was neck height.

Martin quickly turned to the slowly approaching group, checking out their weapons and comparing them to the old man's before making a rash decision.

He grabbed Isabel's hand and dragged her back to the barn. As soon as he moved, so did the villagers, holding their weapons high. The old man was running too, the sharp points of his fork hungry for soft flesh.

Martin ran straight for the barn door. The old man was coming right at him and the fork was less than a second from crossing the threshold. But Martin got there first, and that was all he needed. Martin and Isabel ran into the barn and straight out of the front door of the farmhouse. Martin slammed the door shut, making sure no one could follow them. They were alone.

'You could have told me you were going to do that!' shouted Isabel.

'Sorry, but you called me a coward and I needed to make a point,' said Martin with a smile.

Isabel tisked.

Martin opened the door to the small farmhouse and stepped inside. The tiny doorway that led to the imprisoned Keepers had disappeared. He approached a window and concentrated, searching for any connection that could lead to the Keeper of Portals and the Keeper of Time, but there were none. He went back outside.

'The door's gone.'

'How?'

Martin shrugged. 'The master must have made the Keeper of Portals move it. I guess he knew we'd come looking.'

Martin jogged a little way from the farm. He wanted to see if there was anyone else nearby. Tonight there was a half-moon in the sky, painting the ground with a subtle silver base layer. Without it they could have been surrounded and never known.

Martin ran back to Isabel. 'I don't see anyone else,' he called before taking a quick look inside the house to make sure it was empty. 'Nope, I think we're good.' He took a moment to catch his breath before turning to Isabel. 'So you've seen that before?'

Isabel nodded. 'Yes, once. But never so many. It happened to one of the maids.'

'What happened?'

'She was upset. The master had beaten and scolded her. She cried and kept asking what the point of living was. Then she just stopped.'

'She stopped?'

'Yes. She stopped asking. Then she walked up to the master just to stare at him. I thought he would strike her, but he made no move against her. She then took hold of a knife and said, "There is no point," before plunging the knife into her stomach.'

'She did what?'

Isabel nodded again as a tear slid down her face. 'The master did nothing. He simply watched her like he knew it would happen. Like he was studying her. It was him. The master reached into her head and he made her kill herself.'

Martin leaned against the uneven wall of the small farmhouse. 'That's it!'

'What? What is it?' said Isabel.

'I thought he was the Keeper of Truth. But he's not. He's the Keeper of Questions! You ask a question and he answers it. That's what he does, that's how he can control people. The old man, he asked who we were, but he wasn't asking us, he wasn't asking anyone. He just asked the question. Then he received an answer. That's why he tried to attack us. It was the master. He made him attack us. But if he can do that, you know, get into people's heads, then why doesn't he just do it to us?'

Isabel smiled and stepped closer to Martin. 'You are unaware?'

Martin shook his head.

'Martin, to you this is the past and compared to the people who live in your time everyone you see here must seem stupid. And they are, compared to you. You live in a world where you can create things people here cannot even dream of. Your mind is different to those of us that live here. You have seen so much more, you *know* so much more. The master remains weak, he still looks like an old man. A mind like yours will be too much for him, for now.'

'But…' Martin wanted to say something but it would offend Isabel.

'But what of me?' asked Isabel. 'Yes, I was the same as them: stupid when compared to a girl from your time. I am not ashamed to admit that. How can I compete with someone from the future? I cannot. But that does not mean I am not capable, or I am not strong.

'However, I have changed. Since I saw your world, I cannot stop asking questions. Why? How? My mind has never been this active. But I am not asking questions to the sky. I am asking them to me, because I do not want to just know the answers, I want to be able to find those answers in myself. That is why he is not in my head. I do not ask him the questions so he cannot give me the answers. But he is weak. That still may change.'

A light hovered in the distance. Martin squinted to try and make it out.

'What is it?' asked Isabel.

'A man with a burning torch. God, we really are in the past!'

Martin and Isabel ran for the door of the farmhouse and kicked it open, but the man with the torch was too close behind. They could feel the heat from the flames on the backs of their necks. He had followed them through.

The cries of frightened chickens caused them to pause. Martin had taken them to a chicken coop.

'Do you not have a choice where the door leads?'

Martin noticed the man behind them shake off his confusion and start to come at them again. He swung the torch and sparks flew off and onto the frightened chickens, causing them to squawk in pain.

'I do, but now's not really the time to be picky.'

Martin ran straight into a wall. There was no door at the other end of the coop and the one they'd come through was currently blocked by a man wielding a burning torch. Some of the sparks that had landed on the floor had already lit the straw and flames were beginning to lick at the walls. The man didn't care. Oblivious to the danger he was in, he kept coming forward, muttering to himself with each step.

'There is no door!' cried Isabel in anger.

'Just because I can go through them doesn't mean I know where they all are. Just give me a minute and I'll think of something!'

Martin started to pat the wall frantically in the hope there was a doorway he couldn't see. He could hear the crackle of the burning straw behind him. The flames weren't just making it hotter, they were making it lighter. He stood back; there was no secret door in the wall.

'Got him!'

104

Martin turned around to see Isabel brandishing a handful of eggs. The man had egg over his eyes and was in the process of trying to clear it when he dropped the burning torch. Now it wasn't just the straw that was on fire, the wood was starting to go up too, and fast. The man wiped his eyes as Isabel launched another volley of eggs at his face. But the man was still staggering forward and Isabel was starting to back into Martin.

'What are you doing?'

'Slowing him down! Now impress me, future boy and find a way out of here.' Isabel coughed as she gathered more eggs from the floor.

Martin held his sleeve over his mouth and breathed in. The smoke was getting worse and with no windows there was nowhere for it to go. If they stayed in there any longer the smoke would kill them before the flames did.

There was no door. Martin knew that. If there was no door then they couldn't escape. It's not like he could just make doors out of nothing.

Or could he?

Martin took a step back from the wall and kicked it as hard as he could. His foot sailed through the thin wood to the outside. He looked at the hole and visualised the house's front door and there it was, contorted into the hole left by his foot. The problem was, there was no way they'd fit.

Martin continued to kick a big enough hole in the wall as Isabel tried to hold off their attacker with eggs.

Martin grabbed Isabel and dragged her out of the burning chicken coop. They fell on the front steps of the house. Several chickens flew out of the door on fire. Most made it a few metres before the flames engulfed their wings and they fell to the floor like meteors.

Martin saw the man. He was standing still as the flames rose around him. Then he started to walk backwards and out of Martin's reach. Martin tried to grab him, but the heat was too intense and the flames were rising up like a shield. It wasn't the man's fault the master had control of his brain. Like Isabel had said, he was just a simple villager.

'He won't come,' shouted Martin. 'He's moving away from me.'

'It is the master.'

Flames continued to cover the man but he didn't react, almost like he couldn't feel any pain.

'Time! Make it go backwards!'

Isabel shook her head.

'He's burning! If you make time go backwards then he'll unburn.'

'I cannot! Time does not go backwards. You have to leave him,' shouted Isabel, trying to pull Martin away from the door.

'He's dying, Isabel! You can save him,' said Martin as he fought against Isabel to get back into the chicken coop.

Isabel got a solid grip on Martin's arm and pulled him away from the fire, throwing him to the floor. Then she slammed the front door of the house shut, closing the connection to the burning coop.

'I said that I could not, not that I would not!' Isabel nearly spat the words at Martin, all her sensibilities deserting her. 'Time does not go backwards. Never ever

106

EVER does it go backwards! That is just the way things are. Now get up before the rest of the villagers find us.'

An axe flew through the air and embedded itself into the door. More villagers had seeped into the grounds of the house. They weren't slow anymore; these villagers were running.

Martin scrambled to his feet and threw open the door of the house. They came flying out of the barn window and landed in a pile of mud. Almost instantly they were set upon by another group of charging villagers, waving crude and rusting weapons. Isabel heaved Martin up and they ran hand in hand around the side of the barn.

They went through the back entrance and immediately came out of the front entrance. The villagers were still behind, confused by their sudden disappearance and searched the interior of the barn before they noticed Martin and Isabel sprinting into the silver-hued darkness.

'Where next?' asked Isabel as she flashed a smile at Martin.

'Are you enjoying this?'

Martin pulled Isabel around the side of a log store as an old woman with a garden hoe almost took their legs out.

'Yes! Very much so. I cannot think of the last time I've done anything so exciting.'

'You do know they're trying to kill us,' said Martin.

'Of course! I would not find it nearly so exciting otherwise.'

'But people are dying! How can you go from angry to happy just like that? Are you insane?'

'Do you not have females in the future?' asked Isabel with a smile.

107

Martin stopped by the side of the house next to the outside kitchen door.

'We can't keep running like this,' said Martin. 'Surely they're going to stop.'

'They will,' said Isabel between pants, 'when we have been killed.'

Martin wheeled around at the sound of pounding footsteps. Before he knew what was happening, a man was upon them. He was unarmed, but so large he'd give a bear second thoughts before picking a fight.

Martin and Isabel were rammed into the kitchen door. Martin had to make a connection. If they fell inside they'd have their heads pounded flat by fists the size of microwaves. Martin had no time to think. The cables were joined and a connection was made. As Martin passed through the door, with Isabel pushed into him, he realised it was the wrong connection.

Martin and Isabel fell from a top floor window. The goliath behind them fell too. Just as Martin was level with the top of the first floor, he felt Isabel take his hand.

They stopped falling. The man above them had also stopped, his features frozen in a state of panic. Isabel turned to Martin at normal speed as they hung in the air.

'If it is time you require, you need only ask.'

It was dark, but Martin could pick out the villagers holding torches. They appeared to stop mid-stride, but he knew they were still moving, only very slowly. Isabel had said she couldn't stop time completely.

'You could have done this all along, couldn't you?'

'Of course! I could have transformed the grounds into

a garden full of statues for us to run between, had I wished.'

'Well if we could've done that, then why was I busy pulling us through all those doors?'

Isabel laughed. 'Martin. I am a girl and you are a boy. I had to at least give you a chance to impress me before I went and upstaged you.'

'I wasn't trying to impress you, I was trying to keep you alive!'

'If you were smart you could have achieved both,' said Isabel.

Their subjective speed sped up and Martin and Isabel started to move towards the ground at a faster rate. Everything else started to speed up too. The man above them continued to fall and the villagers that were charging towards them broke into a run, but in a languid manner that made the whole affair appear comical.

As Isabel and Martin's feet reached the floor, Isabel sped up their time once more, allowing their muscles time to brace for the impact, saving them from breaking their legs.

Once on the floor, they jumped out of the way to avoid the man landing on them.

Still holding hands, Isabel and Martin ran from the house.

It was not that they felt like they were running faster, or that running to them became any easier, it was just that with their time sped up they charged through a world in permanent slow motion. With every hundred seconds of their time lasting a mere second in the real world, the pair were gone in a flash, charging at over a thousand miles per hour.

After ten minutes they stopped running. They were over a mile away from the house now. But of course, that had only taken six seconds in real world time.

Isabel let go of Martin's hand and time returned to normal in an instant. They were standing in the middle of a field. The villagers would still be around the house, trying to work out where they'd got to. They wouldn't be able to return tonight.

Martin and Isabel walked into the darkness and towards the distant flickering fires of the closest settlement. They'd have to go further than this, but it would be a start. Martin was actually doing it. He was turning his back on the life he had. Turning his back on his mum. But no matter how much it hurt him, he knew he had no other option.

Isabel poked Martin in the arm. 'Martin, do you know what that is? I have never seen anything like it before.'

For a moment Martin saw nothing as his eyes tried to make the shape out in the darkness, but eventually its enormous structure came into view.

'That's a wind turbine.'

CHAPTER
TEN

The cottages were built in a disorganised cluster around no obvious central location. Each one was single storey with no glass in the small windows. Some had smoke rising from a hole in the roof and hints of firelight leaking through cracks in the closed shutters. The road that separated the houses was just a track of mud, churned up by feet and cattle.

Martin tried to scrape the mud off his shoes using a large stone.

'The only pair of Adidas trainers in the world and they're ruined.'

'What are trainers?' asked Isabel.

'Expensive shoes that don't like mud, apparently.'

Isabel walked up to a few windows and listened. 'Everyone is asleep.'

'But it can't be that late. It was light an hour ago. What is it? Eight? Nine? Why are they asleep?'

'Can you see the Sun?'

'So? They could have a light on.'

'Light means burning oil or candles. The master may be able to afford it, but these people are farmers and fishermen. When it is dark, they go to sleep. When it is light, they get up.'

'I never knew how much I took electricity for granted. I guess I'm going to have to get used to that.'

Isabel pulled a shutter open and wriggled her body through the window before sliding back out.

'Some of these are empty. The villagers will still be with the master.'

'So what? We just stay here?'

Isabel walked over to the door and pushed it open.

'It would be preferable to sleeping outside.'

'But it's someone's house,' said Martin. 'Isn't this illegal?'

'No, these people are poor.'

Martin followed Isabel into the cottage. A fire on the verge of dying sat in the middle of the earth floor of the single room dwelling, the air thick with smoke. There was no bed in the cottage, only a straw mat and an unpleasant looking blanket that would just be big enough for one.

'I'll go find another house and see you in the morning,' said Martin as he made for the door.

'Why, what is wrong with this house?'

'I just thought you'd want some privacy.'

Isabel smiled. 'You must be the hardest person in the world to understand. You shout at me and tell me you hate me, then you act like a gentleman and wish to give me *privacy* of all things.' Isabel shook her head.

'So, I'll see you in the morning,' said Martin.

Isabel sat on the straw mat. 'Come to bed, Martin.'

Martin lay with his eyes open the entire night. He could feel Isabel's body heat through both their clothes. But more than that, he could feel Isabel's body.

Martin had never asked for this. The Keeper of Portals had interrupted his life and some answer he didn't ask for got him stuck four hundred years in the past with no chance of ever getting home. But as he lay there, with Isabel pressed against him and her light breath playfully tickling his neck, Martin realised that of all the places to be stuck, this one was surely not the worst.

Martin opened his eyes to the weak early morning light that teased its way in through the closed shutters. He sat up slowly, not even believing he'd actually fallen asleep. He tried to recall a dream, but none came to him.

Isabel was standing by the window. She turned when she heard Martin stir.

'Most people are asleep. Farmers may awaken at dawn, but while they put on clothes, I prepare breakfast.' She left the window and walked to the mat, running her fingers through her hair. 'How did you sleep?'

Martin's mind bounced back to the night and the reason why his brain had kept him awake for so long.

'Yeah, OK I guess. But I couldn't get comfortable.'

'Really? You did not move at all. I thought you fell asleep straight away.'

Martin just shrugged, he didn't want to explain his nocturnal rigidity.

'Well, we should get going. I know the master. If we wait here too long he will find us. I know where we can find some horses.'

'Horses? We're going to ride horses?'

'Can you not ride a horse?' said Isabel.

'Err, no. Can you?'

'Of course!'

Like her manner of speech, the fact that Isabel could ride a horse seemed to be at odds with her being merely a maid.

Isabel stepped out of the cottage and Martin jumped up to follow her.

'You shall have to learn quickly, because we will have to get as far away from the master as we can, and I do not wish to run!'

Martin hadn't taken to horse riding as quickly as he'd hoped. The problem with it, he found, was that it required controlling a living creature with ideas of its own. Isabel had instructed him as best she could, but even then Martin found himself weaving dramatically.

After a couple of hours on the horses, they reached another settlement. Isabel stopped while they were still several hundred metres away.

'We need food.'

Martin had been trying to overcome the ache in his stomach. With all the travelling through time he had no idea when he last ate, but it was either hours ago or 400 years in the future. Either way, he was hungry.

'I take it we'll be stealing this too,' said Martin.

'We stole a cottage for the night and the horses,' said Isabel. 'I do not see why we cannot steal some meat as well.'

'Will we have to keep doing this? Stealing all the time?'

'Maybe. We could become bandits travelling from

town to town and taking what we want. Why, does it concern you?'

'No. Actually it sounds quite fun. Plus, if there are no laws to stop us, then what's there to be afraid of?' said Martin.

Isabel laughed. 'I said we broke no law sleeping in a farmer's house. We are planning to spend our lives going from town to town stealing. When they catch us, they will most certainly kill us.'

Isabel geed her horse and rode off at full speed towards the town.

'Kill us?' shouted Martin as he followed. 'And what do you mean by *when*?'

Martin and Isabel crossed the small river using a wooden bridge. It was the second bridge they'd encountered. The first one turned out to be a public toilet, constructed over the river so that the waste was carried away to become a problem for the settlement downstream.

The town was ahead of them, and unlike the village they had left that morning, this one was full of people. Today was market day.

Stalls were alive along both sides of the road as people begged and bartered for all manner of goods from vegetables and meats to cloth and animal hide. The atmosphere of the place gave Martin hope. He may be 400 years in the past, but people still acted the same; it was only the stuff that differed. Martin was amazed to see 17th century equivalents of fast food being served and eaten while people browsed the stalls.

'If only you had something amazing from the future that would impress people enough to give us free food. One of those moving pictures would have sufficed. They may think us a witch and wizard pair and fear us.'

'If I could do that at least we wouldn't be killed for stealing.'

Isabel walked over to a fruit cart and picked up an apple. It looked diseased when compared to the perfect apples Martin was used to seeing in supermarkets.

'True, but they would kill us for witchcraft, and that is a *very* unpleasant way to go.'

'I hope you're not thinking of taking that apple, young miss.'

Isabel looked up at the woman with large innocent eyes. 'Of course not. The very thought offends me! I was merely inspecting its fineness,' said Isabel as she held up the apple in front of the lady's face with her left hand while her right hand stole a couple of pears.

'Sadly, I have no money or anything to trade with you. Perhaps when I come back later you and your apples will still be here.'

'I'll be here 'til the lot's gone,' said the lady, completely won over by Isabel's innocent act.

Martin followed Isabel as she walked away from the cart. From behind him, he heard the old lady talk to herself.

'What a pretty young girl, but why do her and that boy wear such strange clothes?'

Martin stopped. He felt the back of his neck prickle.

'Because the children are dangerous and must be destroyed.'

Martin turned around. The old woman was staring right at him. Isabel still hadn't noticed. Martin reached for her hand and she threw a pear at him as she ate the other. Then Isabel spotted the woman.

'Uh oh,' she said with mock fear and mild excitement.

Martin shook his head. 'It's not about the pears.'

'Then what is it?'

The woman was away from her stall now and moving towards them.

'The children are dangerous and must be destroyed.'

Isabel's hand tightened around Martin's and she dropped the pear.

'Run!'

As Martin and Isabel ran through the crowds of people, more and more turned to watch. They asked questions, but not to each other and not to themselves.

'Who are those children?'

'Why do they run?'

'What are those peculiar clothes they wear?'

Each answer was the same. As soon as the question had been asked it appeared as an undisputable fact in their brain.

The children are dangerous and must be destroyed.

Some townsfolk ran after the children unarmed, confident in the ability of their strength alone, while others picked up items from market stalls that could be used to pierce, gouge and cut young flesh.

It didn't take long before everyone in sight of Martin and Isabel was asking the same questions. The answer never varied.

Martin and Isabel ran from the mob, but as more and more people ahead of them turned to discover what the commotion was, the threat began to surround them.

Martin noticed the townsfolk move slower until they all but stopped. Together they ran through the crowd like visitors in a museum of historical mannequins. Soon the anger and confusion on the faces of those they passed was gone and the crowd began to thin. They reached the outskirts of the town and stopped.

Time outside their little bubble sped up again as Isabel let go of Martin's hand and collapsed panting on the floor. He had been wondering if Isabel had needed to hold his hand when she slowed down time or if she did it because she wanted to. The truth was a bit of a blow, but it was fair to say they had slightly more important things to be dealing with at present.

'He can still control people, even out here?'

Martin nodded. They were hiding in a small wooded area near the edge of the town. Isabel was sat with her back against a thick oak while Martin watched for any approaching townsfolk.

'It makes sense, I think,' said Martin.

'You think?'

'All this stuff with Keepers is new to me too, so it's not like I'm an expert, but I think there's just one Keeper for each thing. One Keeper of Time, one Keeper of Portals, one Keeper of Questions, and so on, right?'

'Correct.'

'So if there's only ever one Keeper for each thing, then

it shouldn't matter where they are. The Keeper of Time still has to make sure time is correct, the Keeper of Portals has to make sure the doorways are properly connected and the Keeper of Questions—'

'Has to answer the questions of everyone in the world,' finished Isabel. She dug her finger into the rotting dirt before looking up at Martin. 'So it does not matter where we are, if someone sees us and asks the question, "What are those children wearing?" or "Where are those children going?", he will give them the answer?'

'I think so.'

Isabel stood up. 'So what can we do? If someone sees us they will ask a question, then he shall take control and they will come after us. That will cause a commotion, which will cause more people to ask questions and then they will chase us also.'

'Just like the town,' said Martin. 'Everywhere we go, it'll be the same. There's nowhere safe. Unless…'

'Unless what?' said Isabel.

'Unless we never see anyone again. That's the only way we can be safe.'

'Is it? What if he becomes stronger, strong enough to control us? He would not even need to control both of us, just the weakest. He could control me; make me kill you and then kill myself. We cannot do it. We cannot stay here.'

'What do you mean by here?'

Isabel smiled. 'I mean now. But if we cannot get through the door, then now is all we have. Returning to your time is not possible.'

Martin thought for a moment. Isabel had a limited control over her own time and anyone she touched. The one rule Martin had learnt for certain was that she couldn't make time go backwards. That was simply impossible, and it was probably as impossible for her as it was for the Keeper of Time himself. So far all Isabel had done was speed up her own time, so that for every second everyone else lived, she would live many more. This was what allowed her to move so much faster than everyone else. But that was only going one way. What if she slowed her time down so that every second she lived was many minutes lived by everyone else?

Isabel took Martin's hands. 'Are you certain this will work?'

'Not certain, just hopeful.'

The trees told Martin something had changed. The leaves shook violently in the wind as the outside world played out at speed around them. Birds darted between branches like rockets and red squirrels jumped from bough to bough as the sun rolled through the sky from its noon zenith to a large orange ball that shone through the thick oak trunks.

They caught up with the runaway outside world in a few seconds. Isabel blinked a number of times before letting go of Martin's hands and looking around the golden-hued copse that had been bathing in the noon-day sunlight only minutes ago.

'It worked.'

'Five or six hours must have passed,' said Martin.

'Yes,' said Isabel as she looked around in wonder. 'So what shall we do now?'

120

'We're in the middle of a wood. We can't just stand here for hundreds of years. People'll see us. Things around us will change. The trees will grow. Houses will be built. We need somewhere secluded, somewhere no one will ever find us.'

'I think I know where,' said Isabel.

'Are you sure? We'll be there for a very long time. It has to be somewhere that'll still be around in the future.'

Isabel nodded. 'It will still be there. The only problem is, we need to return to the master's house.'

The horses were where they had left them, tied to a tree on the other side of the town, but they weren't in best spirits and needed feeding before they'd even consider being ridden. Once that had been taken care of, Martin and Isabel left for the master's house.

Martin managed to stop his horse once they reached the edge of the master's estate. He jumped off and walked through the dark field until he was in front of the wind turbine. It was as high as a block of flats and thunderously loud. He placed his hands against its smooth metal surface as Isabel appeared by his side.

'It's really here, isn't it?' said Martin.

Isabel touched the wind turbine. 'What is it?'

'It's a wind turbine. It generates power from the air, kind of like a waterwheel. It turns a dynamo and that produces electricity.'

'What is electricity?'

'Exactly!' said Martin as he moved away from the wind turbine. 'Exactly! We're in the past. Nothing here needs electricity. You don't even know what it *is*! So why is there a wind turbine here? And why did I see a tractor? And why were you cooking at an electric oven? Just what the hell is going on?' Martin looked again to Isabel. 'This *is* the past, isn't it? I mean, really, actually the past and not just some crazy TV show with a massive budget and no eye for detail?'

'Martin, I've told you before. The year is 1623. To you this is the past. I do not know what this thing is nor do I know the other things you spoke of. But I can tell you one thing.' Isabel slapped her hand against the wind turbine, 'this was not here two days ago.'

'Only two days?' mused Martin. 'Isabel, has anybody else seen this?'

'It is somewhat prominent, only the man with a fixation on his shoes should miss it.'

'And have you heard anyone say anything about it, or talk about it at all?'

Isabel shook her head. 'They have not. I know that it has been seen by them, for I have watched them walk past it, but no one speaks of it. They either pretend it is not there or their eyes skip over it without them knowing.'

Martin picked up a large rock from the ground and threw it as hard as he could at the metal structure. It hit, making a very satisfying ding. It was definitely real. A wind turbine was here, in the past. Along with the existence of Keepers and the knowledge that if they stayed there any longer they were going to be killed, this was just something else Martin was going to have to deal with.

'A cave?' said Martin as he stood with Isabel at the top

of the cliffs. They'd tied the horses up at the edge of the estate and ran to the cliffs in less than ten seconds. Their return hadn't been detected, but that didn't mean they were safe. As soon as they were spotted, questions would be asked and, cave or no cave, there wouldn't be anywhere safe for them to hide.

'I found it when I first came here. The master hit me. I had never been hit like that before, so I ran away only to find myself by the cliffs. Then I started to climb down.'

'You climbed down?'

Isabel shrugged. She sat down on the edge of the cliff. 'I was being dramatic, fancying myself as the heroine in one of Mr Shakespeare's tragedies. I wanted to fall, just slip into the sea and sink beneath the waves. But I found the cave, so I remained in there for a time. Eventually my spirits were cheered by the solitude and I climbed out.'

Martin sat down next to Isabel. 'How far down is it?'

'Quite far. This was the middle of the day. The sun was high and the sea was calm. It was not like this at all.'

Isabel sighed and swung herself over the edge. She knocked off a few bits of stone but eventually managed to get a solid purchase. Martin did the same. He'd never had a problem with heights. He'd been climbing on school trips, but there was a big difference between climbing with a harness on attached to a rope and swinging yourself over the edge of hundred metre high cliffs in the dark. If he was scared of this, it was for a very good reason.

Martin heard Isabel slip. He looked down. She was still there, but her right leg was dangling with nothing beneath it. Several rocks fell into the sea, but the noise

123

their splashes made was swallowed by the waves crashing against the cliff's base.

'Are you OK?' Martin shouted down.

Isabel shook her head. 'I cannot do this. I was angry when I found the cave. I cared not if I fell, but now I do. I care, Martin. I do not wish to fall.'

Martin knew it was always going to be a matter of who broke first. He certainly wasn't comfortable on the cliff, and the wind bit into him with jagged fangs. If only the house wasn't so far away, then he could have used a door to get to the cave. But it was beyond his ability. They had no option but to climb.

Martin walked his legs up the cliff so he could lean back and survey its length. He spotted one. It was only a few metres to his left and up a little.

'Come to me,' shouted Martin over the crashing sea. 'I have a short cut.'

Confusion cut through Isabel's fear. 'A *short cut*?'

'Trust me!'

Martin tried to point to the little cave entrance he'd spotted. Isabel saw it and nodded. Martin's foot scraped against the cliff and a shower of stones fell to the sea. His left hand slipped and for a moment Martin was holding his entire weight with just his right hand. He felt the sweat working his grip loose, but he wouldn't let it. He couldn't fall – not here. Isabel needed him to get her to the cave, and he needed her to get them to the future. Either they both survived or neither of them did.

Martin grabbed a new rock with his left hand and kicked against the wall with his feet until they found something solid. Isabel was next to him and it didn't take them long to reach the cave.

It was only as deep as Martin's arm, but that wouldn't be a problem: they weren't staying there. The connection to Isabel's much larger cave was made and Martin helped her through before following.

Once inside, he closed the connection and the cave's true view of the sea appeared at its mouth. They were only a few metres above the crashing waves now. How Isabel had managed to climb here by herself that first time was a mystery. One thing Martin was certain of, if he hadn't created the shortcut, at least one of them would have fallen to their death.

Isabel had calmed down surprisingly fast once she was off the exposed face of the cliff.

'Shall we wait here?'

Martin shook his head. Isabel had already told him the cave was long, extending far from the sea, so he knew it would be a safe place to stay.

'We need to be as far from the sea as possible. You saw the house in my time. All this will go. The sea will erode it until it falls in. If we stay here, we'll fall into the sea with it.'

Martin and Isabel went as far into the cave as it was possible to go. By Martin's reckoning they were probably directly underneath the house. Once they found their spot, Martin insisted on using the loose rocks in the cave to block themselves in. The master had control over the Keeper of Portals. Surely there was nothing to stop him forcing the Keeper to search every doorway and gateway until he found them. If they blocked up the cave, then there would no longer be an entrance and nowhere for the Keeper to enter by.

Once Martin had finished blocking up the cave, he felt his way back to Isabel. They were already so far into the cave that all light had long since gone. But with the rocks in place, the lack of possible escape made it seem even darker.

'So what do we do now?' asked Martin.

'I slow down time and we wait.'

'Do you think you can do it? We'll need to be here for 400 years for this to work.'

'I think so. But do we really need to go that far forward? Could we not go fifty years into the future? The master will surely have forgotten us by then.'

Martin tried to make himself comfortable, but he couldn't find anywhere to sit that didn't have something poking him.

'He's a Keeper, not a human. He won't get old and die, he'll still be there in fifty years. We need the Keeper of Portals. My Keeper of Portals. He must know the master, the Keeper of Questions. He'll know how to help us.'

'Do you think the master still lives in your time?'

'I don't know. Maybe. But he'll have killed me as a child if he knew I was going to grow up to be a problem for him.'

'But the Keeper of Portals went missing? How will we find him?'

'He told me he'd been waiting in that house for 400 years. But he also said he hadn't spoken to anyone for

126

almost that long, so we can't see him during that time. I suppose he must also get freed by the master at some point, but I don't know when that is.'

'Well, we should go to the last time you saw him.'

'Yeah,' said Martin. 'Maybe I'll run into myself and tell him not to go through that door in the first place.'

Martin waited for Isabel to make some kind of comment, but she remained silent. Martin had meant it as a joke, but it didn't appear to have been taken as one. It was a while before Isabel spoke again.

'What was the time and date you last saw the Keeper of Portals?'

Martin felt Isabel take his hands as he told her, just before he'd fallen asleep on the night he found the crystal. The crystal that was so similar to the one now embedded in Isabel's forehead.

'When I slow down our time,' said Isabel, 'it will make everything around us appear to travel much faster.'

'OK,' said Martin.

'So if our time is slowed down ten times and someone throws a stone at us, it will feel like that stone is hitting us ten times faster than it had been thrown.'

'That sounds pretty dangerous.'

'It is.'

'So why are you telling me this?' said Martin.

'Because I shall slow down our time *a lot* more than ten times.'

'And?'

'And I hope these caves are not prone to falling rocks.'

CHAPTER
ELEVEN

Waves battered the solid cliffs that refused to yield. Though as time sped past, the cliffs found themselves losing to the sea's persistent attack. Massive overhangs would form and quickly lose their grip, tons of rock disappearing in an instant. As hundreds of years passed in the waking of a kitten, the sea's assault appeared relentless and the land retreated without a fight.

Life in England continued. Monarchy changed from James I to Charles I, through the Protectorate, on to Charles II, James II, Mary II and further. Countless battles were fought and lives lost across the country. The Great Plague of London swept the city in 1665 before the Great Fire finished it off in 1666. Newton's *Principia* was published in 1687, 1756 was the start of the Seven Year War with the French and in 1789 the last execution by burning occurred. In 1819 Queen Victoria was born, in 1837 she was crowned and in 1901 she died. World War I started in 1914 and ended in 1918. World War II started in 1939 and ended in 1945. In 2006, Darwin's tortoise died at the age of 176 and on the 9th of September 2015, Queen Elizabeth II of the House of Windsor became the longest serving monarch in British history.

History charged forward with no concern for Martin and Isabel trapped in the cave. But as this history continued, there was another one fighting for dominance. It was a history that was not supposed to exist. A history that was growing in strength. Powerful hands were keeping the competing timelines apart, but those hands were growing weary and it wouldn't be long before they surrendered.

Martin fell backwards as Isabel let go of his hands. They were together in the cave and light was coming in through the cracks in the wall.

Martin moved over to Isabel and helped her sit. She appeared dazed, like she'd spent ten rounds in a boxing ring. But she had managed to slow down their subjective time so much that 400 years had passed in less than a minute.

'How do you feel?'

Isabel nodded in the weak light. 'Tired, but uninjured.'

'I can't believe you did that! We literally travelled forward in time 400 years! It makes my power seem like nothing.'

Isabel tried to stand, but she was still too weak. Martin caught her and lowered her back to the cave's floor.

''Tis strange. I knew exactly when to stop.'

Isabel stood with a little assistance and stumbled towards the wall of rocks Martin had created. They had been there for 400 years and were now solidly in place. No amount of grunting or straining was going to budge them.

Isabel punched the wall with the side of her fist.

'Caves do not appear to have changed much in 400

years. Would I be correct in assuming we have no other means of leaving?'

Martin walked over to the wall. He pushed a few rocks, pulled a few more, but none of them moved. Through a large crack he was able to see the sea. The tunnel they had travelled through had long since vanished. All that remained of the cave was an area no longer than a car and only just tall enough to stand in.

Now that some light was coming in through the cracks, Martin could see there were still quite a few rocks remaining.

'I can get us out of here,' said Martin with a slight note of unease.

'But?' said Isabel.

'But I'm going to need your help.'

Martin picked up another rock and sized it up before going for a different one. He walked over to Isabel and placed it near the top of her back. She strained slightly under the weight.

'I know I have told you this many times before, but these rocks are astonishingly heavy!'

'Sorry,' said Martin as he placed another rock near Isabel's neck. 'It's all I could think of.'

'Fine! But next time you shall do this part!'

Martin had asked Isabel to crouch down on the floor and then rise slightly. He had then placed rocks around her, creating an arch that would hold itself together under its own weight.

Once the closest thing Martin could find to a keystone

had been placed in the centre, Isabel slipped out from underneath the arch. 'If you had told me you were going to build a bridge around me then I would have considered hiding somewhere else,' she said as she rubbed her back.

'I thought I'd be able to take down the wall. Sorry.'

'Do not concern yourself. So, shall we use this to get to your house?'

'That's the plan.'

Martin sat down in front of the stone arch and concentrated. Bright light appeared in the cave, streaming in through the open windows of the room on the other side of the newly created portal.

Martin decided to crawl through first, just to make sure the connection was safe. He came out into a room of the house he hadn't seen before, or if he had, it hadn't left an impression. At the windows, Martin surveyed the remains of the once proud garden. He even spotted his mum's car parked under a dead tree. Something tugged at his insides. He was home.

'Is it safe?' called Isabel from inside the cave.

'Yeah, it's safe.'

Martin watched as Isabel wiggled herself through the arch. She was coming in too fast and not paying attention to what her limbs were doing. Her elbow knocked a stone at the bottom of the arch. The distorted image of Isabel in the doorway wavered dramatically. The rocks were going to fall.

Martin ran across the room and grabbed Isabel's hands. He pulled her as hard as he could and Isabel came flying out of the door and straight on top of Martin. The image of the cave crumbled the moment Isabel was through.

Isabel looked down at Martin, her hair falling over his face.

'One is supposed to proposition a lady first, Martin.'

Martin took a moment to catch his breath.

'Your elbow,' he said between breaths, 'it caught the arch. It was falling.'

'The arch was falling? Oh. So if you had not so gallantly leapt to my aid, what would have become of me?'

'Well,' said Martin. 'You'd still be here.'

'But?'

'But only your top half.'

Isabel made a face and stood up. 'Well, I suppose you did owe me for building a bridge on my back,' she said as she banged the cave grit from her clothes. 'By my reckoning that makes us even. What say you?'

'I wasn't really keeping track.'

'You weren't?' said Isabel with a smile. 'Well in that case I retract my previous statement. Now that I think about it, I believe you still owe me.'

Martin walked with Isabel towards his bedroom. He couldn't believe it, he was actually going to meet himself face to face. What would he say? He was the one from the future, so surely he must spout a prophecy of some kind, probably something along the lines of *don't go through that door, an insane Keeper will lock you away and try to kill you by controlling the minds of peasants.* But if Martin said those things, then what would happen? He'd never go through the door, never meet Isabel and life would continue as normal. Sure, things were dangerous now, but he couldn't say it wasn't exciting. Did he really want to go back to his old life, just him and his mum in this massive house, alone with no friends? And what about Isabel? He wouldn't just not meet her, he would un-meet her, if such a thing were possible. Martin turned a corner in the corridor and passed by the stairs where the portrait of the old lady hung. Then he entered a different corridor with very little light and doors on either side. He was surprised by how well he knew the house. Isabel had paused to marvel at the painting for a moment before returning to Martin.

Martin realised that if he did try and talk to his past self he would create a paradox, an event that's very existence is a contradiction. As every science fiction film he'd ever seen told him that would be a bad idea, he decided not to bother.

Walking became difficult as Martin got closer to his room. It felt like someone had tied bungee cords to his back and after a few steps he had to stop completely. He turned to Isabel. She had stopped walking as well, but stranger than that, her feet were actually sliding backwards. Martin looked down and realised his were too.

Eventually they stopped sliding and stood at the far end of the corridor. It didn't look any different. Even when they had felt like they were walking through treacle, the air was still transparent. It was only the feeling that was wrong.

'What just happened?' said Martin.

'I have no idea. I believe we were pushed.'

'Well I didn't see anyone. Did you?'

Isabel shook her head.

Martin walked down the corridor again while Isabel waited. He made it further this time, but eventually he got to a point where he had to stop. Once more he was pushed away and back to Isabel.

'I don't get it,' said Martin.

'Neither do I. Could you not create a doorway to your bedroom?'

'Good idea!'

Martin went up to a room, concentrated and tried to open the door.

'It won't open.'

Martin was turning the handle as hard as he could, but it refused to move.

'Maybe it is stiff,' said Isabel. 'Try a different one.'

Martin walked up to another door, visualised his bedroom door and tried to open it. Nothing happened.

Without using the power from the Keeper, Martin tried the door again. This time it opened with ease and Martin almost lost his balance from pushing too hard.

'Well the door opens, so that can't be it.'

Martin tried again, but not just his bedroom door. He tried his bedroom windows, wardrobe, drawers, he even tried an unpacked box, but nothing would open.

Martin wiped away the sweat that was beading on his forehead and without a word, sprinted as fast as he could.

This time he didn't feel the treacle. There was no gradual build-up of resistance, instead it felt like he'd run into an invisible brick wall. The next thing he knew he was being flung back the length of the corridor, not even touching the floor until he reached Isabel.

Martin stood up. He dusted himself down, lowered his head, and charged again.

Martin kept on running down the corridor, and each time he did he was met with an invisible resistor that tossed him back the way he'd come.

After his sixth attempt, Isabel grabbed his hand and pulled him away.

'You are being an idiot. All you will achieve is hurting yourself. We will have to get to your room another way. Follow me, I know where to go.'

Martin was following Isabel when the reality of what had just happened dawned on him. He stopped Isabel and spun her around. 'I can't get to the room,' he said.

'At all?'

'At all. I'm being stopped, and I'm being stopped for a reason.'

'Why would someone stop you? This is your house.'

Martin shook his head. 'It's not like that. I never saw my future self when I was with the Keeper. I didn't see you either. If I went into that room and saw myself, then it would be a paradox. The me that's in the room saw his future self, but the me that went into the room never saw *his* future self when he was in that room. Does that make sense?'

'Absolutely not,' said Isabel.

'Basically, if I go into that room, then I'll be making something happen that never happened. That can't be allowed, so something's stopping me from doing it.'

'Another Keeper?'

'I think so. When I was pushed back, I definitely felt hands on me.'

Isabel looked back to where they'd come from. 'So what do we do, wait for the Keeper to go somewhere else?'

'I think he was with me until I fell asleep, so we'll have to wait until then.'

'What do we do now?' asked Isabel.

'Well,' said Martin, 'it's been 400 years since either of us ate.'

After raiding the kitchen, Martin and Isabel took their carefully cradled armfuls of food into a room on the first floor on the side by the sea. Isabel had been equally impressed and disgusted by modern food. While she delighted in such things as chocolate and sliced ham, she complained the bread lacked flavour and that fizzy drinks actually hurt her mouth.

Once they'd eaten as much as they could manage, Isabel got up and started to look around the room.

''Tis sad to see the house look as it does. If it were a person then it would be ready to die, having already lived the most exciting years of its life. All that is left is for it to fall quietly into the sea.'

'It doesn't fall quietly anywhere,' said Martin. 'A few nights ago my mum said some of it fell in and it woke her up. I didn't hear it, though. Oh wait, that wasn't a couple of nights ago, that's tonight, or tomorrow. I'm not sure which. I'm still trying to get my head around when I am.'

Martin heard Isabel rummaging through an old chest behind him.

'What're you doing?' he called.

'I have found some clothes.'

Martin turned around to see Isabel in a half state of undress. He didn't see anything he wasn't supposed to, but still more than he'd expected. He quickly turned away, hearing Isabel laugh behind him.

'I shall become complacent if you keep blushing and giving me privacy. I may start expecting other things.'

'Like what?' said Martin.

There were a few rustling noises and the sound of fabric being torn before Isabel strode into Martin's view.

'Compliments.'

Isabel stood in front of Martin wearing a hideous dress that had probably been sitting in that trunk since the Victorian times. There were moth holes in the arms and a stain that may once have been wine, or was possibly blood, over the chest. Isabel twirled.

'I have never seen a dress so beautiful!'

Martin just stared. There was nothing he could say to that. The dress was awful: unequivocally, unabashedly awful. But Isabel was happy, and in part, that made Martin happy. She knelt down in front of him, tucking the dress beneath her knees.

'Do you not think it pretty?'

There was something pretty in front of Martin, but it certainly wasn't the dress.

'It's seen better days, that's for sure.'

Isabel picked at the fabric. 'Perhaps, but compared to my clothes it is elegant, if not somewhat impractical for my needs.'

'So what's it like being a maid?' said Martin. 'You know, apart from dealing with the master. Like, what do you do for fun in the past?'

'Fun?' said Isabel as she cocked her head to one side. 'What do you mean?'

'Like hobbies, or playing with friends. Did you get to do anything like that?'

Isabel thought for a moment.

'I used to press flowers.'

'Press flowers?'

Isabel nodded, her face lighting up as she reminisced. 'This was when I was younger, before I was with the master, when things were… different. I would go out and pick flowers and then press them between the pages of a book. The only book I had at the time was the Holy Bible. We had many bibles in the house; they were all very religious. Sometimes they would go to read the bible and all these flowers would fall out. They never knew it was me.'

'Your hobby was making flowers flat?' said Martin.

Isabel stared at Martin with a hint of disdain before speaking.

'You think my hobby buffle, don't you?'

'Buffle?'

'Foolish,' Isabel clarified.

'No, no, it's not that. I mean, well, yeah, it kind of is. It's just, I don't really see you as the type who goes around picking flowers.'

'I was,' said Isabel, 'back then.'

Nothing more was said. Martin had clearly forced Isabel to open a part of her history she'd wished to remain shut. While she hadn't divulged anything about her past, Martin was glad that she'd allowed something to slip through. He didn't just want to know her as the girl who worked for the master and could slow down and speed up time; he wanted to know her as Isabel, the supposedly sixteen year old girl who'd saved his life, whose life he too had saved.

'And you?' said Isabel. 'What occupies your free time?'

'Not a lot right now. My mum and I only just moved here and so far you're the only person I've met.'

'Your father, where is he?'

'Dead,' said Martin.

The word lingered in the room for a few uncomfortable minutes before Isabel spoke.

'Did he die recently?'

'I guess. Ish. I don't know, really. Sometimes it feels like it was last week but then other times I can't even remember what he looked like, or how his voice sounded or what his aftershave smelled of. I don't know. I guess that part of me thinks in here,' Martin tapped his head, 'it will always be recent.'

'We do not have to talk about him, if you do not wish to.'

'No, I think I should. I think that's been the problem… not talking about him, I mean. I guess I've just never found anyone I wanted to talk to.'

Isabel took Martin's hand. Their time didn't change.

'His name was Graham and he died when he was forty-four. I was thirteen. It was pancreatic cancer. You probably don't know what that is because in your time everyone dies of dysentery or typhoid before they even get the chance to develop cancer, but that's what killed my dad and it was fast.'

Martin let out a long breath. He knew he needed to do

this, but that didn't make it easy. Isabel remained quiet and continued to hold his hand.

'He was hospitalised as soon as he was diagnosed. My mum left her job straight away so she could be with him, but I just kept on going to school.'

Isabel's eyes widened at Martin's mention of school, but she didn't voice her amazement.

'My mum begged me to go to the hospital and see him, but I never did. It's not that I didn't want to see him, I just didn't want to see him in there. I can't explain it well, but I just thought that hospitals are where people go to die and if I saw him in there then that would be it. If I didn't then it was just like he was away on a work trip or something. Even though I knew the truth and knew he was going to die, I wouldn't go and see him.'

Isabel squeezed Martin's hand and he squeezed it back. Martin saw the countless questions simmering under the surface of Isabel's skin, but she continued to remain quiet and let him speak.

'I tried to talk to people at school about it, but no one really understood. They weren't going through what I was going through so just found it awkward and tried to ignore me. When I did find people who would speak to me, they didn't help, even though at the time I thought they did.

'They told me he was going to a better place and that one day I would be there too; then we could spend all of our time together, just me and my dad. I believed them. It wasn't hard because I wanted to believe them so much it just happened without me realising. All the time I was talking to these people my mum was pleading with me to see my dad. She would scream at me and threaten to call the police to take me to the hospital by force, but she never did. I refused to go, telling her that I would see my dad again in this better place.'

Martin let go of Isabel's hand and closed his eyes. He wanted to believe he was telling this part only to himself.

'Then my dad died. It was a Sunday. My mum was in hospital and I was at home watching a movie on TV. It was a James Bond film, *Casino Royale*. Bond revealed his straight flush when the ringing started and Le Chiffre had left the table when she hung up. *He's gone.* That was all she said.'

Martin opened his eyes again. 'I was wrong. I should have listened to my mum. There's no *better place* where I'm going to see my dad again. He's gone forever and I have to live knowing that I didn't go and say goodbye to him when I had the chance.'

Isabel wiped away her tears with the torn fabric of the Victorian dress.

'Me not seeing my dad must have broken my mum apart. I can't be trusted to make the right choices, that's what I've learned. When something big comes up, I just take the easy option and then have to deal with all the shit later.'

'Do not be so hasty,' said Isabel. 'You knew the master was evil and that he wished to do me harm. I would not hear of it but you were determined to pull me away, even when you professed to hating me. You saved me from him, Martin, and in doing so you saved my life. So perhaps not every decision you make is ill-fated.'

141

Martin smiled. 'Thanks. And, you know, thanks for listening.'

'You're welcome,' said Isabel. 'And thank you for telling me. I know it was hard.'

The only sound in the room was Martin's breathing as he slept. Inside the wardrobe, the future version of Martin and Isabel sat in wait for the Keeper of Portals. Upon entering the room, it was the only place they were able to remain without the hands of the unknown Keeper pushing them out, though that didn't mean they felt nothing. Martin was asleep in his bed, so would not be aware of a presence in his room, but the force on Martin and Isabel was evident enough and the message was clear. *You may stay in this room, but remain out of sight.* Clearly, if the Keeper of Portals were to return, then they were not to meet him that night. But Martin had elected to stay, because this was the night the door would be opened for the first time in 400 years.

The Keeper of Portals stepped into the room through Martin's bedroom door. Behind him was a bright beach with a rich blue sea lapping at its shore, but that disappeared as soon as the door was shut.

The Keeper crept forward and regarded the sleeping Martin for a moment. He bent down, ready to shake him awake, when he noticed something on the table next to Martin's bed.

Martin moved his shoulder slightly to wake Isabel. She had been asleep for the last hour, curled up against him. Martin held a finger over her lips to silence her. Isabel nodded. Together they watched from inside the wardrobe as the Keeper of Portals bent down and picked up the glowing crystal from Martin's bedside table. It was the one he had found in the sealed room, the same room the master had locked him in.

The Keeper of Portals held the crystal level with his face, watching as the mix of cerulean and turquoise light swept over the walls. He turned to the end of the room, where the door was, before looking at the crystal once more.

The Keeper of Portals opened his mouth and swallowed the crystal whole.

As he walked to the end of Martin's bedroom, a gash appeared in the centre of the Keeper's perfectly white forehead before the tear shaped crystal started to protrude from his skin.

At the door, the Keeper of Portals reached out his hand and grasped the handle. He waited for a moment before turning it.

The fabric of the room started to fold in on itself over and over again. The Keeper of Portals struggled against the door, fighting its unwillingness to form a link.

As Martin watched, he could partly understand what was happening. When you make a connection, you have to seek out an exit door. The same must be true with a doorway through time. The Keeper of Portals was searching for an exit *time*. But he was the Keeper of Portals, not the Keeper of Time. He had no control over when the door led to. There must be another force controlling that, maybe even the crystal itself.

Then, suddenly, two things happened.

The crystal on the Keeper of Portals' forehead exploded in a shower of blue sparks that shot, spun and twirled their way around the room, illuminating everything in perfect detail. The other thing that happened was that the door at the end of Martin's bedroom opened for the first time in almost four hundred years.

Martin had to reposition himself in the wardrobe to get a better view, even though the Keeper of Portals was blocking most of it, but he just about managed to make out the master's study on the other side. And more than that, there was someone in the room.

It was Isabel.

CHAPTER
TWELVE

Isabel approached the shuttered shelves at the end of the master's study. Pausing for a moment, she checked the door before focusing on the bronze clasp. Isabel took a deep breath, and like lightning, her hand shot up.

The noise of the unhitching clasp was almost deafening. Isabel's head flicked involuntarily towards the door. No one came in. She grabbed the shutters and threw them wide open.

On shelves that reached from the floor all the way to the ceiling were jars larger than Isabel's head, and in each of them was a creature unlike any known animal.

At first the creatures cowered, pushing themselves as far back into their jars as possible, but soon the apprehension faded and the creatures moved forward. Some of them pressed their hands, or hand equivalents, against the glass while others tried to call out to Isabel with voices too quiet to discern.

Isabel walked towards the creature directly in front of her. It was small, no bigger than her hand, and appeared to be almost human in design, but with longer limbs and a head that appeared part rodent – not brutal like that of a rat, but kind and inquisitive like a field mouse. The creature was naked and its body was covered by a shimmering fur. Wings grew from its back, made from many strands of thick golden hair that danced behind the creature in a manner that managed to keep it afloat. Isabel smiled.

'Good day.'

The creature looked back at her, confused for a moment, before smiling and performing a little bow.

Isabel reached out her hands to remove the jar from the shelf when she heard a noise behind her. She spun around to see the door at the end of the master's study open. Immediately Isabel ran for the shutters and closed them, locking the clasp back in place. She walked towards the open door and the bizarre creature that stood on the other side of it.

Martin watched as Isabel walked towards the door where the Keeper of Portals stood. Beside him was the other Isabel who looked on silently. There was a difference between the two Isabels, aside from their attire. The Isabel who now stood in the master's study had no crystal on her forehead. This was Isabel from the past.

'Who are you?' asked Isabel

The Keeper of Portals was about to speak when Isabel's eyes dulled over.

'*You* are not supposed to be here.'

Isabel ran back to the fireplace as the Keeper of Portals stepped through the threshold and into the past. Suddenly the Keeper hunched over. He managed to straighten himself slightly, looking around the room with large confused eyes before taking another step forward. His long, blue feathers fell to the floor like autumn leaves as he stumbled forward another step, too disorientated to see Isabel advancing on him. By the time he noticed her it was too late.

The poker speared the Keeper of Portals right through the middle, tearing his rubber-like skin and spilling his blood onto the floor.

Martin watched in shock as Isabel yanked the poker from the Keeper's body and used it to repeatedly beat his head. Beside him, the other Isabel started to scream. She was shaking and clawing at the wardrobe door, trying to open it fully as she watched a past version of herself attack the defenceless Keeper of Portals.

'What are you doing?' shouted Martin.

'That is not me! I am not doing that!'

'Yes you are!' cried Martin. 'You're killing him!'

'It is the master, he must be inside my head! He is controlling me!' Isabel wiped the tears from her eyes. 'It is not me doing that. 'Tis him. I promise!'

Martin burst through the wardrobe doors and dragged Isabel with him. This couldn't be it. The Keeper of Portals couldn't just die here. If he did, then there would be no one to help them. They would be alone. And what's more the door was open. Maybe the only reason they had been able to survive for four hundred years was because the master had used the door to Martin's time to kill them. Just because the master wasn't able to go through, that didn't mean he couldn't send a hoard of brainwashed villagers into the future to massacre them as they slept.

Martin pushed Isabel towards the door.

'It's *your* past self – you stop her!'

Isabel ran to the door that led to the master's study, but as soon as she got near she was forced back into a pile of boxes stacked by the side of Martin's wall. She picked herself up again and ran for the door as fast as she could, aiming at the past version of herself that continued to brutalise the cowering Keeper. Again she was flung back into the room, as if what was preventing her access actually wished her harm. This time when she stood, Isabel was serious. She ripped off the Victorian dress to reveal a silk underdress and ran for the door. Time around her slowed down as she dramatically ramped up her own subjective time as fast as she could in an attempt to overpower the Keeper trying to stop her.

The hands caught her before she even managed to cross the threshold into the other room. Isabel flew through the air in slow motion as Martin watched horrified. Before she made contact with the floor, she twisted her body so her feet were down and returned her time to normal.

'I cannot get through,' panted Isabel. 'That thing stops me.'

Martin had no other option. He ran for the master's study. Would he too be pushed out and forced to watch as the Keeper of Portals was beaten to death?

Martin made it through the door. He could enter the room, but then there hadn't been a conscious past version of himself in there. Martin ran for the Keeper who lay crumpled on the floor as Isabel stood over him, beating him with the blood-stained fire poker.

He wrenched the fire poker from Isabel's hands and threw it to the floor as he pulled Isabel away from the

Keeper. She fought him, punching and kicking, but her relentless attack on the Keeper had made her weak so most of her strikes failed to connect and the ones that did lacked power.

Martin grabbed hold of Isabel's shoulders and started to push her away from the Keeper as she continued to pummel him.

'What should I do?' shouted Martin into his bedroom.

Isabel was as close to the door as she could get; the invisible force constantly pushing her away made it look like she was running on the spot. She looked at the Keeper of Portals, who lay barely alive at the side of the master's study, and then at the younger version of herself with hatred in her eyes as she tried to fight her way free. Finally she turned to Martin, her gaze firm. She rubbed the side of her face and smiled.

'Punch her!' she cried.

There was nothing Martin could do to the Isabel he fought that hadn't already been done to the other Isabel. That was how paradoxes were kept at bay. Surely that meant he couldn't actually hurt her, even if he tried to. The attack would be stopped by a power much greater than his own.

Martin clenched his fist and brought it up. He swung at Isabel with all the strength he could muster, twisting his hips as the swing came around to provide it even more power.

Martin's fist connected with Isabel's face, the full force of his punch smashed into her right temple. Isabel instantly lost consciousness and collapsed to the floor.

Isabel ran through the door and into the master's study. Now that her past self lay in an unconscious heap on the floor, there was no longer the threat of the two of them interacting.

She cradled the broken body of the Keeper of Portals in her arms. Despite his height he was amazingly light and Isabel was able to hold him with ease.

'He is still alive, but badly hurt. We must do something.'

Martin walked over to Isabel. 'We have to get out of here before the master sees us.'

They ran to the door, the Keeper trailing blood and feathers as they went. As Martin approached the door he felt the familiar push impeding his progress. He saw his past self fidgeting in bed. He was beginning to wake.

Isabel was back in Martin's bedroom. The Keeper of Portals was limp in her arms and so long his feet and head almost touched the floor. When Isabel moved the Keeper, blood was flicked over the walls and the wardrobe and when she was still it fell in thick globules along with the ever shedding blue feathers.

'Martin, what is wrong? Why won't you come?'

Martin forced a foot forward but it refused to stay.

'It's the past me, he's waking up. I remember this. I woke up in the middle of the night. You need to go.'

Isabel held his gaze for a moment then nodded. In an eye blink she had vanished, accelerating her subjective time and running from the room.

Martin watched as his past self tossed and turned. He too was being moved in the bed. They were like magnets of the same polarity, forcing each other apart. The more

150

Martin moved forward, the more he pushed his other self against the wall. There was nothing else for it. Martin went further into the master's study and away from the door until he could feel the repulsion no more.

He watched, hiding behind the large bookcase in the far corner of the room. He knew his past self would not see him because he had no memory of that.

The waking Martin rolled over and surveyed his bedroom with eyes that resented being pulled from their rest. Then he saw the blood and jumped out of the bed.

Martin watched as his past self picked up one of the curly feathers shed by the Keeper of Portals and studied it for a moment. Then he noticed the door.

He walked forward, previously half-closed eyes now fully alert as they shot around the room on the other side of the door. Then they fell upon Isabel and her crumpled body lying unconscious on the floor.

Martin remembered. Isabel didn't stay unconscious.

Her dress moved first before she rolled over and checked her apron and headscarf. She stood slowly and Martin saw his past self take a few cautious steps forward before he started to jog into the room.

'What happened?' said a voice Martin knew as his own.

Isabel was facing the window and turned to watch Martin's past self enter the room. Suddenly she lunged forward, grabbing the fire poker as she ran and holding it high and ready to spear.

Martin tried to recall what had happened after Isabel had charged at him, but the memory wasn't there. Then it came, someone had moved at the back of the master's study.

Without even thinking, Martin understood what he had to do. He sprinted for the open window on the other side of the room. As soon as he was out from behind the bookcase he could feel the hands of the invisible Keeper begin to crush him harder than ever before. His past self could see him now, and that was a problem.

The hands suddenly switched, now they were pushing Martin faster than he could run. He jumped onto the desk and was practically thrown out of the second storey window in order to avoid him interacting with his past self.

Martin smiled as he sailed through the air: he had no intention of leaving the room.

The connection took him back inside and out of the wardrobe his past self was standing next to. As the wardrobe doors flew open he could see himself in the middle of the room and the tip of the fire poker that was nearly touching his chest.

The force of the mysterious Keeper threw the two Martins apart before they could collide. His past self was hurled at the wall while Martin shot back into the open wardrobe and in through the window at the far end of the master's study. He sailed over the desk and managed to curl himself into a ball and protect his head before he too crashed into a wall.

Picking himself up, Martin realised there was no time left to waste. His past self may have avoided getting skewered, but Isabel was still in the room, armed and angry.

Wincing with the pain, Martin ran for Isabel. Her back was to him and she hadn't moved, probably in shock over the two Martin's flying through the air. Before she got the chance to advance on the unconscious form of Martin's past self, he had grabbed her by the shoulders and thrown her into a wardrobe, connecting it to the first doorway he could find.

Martin never knew he was this heavy. Maybe it was because his past self was asleep that made carrying him so awkward. He wasn't sure. It was strange to think that if someone had told him a week ago he would be carrying a past version of himself and putting him to bed, he would have said they were completely insane, but with everything else that had been going on, this was considered downtime.

He dropped his sleeping self onto the bed and pulled the duvet over him. Martin faced his bedroom door, the one that led to the corridor and not to a different time. Isabel had left through there with the injured Keeper of Portals to take him somewhere safe. Martin wanted to follow, but knew he couldn't, not yet.

He'd thrown Isabel into that wardrobe and made a connection with the first doorway he could find. She may not be the Isabel that Martin knew, but she would become her. That meant he had to find her and make sure she was safe. And if she was safe, he had to stop her from going back into the master's study and through the door at the end to butcher his past self while he slept.

The Keeper of Portals was away from danger now; that

was all that mattered. And Isabel would keep it that way, Martin was sure of it.

Martin left his sleeping self and walked across his blood-splattered floor to the door at the end of his bedroom. He stepped back into Isabel's time, closing the door behind him.

Martin ran from room to room trying to find where he'd dumped Isabel. She was in the house, he knew that much, but in a building that had more rooms than most villages that wasn't overly helpful.

Martin searched bedrooms, parlours, sitting rooms and dining rooms, but even after looking through over 100 rooms, he still hadn't managed to find Isabel.

Martin flung open the door at the end of the cellar and burst his way into the largest living room he had ever seen. The fire in the oversized hearth was roaring away and sitting in front of it in an equally oversized chair and reading a book was the master of the house.

'*Who* are *you* and what, pray tell, are you doing in my house?'

He was young, before he had weakened himself by opening the door to Martin's time.

'I said, what are you doing in my house?'

Martin closed his mind. If he started asking questions then he would become just another of the master's puppets. This master was young and strong. It wouldn't take much for him to get inside Martin's head.

Martin shrugged his shoulders as the master rose slowly from his seat, leaving the book on a cushion, and walked over to Martin before grabbing him by the shoulder. He moved his face close. His skin was perfect and he even smelled pleasant, though Martin tried not to think about that. A frown crested the master's brow.

'Do you not have a question? Do you not wonder who I am?'

The master studied Martin once more, but when it was obvious that Martin wouldn't respond he pulled him by the shoulder and marched him out of the house.

'The girl brought you in. I was always concerned that one so young and pretty would attract the attention of local dullards.'

The master stopped at the door and bent down to Martin's level. He looked confused for a moment and fingered Martin's T-shirt before whispering in his ear.

'What transpires in this house is of no concern to you or anyone else from the village. They have the sense to keep away.' The master rapped on Martin's head as one would a door. 'Perhaps there is a brain so dim that even I cannot reach into it. Usually stupidity welcomes me, but it appears that at some point it grows so encumbered it is unable to even open the door.'

The master patted Martin on the back.

'One more thing before you leave. If I am to ever see you in my house again you will find yourself starving to death within its bowels. This is a fate which I would find most intriguing. However, the work of someone as busy as myself is never complete. Of this fact, you are most fortunate.'

With that the master grabbed Martin by the arm and hurled him through the door.

CHAPTER
THIRTEEN

Martin waited a moment before running back to the front door and opening it into a spare bedroom. He still needed to find Isabel before he could return to his time, threats from the master or not.

Eventually he found her curled up in a heap inside a wardrobe. It was after searching every one of the house's 354 rooms that he realised he needed to look in everything that had a door, not just the rooms. And there she was inside the wardrobe of the 232nd room, sleeping peacefully.

Martin reached in and carefully picked her up. She felt small beneath her thick, dirty clothes and her head fell against his chest. She didn't wake, or make any noise except for her soft breathing. Martin had to stop himself from staring at her too long.

The room didn't contain a bed, but after going into every room of the house, Martin knew which ones had furniture and stepped through into a modestly sized room with a neat little bed in one corner.

He set Isabel down and tucked the blankets around her. A few locks of her hair had worked themselves loose and Martin brushed them back under her headscarf. The bruise that Martin had seen when Isabel was in the kitchen was starting to come through. After all the anger he'd felt towards the master, he couldn't believe that he'd been the one to cause it.

Martin left the room where Isabel slept peacefully and made a connection to the master's study, ready to return to his time and find his Isabel and the Keeper of Portals.

The room was still dirty. Thinking back, he remembered it being clean that first time he'd stepped into the past. He knew that if he didn't clean it now, it would be Isabel that had to do it. And that would be after she received a beating for making the mess in the first place. Leaving her to take the blame was as bad as hitting her himself. Martin found a cloth and some water and cleaned the master's study as quickly as he could. Once he was finished he surveyed the room. It looked exactly like it had that first time he'd stepped into the past.

Martin's hand was on the handle when he turned around and saw it at the far end of the room. He left the door and walked back into the master's study.

As soon as he'd decided what he had to do, he was shoved halfway across the floor. He picked himself up and faced the shuttered shelves. Isabel had closed them after her snooping, but all he had to do was unhook the clasp and slide back the shutters, then he'd be able to free the Keeper of Buttons and the rest of the Minor Keepers before the master was able to consume them.

Martin didn't bother trying to walk towards the shelves. If he was going to do this, he needed to run.

Martin charged. As soon as he was within a metre of

the shelves he felt the hands on him and he was hurled to the back of the room. He instantly jumped up and ran, but again he was pushed away.

'I know you're in here,' said Martin, 'so there's no point hiding.'

Martin looked around the room, but no-one new appeared. He focused on the shelves again and flew towards them. This time when he was pushed back it was with more force.

'That wasn't very nice,' said Martin. He'd tried to roll when he landed but he hadn't timed it quite right. A snake of pain ran from his right shoulder all the way down his back.

'I don't get it,' said Martin. 'He's a Keeper like you. I'm just trying to save his life.'

Martin ran again. This time when he was pushed back it was gentler and Martin landed on his feet.

Martin focused on the death of the Keeper of Buttons, how his tiny faery body had been snapped backwards by the master's tongue and his black eyes went dull as life deserted him.

'I don't care that I saw him die. If that's the only difference I'll just forget it.'

Martin charged once more. This was his fastest yet, but again he was pushed away, this time not so gently.

'You're a coward!' shouted Martin. 'You can let me save him, you know you can!'

Martin started to run, shouting to the invisible Keeper as he went. 'The world won't end just because I saved his life!'

As he approached the shelves, a figure appeared before him. She was beautiful and dressed in white robes that moved as if she were underwater. Her hair was long and purple and reached to the floor. Behind the woman's translucent form Martin was still able to make out the shelves. The lady slowly held up her hands as anger ran across her face.

Martin's chest collided with her palms but the woman didn't move backwards. Her arms bent slightly and Martin's face was only millimetres from the apparition in front of him. Her eyes were completely blue, resembling oils swimming around each other, and her skin was the colour of alabaster, making her look like a living statue.

The Keeper's gaze penetrated deep into Martin and he felt a presence unlike any he had experienced before.

For a moment they stayed there, as if Isabel had paused them. But time continued and Martin felt his feet begin to rise off the floor.

Please, just this one, just let me have this one, thought Martin.

The Keeper's eyes narrowed.

'No!'

Martin was thrust towards the far side of the room at an incredible speed. He flew through the master's study, into the open doorway to his bedroom and crashed onto the unforgiving wooden floor.

Martin stood up. By some miracle he didn't think he'd broken anything, but he had received some serious scratches from the landing and pulled more muscles than he'd care to think about.

He was leaning against the wall by his bedside table, exactly the same place the master had the Minor Keepers locked up. His past self was still in bed asleep, but it wasn't long off morning now, and he'd probably be waking up in less than an hour. He felt a gentle push, slowly sliding his feet away from the bed.

'Oh, so now you decide to play nice.'

The door to the master's study had been closed. This morning, after breakfast, his past self would step through it for the very first time and meet Isabel and the master. He desperately wanted to be able to tell himself something, but there was no way that could happen. A part of him almost felt jealous. It was like the boy in the bed wasn't even him, just some new guy who was going to steal his adventure. It wouldn't be long before that boy in the bed became the Martin who stood watching over him. It was a strange little cycle.

Martin's mind turned to the Keeper of Buttons once more. He had tried so hard to save him and still he had failed. There was nothing more he could do. The Keeper would be killed by the master and his body would be crunched inside those tar-filled jaws. If Martin went back to the master's study now, then he'd only be thrown in here again, and the longer he spent doing that the closer he'd come to finding himself barred from his own room because his past self had woken up. Plus, deep down, he knew. No matter how hard he tried, no matter what he did, the Keeper of Buttons would die. Martin may have the power to travel through space by connecting doorways, but changing the past was just too much, even for him. He

160

turned and left the room, wishing his sleeping self good luck as he did. He was going to need it.

Martin charged through the house, creating a passageway into one room, finding it empty and then creating a passageway into another. He tried to do this in a systematic manner, moving through the house in a logical order, one floor at a time, working through the rooms in rows, but his order was breaking down and he was starting to panic. The Keeper of Portals could be dead, and then what?

Martin burst into a room. There was a bed in there and unpacked boxes on the floor. A wardrobe stood half-filled and a detective novel lay pages down on an upturned box that was being used as a bedside table. His mother was still asleep in her bed. Martin approached carefully. His mum had yet to hang any curtains so the summer morning light poured into the room unobstructed.

Martin watched his mother sleep. What would she have done if he'd been unable to return to the present? He would have tried to leave a message for her, telling her that he was safe, but even if he'd done that, it would've been poor consolation when it meant she'd never get to see him again. Martin was his mother's only child and her husband was already gone. If Martin was to leave too, then it didn't bear thinking about what would happen. The house being so close to the cliffs made Martin shudder. He resolved himself to stay positive. Whatever happened, he would come out of this alive and in the right time period. Plus, he would have Isabel with him. He knew his mum would be more than happy to have her living with them, even if explaining her origin might prove somewhat difficult.

Martin turned to leave but he stood on a loose floorboard, causing it to creak. He heard a rustle behind him but didn't dare turn around.

'Martin, is that you?'

He quickly lunged for the door and opened it into the kitchen.

Martin was on the third floor. The door in front of him had been nailed shut. This corridor led to the part of the house that overhung the cliff. He'd ignored it before because he couldn't think of any reason why Isabel would come this way, but he had been everywhere else and there were no signs of her.

The door wouldn't open to Martin so he retraced his steps down the corridor to find one that would.

Martin could feel the doors; the connections were there, but while he could connect to them, he couldn't open any of the doors that had been nailed shut. Eventually he found something. It was small, possibly an old clothes hamper.

Martin created the gateway and saw the top of a room through the door in front of him. He knew he wouldn't be able to step through because the gravity in the other room would pull him down again.

Martin took a couple of steps back and dived into the door. His body shot through the open clothes hamper and up into the room before he was dragged back down again. He stuck out his arms and grabbed onto the sides of the hamper before falling back into the corridor. He pulled himself up and into the room.

Martin was on the other side of the nailed door now. The bedroom doors coming off either side of the corridor were also nailed shut, but they were much thinner than the one in the corridor so Martin had been able to kick his down and get out. At the end of the corridor there was a bright blue light. That was where the house ended.

The floor extended further than the roof, remaining level before vanishing altogether. There was no wall on the far side, opposite the entrance Martin stood in. The side walls extended out with the roof, providing support.

It was a large room, though Martin couldn't tell what it had been used for: probably many things in the hundreds of years the house had stood. Many of the rooms in the house had no furniture in them, but this room appeared almost full. There were old bookcases along one wall and paintings hung on the other. A grand piano was pushed against the wall furthest from the sea with a chaise longue in front of it. Other chairs and seating from various periods were also dotted about the large room. However grand such a description may sound, the room was anything but. Being open to the elements, especially the sea wind and the salt water brought with it, the furniture in the room had grown bloated and disfigured. Many items were swollen to the point where the stitching had been ripped open, while others had contorted like melted plastic. The stench in the room was also foul. The sea breeze managed to cover most of it, but the scent of decay could never be erased.

At the far end of the room stood Isabel. She was facing the sea, holding the Keeper of Portals in her arms.

'Isabel, what are you doing? It's not safe here.'

Isabel turned around at the sound of Martin's voice.

'I remember it, Martin. I remember all of it.'

'What? What do you remember?'

'Attacking the Keeper. I was so angry. I wanted to hurt him so much. I wanted to spill his blood until it was splattered across the room. I wanted to kill him, Martin. I genuinely did. Then I woke up in a strange bed. I thought it must have been a dream. I saw you the next morning in the kitchen and I remembered you from that dream, but I said nothing. It would sound stupid, would it not, to tell you that I had seen you in a dream? Even after we grew closer, what good would come of you knowing I had dreamt of you apart from you thinking me a lunatic or love-struck?'

'But that wasn't you,' said Martin. 'The master got inside your head. He was the one that made you do those things. It wasn't your fault.'

'But I still felt it!' Isabel cried. 'It was still these hands that beat the Keeper. He couldn't know, you see. The master's knowledge came into my head. No other Keeper could know he was planning something; they would only tell others and try to stop him. That was why he wanted the Keeper of Portals dead.'

'Isabel, just come away from the edge. We can talk about it over here,' called Martin.

He was getting closer to Isabel, passing beneath where the roof ended and the floor continued on by itself for a few metres before reaching the sky. There was no furniture here, it had either been blown back into the room or out to sea. The floor was weak; only now did Martin realise that parts of it were curving downwards, meaning there was no solid support beneath them. Would it really be able to take his weight as well as Isabel's and the Keeper's? Despite his doubts, Martin continued on until he was just behind Isabel. He could see the sea below, many metres down. They were overhung so far he couldn't make out the cliffs. He stood next to Isabel, stealing a glance at the Keeper of Portals. Illuminated by the morning sun he looked even worse than he had before, but he was still breathing. That, at least, was something.

'My bedroom was out there,' said Isabel staring straight ahead. 'After this room there was another small corridor and at the end of that there was a place where you could get into the roof. That's where my room was, tucked away in the corner.'

'Is that where you were taking him?' asked Martin.

Isabel nodded. 'I wanted to heal him and just ran to my room. It has always been a safe place for me, so I thought it would be for him too. It was difficult to get here. Many of the doors had been sealed shut, but I found a way. I just forgot that this is not my house nor is it my time. My room is no longer here. It fell into the sea many years ago. I just wanted to help, but now I cannot move. I do not wish to be here, Martin, I do not want to be the one who did this.' Isabel gestured to the wounded Keeper in her arms. 'Pray don't hate me. I've never met anyone like you. Boys like you, they do not exist in my time. You are brave and selfless. You helped me without even knowing anything about me. I just couldn't bear for you to hate me.'

Martin moved closer to Isabel, ready to reassure her, when something gave way beneath his feet.

He wasn't touching Isabel. He turned around and saw the fear explode in her eyes. They were both starting to fall.

Isabel swung her arm around and caught Martin in the stomach with a fierce punch. The brutal impact forced Martin backwards into the room as Isabel was pushed down even further. Martin hit the floor and rolled. He looked back but Isabel was nearly out of sight. He was about to run to her when he realised that it wasn't just the end of the floor that was giving way, but the entire room. Their weight had thrown it off balance, starting a cascading effect that was forcing the overhang into the sea.

Martin sprinted for the door, feeling the floor slope beneath his feet. At first it was at 10 degrees, then 20, then 30. Furniture zipped passed him, beating the room in the race to the sea. He had to jump over the chaise longue and quickly sidestep the grand piano. Everywhere around him furniture was falling as the walls gave way and dropped the heavy wooden beams that held up the ceiling.

The entire room was going down, door and all. There was nothing on the other side of it now. The room and all those below it were falling into the sea with Martin still inside. He leapt into the air. The door was above him and falling with a section of wall. Luckily for Martin it was still open. He concentrated and made a connection. The doorframe whacked his shoulder as it and the wall fell around him to the sound of the house tearing itself apart.

Martin landed in a heap in a random room. He saw the view through the door, of the room and many others falling towards the sea. The connection was still there, which meant that if the door went underwater, the sea would come flooding in and fill the room. Martin quickly slammed it shut.

There was a massive crash as the house's overhang reached the sea and disintegrated. Martin breathed a sigh of relief. He was safe, but that meant nothing when he knew that Isabel and the Keeper of Portals had certainly fallen to their deaths.

CHAPTER
FOURTEEN

Martin ran out the front door and headed straight for the cliffs. The ground was strewn with bricks, tiles and smashed furniture while thick beams that had been left hanging in the walls were still falling into the sea. Looking down, Martin could see vicious waves forcing the wreckage against the cliffs. Then he spotted something strange floating above the water. Martin leaned over the edge to try and get a better view and his heart nearly stopped when he realised it was Isabel and the Keeper of Portals.

They were completely motionless, just like the villagers they had sped past when Isabel increased her subjective time. But how was that possible? Isabel could only slow her own time down, not everyone else's. She controlled a little bubble of time. When she ran, the bubble went with her, making it appear like she could move at inhuman speeds. But Isabel couldn't control her descent. Gravity would pull on that bubble at the same rate regardless of what Isabel did inside it. Increase time or decrease time, it didn't make a difference. She and the Keeper should have fallen into the sea along with the house.

Martin swung a leg over and lowered himself down the side of the cliff. The weather was calmer than the last time he'd attempted this, but that didn't stop him from freaking out slightly. He tried to ignore the fear as best he could. He needed to get to Isabel and the Keeper and work out how to save them. Nothing else mattered.

It was only when he was a couple of metres from the top that Martin realised gravity was working against him. He was going down, so it should have been pulling him, helping him even if he didn't want the help, but as he lowered his foot to find another hold, it almost felt like something was pushing it back up.

Soon he was literally kicking his feet into the air only to have them spring back and it wasn't long before he felt himself start to float up the cliff. His hands grabbed for anything they could and showers of tiny rocks were dislodged as he tried to stop himself from going any higher. Eventually Martin was back where he started. He felt a push as he was shoved over the edge and ended up lying on his front, face in the grass.

He stood up and looked over the edge of the cliff. There it was again, a push, gentle like before, moving him backwards. His feet slid across the brittle grass as he tried to get closer to the sea. He was ten metres from the edge when he came to a rest.

He started to walk forward again, but the force was still there. *She* was still there, that mysterious Keeper. Martin turned around and feigned disinterest.

What he had in mind was ridiculous and possibly even suicidal, but he just couldn't help himself.

Martin ran towards the edge of the cliff as fast as he could. He couldn't feel the resistance, not just yet. His feet left the ground and after a couple of seconds of falling through the air Martin just stopped. He hung over the sea like he too had been paused. The morning sun was rising in the east and there was still a slight chill in the air that would quickly be eradicated as the morning wore on.

Martin knew he wouldn't fall, not when that Keeper wanted him to be somewhere else. He had to stop a paradox from occurring. The entire history of the world depended on that and he wasn't going to get out of it by doing something as trivial as dying.

Then he heard a voice, spoken like an exasperated mother.

'Foolish boy.'

Martin was thrown back into the air and up the cliffs. He expected to land on the grass at the top, but he kept on going, higher and higher and up to the top floor of the house. He was hurtling towards the wall of a room that faced the sea. Before he hit it, the wall shattered inwards, throwing bricks across the room. Inside the house, Martin flew along the corridors, suddenly being thrust left and right as they twisted, split and re-joined. Martin was being taken somewhere, directed to the place where the paradox would occur if he didn't intervene. Doors were flung open for him as he was pushed deeper into the labyrinthine house. Then he stopped, floating a few inches off the floor, and was lowered gently to his feet.

He was in his bedroom, his sleeping past self still in bed. Martin tried to work out what disastorous paradox could possibly occur here, but came up with nothing. He was about to leave when he collapsed to his knees and his head was forced down to look at the floor. A bucket and a mop shot through the door, pushed by invisible hands too, and stopped just in front of his face.

'OK, OK, I get it!' said Martin.

His bedroom had been clean when he woke up – when he would wake up in about an hour's time. That meant someone had come in and cleaned it. Apparently not all paradoxes were as interesting as dinosaurs still being alive or Hitler winning World War II.

A wardrobe on its side was connected to an open CD case Martin had propped against the wall in his bedroom. An image was stretched to the full size of the open door so the view played out like a cinema screen, only with distortion and warping around the edges.

His past self was standing at the end of his bedroom in front of the door. Martin still couldn't help the compulsion to shout *stop*, but he knew he wouldn't do it. He also couldn't do it and, ultimately, hadn't done it.

His past self grabbed the handle and waited. Then he turned it and opened the door.

Martin watched as he stepped into 1623 for the very first time. He would be back in an hour with the past version of Isabel. That meant Martin wouldn't be able to return to his room until much later, not if he didn't want the mysterious Keeper throwing him about at her whim.

The door closed and Martin of the past was gone.

After watching his past self set out on his adventure, Martin went back to the cliffs to try and work out how to save Isabel and the Keeper of Portals, still frozen in time.

He'd tried to climb down a few times, but without the adrenalin of when he'd first found them pumping through his body, or the mysterious Keeper there to act as a safety net should he fall, Martin never got lower than a couple of metres from the top before giving up. At 6:00pm, feeling like a failure, Martin realised that he had to go back inside. His mum would start to worry about where he was. He didn't want her to come looking for him and find Isabel and the Keeper. He stood up and shook the brittle grass from his clothes, then found a portal and stepped back into his bedroom. He needed to change.

The cracks around the door at the end of his bedroom appeared to have stopped growing. Martin stood and listened, waiting for the sound of old wood being pulled apart, but all was silent.

He reached for the handle. It didn't move. The connection to the past must have been severed by the Keepers of Time and Portals at the order of the master. At least the cracks were no longer growing, which meant the house wasn't in danger of tearing itself apart right this minute, even though its future still remained bleak.

The cracks radiated from around the doorframe like the tentacles of an octopus and were so thick that the wall appeared to be more cracks than wood. Even the outside wall was riddled with so many of them that a breeze blew in. The cracks reached all around the room, splitting in two again and again. They travelled up into the ceiling to infect the loft and down to the floor, spreading through the rooms below.

Many of the cracks were so large Martin could actually put his arm through them. The door had been open for five hours at most and the damage it had done to the house, especially Martin's room, verged on catastrophic. It would take very little for a person to kick each one of the four walls to the ground. If the master hadn't ordered the door to Martin's time closed, then the house would have collapsed within a day.

Martin took his hand out of a crack, it was so large that part of him could actually pass through it. That made it a portal. Martin placed his palms against the wall and concentrated. He could feel them. They were connections like the doorways and windows, but there was something different about them. He wouldn't be able to walk through them, they were too small for that, but that didn't mean he couldn't manipulate them.

The cracks around the door started to close, knitting themselves together like gaping wounds healing in fast forward. The end result wasn't the wall that had once stood, but it was the structural integrity that Martin was trying to repair, not the decor. Martin took his hands off the wall; a patch about a metre square had been repaired, leaving a swath of scar tissue in the wood. He moved over to another area and concentrated. It would take a long time to fix them all, but if Martin wanted any sense of privacy in the room he spent the most time being naked in, then he'd better get to work.

The TV was unpacked and a sofa shoved in front of it, but the rest of the living room, one of many, was completely empty. This made the little television arrangement in the corner look somewhat absurd.

Martin collapsed onto the sofa. It was dark outside. He'd wanted to go back to the cliffs in case inspiration happened to strike, but he knew it wouldn't. There was nothing he could do for Isabel and the Keeper and he needed to spend some time with his mum to stop her from growing suspicious. He felt like he'd done something terrible and spent every second dreading someone would find out. He'd abandoned them. But what else could he do? Isabel and the Keeper were safe, he knew that, protected by someone or something more powerful than himself. Martin might even make things worse by trying to help them. Until he was certain what he had to do, Martin could only wait, and worry.

'Seriously, mum, here?'

'What's wrong with here?' said Jo.

'Couldn't find anywhere further from the door?'

Jo shrugged and put an arm around her son. 'Any reason you're wearing a hat?'

Martin touched the hat that covered his feather. 'Any reason you're not?'

Jo rolled her eyes. 'Better than piercings and makeup, I suppose. Anyway, what are you doing here?'

'I just thought it'd be nice to spend some time with you, that's all.'

'Well, I suppose living in a house this size we probably won't run into each other much.'

'Exactly. Plus, you are my mum, I mean, we *can* still hang out.'

'How considerate. I take it Isabel's gone home.'

'Yeah.'

'Do I need to bring up the bath thing?'

'Trust me, mum, it's not what you think.'

Jo sipped her tea. 'You're sensible, Martin. Well, sensible enough when you need to be. It's just, I know there's not much to do out here.'

'Seriously?'

'Just hear me out,' said Jo, holding up a hand. 'I'm glad you've made a new friend already, and I know you think you're grown up now you're fifteen—'

'I really don't,' said Martin.

'Let me finish. I know you think you're grown up, but that doesn't mean you're ready for the responsibility of fatherhood.'

Martin buried his head in his hands. 'Mum. Please. Shut up.'

'Don't think I didn't notice how pretty she is.'

Martin sighed. '*That* is not going to happen. We're just friends. Plus, I'm not sure when I'll see her again.'

'OK. It's just, I know your father's not here to have these kinds of talks with you.'

Martin rested his head against his mum's.

'You're my mum. I don't need you to be my dad as well.'

'I know, but it's difficult being a teenager.'

'It is when you make me talk about it.'

Jo nodded and turned up the volume on the television. The sound of the news filled the room.

'…strangest story of the week comes from Doncaster

where a woman opened the door to her downstairs toilet only to find it led to a remote village in the south of France. She claimed she was able to step through and even spoke to a few locals who were apparently surprised to see her walking around in a dressing gown and slippers. She had time to buy herself a baguette and some cheese before she returned home to her husband. The husband, Mr Miller, went to check the door immediately after his wife came back, but found it led to the downstairs toilet. However, he couldn't explain why the bread was still warm or why there was a lost French boy in his house. The police were called and the parents of the child were eventually tracked down. The boy has now been flown back to his home in St Guilhem-le-Désert.'

'She must have been drunk,' said Jo as she grabbed the remote and put on a soap opera.

Martin tried to think as his mum lost herself in the television. With the Keeper of Portals still falling from the cliffs outside his house he wasn't able to do his job. Perhaps this was just a one-off. The door went to France that one time and then went back to the toilet, like it was supposed to. It could have been a freak occurrence, but then again, it could just be the start.

Jo grabbed her shoes and ran after Martin.

'Are you going outside?'

'Huh?'

'To see if the house fell in the sea? I was so busy trying to arrange rooms yesterday I forgot to go and look.'

Martin was standing by the front door. It was smaller

than the one in the master's house, like a standard door cut into a massive one.

'Oh right, yeah, I guess.'

He was planning to check on Isabel and the Keeper, though part of that would include assessing the damage caused to the house and whether there was anything he could use to create a doorway. He had one idea involving making a square out of floor and roof joists that were still on the cliff top and floating it in the sea. But the practicality of building it and actually getting it to the sea without it falling apart were probably beyond him.

Martin walked away from the door. He couldn't take his mum to the cliffs and risk her seeing Isabel and the Keeper. Who knew what she would think? Even if he decided he didn't want to go anymore, there was nothing to stop her from going herself. He needed a way to keep her inside. Luckily he had an idea, even if it was a touch on the devious side.

'Actually, I know a short cut through the house.'

Martin left the door and jogged back into the house. His mum followed, running to catch up. Martin sped up and charged along the corridor before diving into a door to his left.

'Martin, why are you running? There's no rush.'

There was another room at the end and Martin burst into it.

'I just wanna see the mess,' Martin shouted back. 'I've been sitting around here all morning, it feels good to move.'

All he had to do was get one room ahead. He looked

back; his mum was still there. She didn't look tired or angry, and actually seemed quite excited to be running through the house, throwing the doors wide each time just before they closed. This is what she needed, Martin thought: to have a bit of fun. It was a shame she wouldn't be going outside.

Martin flicked the door shut behind him. His mum was far enough back that it wouldn't physically hit her in the face, even if the gesture would.

On the other side of the door, Martin stopped. He'd never actually done this before, but the concept made sense to him. Once it had been made, there wouldn't be any additional effort required on Martin's part to retain the connection. It would be there until he chose to do something with it. It just so happened that what he did most of the time was close the connection within a few minutes, either by shutting the door or by disconnecting the cables he visualised in his mind.

The door Martin had just ran through led to a room on the far side of the house, close to the cliffs but not close enough to be missing a wall and exposed to the brutality of the sea. There was a second door in that room which now led to a forgotten kitchen further along the hall. That kitchen had two doors leading off from it: one went into the living room and one led to the first room Martin had run into. In total, twenty-six rooms had been connected unnaturally in a circuit without an exit. Martin hadn't made the connections in an instant, but instead had been piecing them together as he ran; all he needed was to close the door behind him and then it would be complete.

Martin opened a different door and stepped into the garden. He would free his mum later, once he'd checked on Isabel and the Keeper. He'd probably have to make up some lie about the sea washing all the debris away, but that would only work for today. Martin would have to keep his mum away from the edge of the cliffs until he'd managed to save Isabel and the Keeper, and that could take days.

The overhang had completely gone and the outer wall of the house ended with the land. Martin grabbed onto the frame of a window and swung himself over the drop down to the sea and back into the house.

The room was now only three metres long. The rest had disappeared in the night along with the rooms of the two floors above it. Martin stood at the edge, among the remains of furniture and the burgundy carpet that rolled over the end of the cliff and down its face like a tongue.

He could see the Keeper of Portals, draped in the arms of Isabel. If only her control of time was greater and she could reverse its flow. Then she and the Keeper could just leap back up the cliffs to safety. But such a power had not been bestowed upon her because it was not possible. Time doesn't ever go backward. Things dropped never fall up, even by accident, in the same way that a smashed vase never reassembles itself. It was entropy, pure and simple. There was probably a Keeper for that.

Martin walked to the wall and swung himself over the drop and back onto the rough grass outside the house.

As he walked, the scenery changed. The midday blue of the sky suddenly shifted to a foggy grey and the air felt thick and stagnant in his mouth. The house disappeared completely and all vegetation along with it. In the distance, Martin could see a series of enormous structures. Some billowed black clouds into the air while others rose even higher, threatening to pop the earth's bubble of atmosphere with their pointed spires.

Martin spun around, trying to take in everything he saw. But as soon as it appeared before him it was swept away. The house returned, standing in the middle of a once grand garden back-dropped by the rising green tops of the cliffs behind it. The grey sky, hot and thick with pollutants, was once more the blue of a summer's day with white clouds drifting across it.

Martin ran back to the cliffs. Isabel and the Keeper of Portals were still there, still unmoving. As he stepped away, he patted himself down, just to make sure he was still real. Martin had been shown something. Something he never wanted to see again.

CHAPTER
FIFTEEN

Martin stood in front of his bedroom window looking out over the garden. He was searching for inspiration, but found none. Two weeks had passed since the house's overhang had fallen into the sea and Isabel and the Keeper of Portals had started their descent. Every day of that fortnight he had spent hours hanging over the edge of the cliff, trying to work out how he could possibly save them. He'd come up with hundreds of ideas as he watched their still bodies, but every single one carried a risk: of cutting them in half; of the gateway breaking when they were only partway through; of him only being able to save one of them. As long as they were still alive, the risk would always outweigh the benefit. Until Martin could find a way to save both Isabel and the Keeper of Portals without harming them, they would have to remain where they were, slowly falling into the sea. And they were falling. Two weeks ago they had been ten metres from the violent waves beneath them. Now they were only two.

A figure appeared at the far end of the estate by the line of redwoods. Riding a horse, Martin's mum approached the house. She stopped, jumped off gracefully and untied the shopping bags she'd attached to the saddle.

Nothing had been said three days ago when the red Ford Focus was no longer parked by the door and a horse stood in its place. Martin had waited for his mum to comment, but instead she jumped on and headed into the local village. He wasn't sure if she'd been playing a game with him, going along with the ruse just to see when Martin would crack, but after all the lights were replaced by candles and the television exchanged for an antique bookcase, it became obvious this wasn't a test. Items were being swapped with those from another time and his mum remained completely unaware. Ever since his dad had died, Martin's mum had been slightly detached from reality, but it had never been this bad.

Martin opened the window in front of him and leapt out of his second floor bedroom.

Jo jumped and dropped the shopping.

'Where did you come from?'

'Sorry, mum. Saw you were back and thought I'd give you a hand.'

'Did you just jump through the door?'

'It's OK. You didn't close it.'

Jo picked up the shopping and walked to the kitchen.

'Even so, you need to be more careful. This isn't a game, Martin. Something strange is going on and while it may seem cool to you, people are dying.'

Martin kicked the door shut and ran after his mum.

'I told you, it wasn't closed. It wouldn't have taken me anywhere.'

'I don't care. You're too reckless. You don't know where

182

these doors could lead. You think you're running for the loo, next minute you open the door and you're falling into a well!'

'I know, mum. But what do you want me to do? Stay in my room all the time? I thought that's what you *didn't* want me doing this summer.'

'You don't need to stay in your room, just *think*. I know it's the summer, so you've probably forgotten how, but at least try, Martin. You're all I have.' Jo put the shopping down on the kitchen counter. 'So I'd rather you didn't die. OK?'

'Sure thing, mum.'

Martin started to empty the bags. There was very little food in them. They'd managed to buy a ten kilogram bag of rice when they moved in and had slowly been working their way through it, but it wouldn't last forever.

Everyone was too scared to leave their houses through fear of stepping out the front door only to find death on the other side. Most of the time when the connection went wrong, which was not every door every time it was opened, the person would find themselves in a different room of their house, or strolling into their neighbour's kitchen. The mis-wired connections were mainly local, especially in housing estates where the houses were identical and mistakes were easily made. At times like those, the houses were often so similar that people didn't even realise they were in the wrong place. They'd leave their room in the middle of the night to go to the toilet and then return to bed only to find they'd stepped into someone else's room and cuddled up with the wrong wife. Other times, the connections travelled to other countries, providing instant access to a tropical paradise by simply stepping through a dining room door.

While most misconnections were harmless, or even beneficial, there were undesirable effects of doors swapping. In Ireland, a fire drill in a primary school led to half a class evacuating into the tiger enclosure at a local zoo. Three of the children died before the teacher was able to run in and bring the rest back, losing half of her arm in the process. Other accidents were more predictable: people running through a door only to find it led to a window near the top of a tall building. The Willis Tower in Chicago appeared to act as a hub, with someone falling through a window every few minutes.

Martin picked up a big bag of rice and heaved it onto the worktop.

'Well, at least we have more rice.'

'Sorry, it's all they had,' said Jo as she checked their food stock. She took two biscuits from their dwindling supply and gave one to Martin who shoved it in his mouth.

'It's OK,' said Martin through the biscuit crumbs. 'I don't mind rice. Anyway, why break a habit?'

Martin flopped onto his bed. People were dying. That fact had been with him for over a week now. People were dying and it was his fault. If he could save the Keeper of Portals, then the connections wouldn't be falling apart. The worst part was, Martin was safe. And when she was with him, so was his mum. He had control of all passages in a radius of a few hundred metres. Even when she went to town, Martin would follow her, jumping from gateway to gateway to cover the distance. She was always within his sphere of influence, so was never in any danger from a rogue connection. But she was the only one he could save. There was still an entire planet out there in danger of stepping through a door to their death. Until Martin figured something out, it would only get worse.

The sky flickered as Martin stood by the cliffs, flashing a dark grey before returning to blue. Martin didn't move. It did it again, then one more time before the grey finally stuck. Martin waited for the image to disappear. Nothing changed.

Martin turned around. Before him were the tall spire-like structures reaching into the sky. Interspaced between those were industrial buildings like power plants, each one belching dark plumes of exhaust into the air to mingle with the already brown clouds.

The house had gone, but there were other buildings a short walk from him; one of these billowed toxins into the air, while another one rose up into a mighty pointed tower.

A quick glance over the cliff revealed that Isabel and the Keeper of Portals were not here. Whether that was a good thing or not, Martin wasn't sure. Coughing as the thick air attacked his throat, he walked towards the settlement.

The ground beneath him was dead and it sounded like he was walking on a field of crisps. Between the petrified remains of dead trees, Martin could see buildings in every direction. As he got closer he began to make out people moving between them, all dressed in brown robes with their heads bent low. No one spoke.

Martin started to wonder if he'd accidentally stepped into the future. Was this related to the horse his mother now rode and the wind turbine he'd seen in 1623?

Once at the settlement, Martin was struck by the size of the buildings. They were higher than anything he had ever seen and yet there was nothing remotely futuristic about them. They were all built from stone and mostly blackened from the pollution. There were no cables slung from roof to roof, no cars or obvious futuristic modes of transportation; in fact, no visible signs of modern technology anywhere. Even the clothes appeared homemade and were barely holding together. If this was the future, then something had gone terribly wrong.

Martin stood in front of the first large building he came to. It was the monstrosity with an enormous spire built from brick that had long ago turned black. From inside, voices could be heard chanting in unison, but what they said, Martin could not decipher, nor did he care. There was something much more captivating vying for his attention, the only slash of colour to be seen aside from the clothes Martin wore. A figure wearing flowing white robes with long dark purple hair was sprawled on the steps before him. Martin instantly recognised her as the mysterious Keeper.

The Keeper lay on her side halfway up the steps. She watched Martin approach, but made no effort to stand. Only when he was two steps below her did she raise her head and prop it up on her hand. For a moment neither of them spoke. The Keeper stared at Martin, who in turn stared back.

'So,' said the Keeper, gesturing in front of herself with her free hand, 'what do you think?'

'Is this the future?'

'*The* future? No. This is only *a* future.'

'What year is it?'

'The year is 396 AR.'

'AR?' said Martin.

'After Rebirth.'

The Keeper sat up on the step. Her hair continued to flow behind her as if being washed by the current from a gentle stream. 'Like I said, *a* future, not *your* future.'

'Why am I here?'

'Why? Because I need to show you this, or maybe I just wish to. Perhaps I feel I owe it to you. Perhaps I'm merely curious how you'll react. Which of these it is, I am unsure. The truth is most likely a mixture.'

'You feel you owe me because you let the Keeper of Buttons die, is that it?'

The Keeper sighed deeply and brushed the step she sat on with her fingertips.

'You have become embroiled in a world that by its nature is hidden from your view. You witness actions of those you refer to as Keepers and become angered when they do not conform to your own human decencies.'

'So what, you're telling me it was OK for him to die because you're a Keeper?'

'I am not telling you that it was OK for him to die. The

187

truth was that it was necessary for him to die. This is a fact you know.'

Martin's shoulders relaxed slightly. Upon seeing the Keeper he had become tense, but now that was starting to fade. The Keeper was right. Martin understood that if he'd saved the Keeper of Buttons a paradox would have occurred, but he didn't understand why that was such a bad thing.

'Tell me who you are,' said Martin.

The Keeper smiled. 'How demanding of you.'

She stood up. Though not as tall as the Keeper of Time or the Keeper or Portals, she was a good head taller than Martin. 'I am the Keeper of Causality,' she said with obvious pride. 'I exist to maintain the link between cause and effect. I make sure that once an effect has occurred, the cause that produced it remains. In that way I prevent paradoxes from occurring, where the effect produced by the cause manages to interfere with said cause before the initial interaction occurred. Do you understand?'

'I think so. Like with the Keeper of Buttons?'

'Indeed. The cause was the death of the Keeper of Buttons and the effect was you becoming angered. However, you, spurred by the effect, and with the ability to return to a time before the cause had occurred, attempted to free the Keeper of Buttons, which would result in him never dying and removing the cause that initially angered you so.'

The Keeper of Causality smiled. Despite Martin's first impressions of her, he actually found this smile to be pleasant and warm. Plus, he couldn't deny that she was very beautiful, even if she was eerily ageless. The Keeper of Causality descended the steps. As she walked past, Martin could feel a comforting heat emanating from her. He followed.

'It is not that I am evil in allowing the Keeper of Buttons to die, it was merely the case that I was required to preserve that which I exist to maintain. I had no wish for him to die, nor did I relish thwarting your efforts to save him.'

The Keeper of Causality walked the dark streets of the town, if that in fact was what it was. Martin saw no end to it from any direction. It was like many towns had merged, eating into the spaces between them to create a single urban sprawl. As they walked, crowds of people dressed in hooded robes passed by without displaying awareness of the strangers. Deep within one of the throngs, Martin was convinced he saw someone looking his way. He snapped his head around but only saw a group of figures marching away from him as they mumbled unintelligible verses.

'You said this isn't the future,' said Martin, 'that it's only *a* future. Does that mean this is some parallel universe?'

'There are no parallel universes. There is only the one universe and mistakes. This place, this existence, is a mistake.'

For a mistake, Martin thought it was very ordered.

The Keeper of Causality stopped in the middle of the road and people naturally flowed around her as if she were a rock in a river. 'There is much I should explain, much I am sure you wish to understand. I am unsure though, you see, if it is worth the effort.'

The Keeper sat down, her robes flowing around her as she descended. Martin did the same.

'This place. This mistake,' said the Keeper while gesturing around her feebly, 'is a result of many things: of rules that cannot be broken, of childish Keepers and also, of you.'

'Me? What did I do?'

'That whom you call the master received information that he was not supposed to regarding his future. We have been concerned over him for some time now. His handling of what he is transformed him into something that he was never meant to be. He is scared, you see. His role has allowed him to learn too much and because of that a great amount of fear has accumulated within him. Our observations determined that he needed to be reborn, but until that time he would most likely remain a nuisance. His kidnapping of Portals and Time, however, was... unfortunate. Of course, they were to blame for trying to interfere, so the amount of pity I have for them is minimal.'

'Why is he scared?' asked Martin.

'When your human ancestors achieved awareness of themselves, a new Keeper appeared. The Keeper of Sentience existed to monitor this awareness. However, as humans continued to multiply and develop, the role of overseeing this awareness became too large for Sentience alone. Over 20,000 years ago, Sentience split into multiple Keepers, each bestowed with a different facet of human sentience: love, vengeance, pride, cruelty. These Keepers, of which there are thousands, are collectively known as the Keepers of Sentience. Questions is one of these.'

'I still don't get why he's scared.'

The Keeper of Causality looked annoyed, as if she were just about to explain that very point.

'The role of a Keeper is not to interfere. It is simply to monitor, to observe, and when something breaks, to fix it. He was different. By virtue of his existence he was curious. This curiosity led him to do something that should never have happened, especially to one he was so close with. After that he changed. He began to understand the questions humans asked. In those questions he learnt something about the humans, and about the universe. It is that which has scared him. This fear has affected every part of him, turning him cruel and hungry for power.'

The Keeper of Causality brushed her fingers through her long hair before inspecting the ends with indifference. 'He sought fundamentality. He is a Major Keeper, so the universe's requirement for him is limited. In truth, it is ephemeral when the entirety of existence is considered. He believed that greater power would allow him to attain that which he desired, so he trapped Time and Portals and used them to create a doorway to the past. He hoped to leach the energy at the beginning of the universe, the limitless potential for everything that was so abundant in early existence. By absorbing the energy, he would gain power. However, it would never make him fundamental.'

Martin was about to open his mouth but the Keeper of Causality shot him a look. Of course, she was going to explain his question.

'One is deemed fundamental based on the universe's need, not on the abundance of that which is maintained.

191

Most Fundamental Keepers are the most powerful; however, there are some as small as a Minor Keeper. If that which you exist to observe spans the full lifetime of the universe, then you are Fundamental. Because of this, Fundamental Keepers can never die, this also means that they can never be born. He can absorb all the energy there is, but by the very rules that define the universe he will never be a Fundamental Keeper.'

Martin watched the Keeper as she gazed at him with her intense blue eyes of swimming oils. A small red ribbon was tied to her right-hand index finger. As she spoke, she waved her finger in a circle. The ribbon followed like a tail so it looked like she was spinning a red ring.

'But he's a Keeper. Doesn't he know this?'

The Keeper of Causality sighed. 'The fear has driven Questions mad; either that or stubborn. Rules are no longer relevant when you feel your survival is at stake. However, this is pure conjecture. We do not know if he fears for his life or if he merely wished to grow stronger so the fear could no longer control him. In the same way, we do not know what he learnt from listening to the questions of humans to implant that fear in him. At the point where you appeared, our concern became grave. Though, unfortunately, we are not able to interfere.'

'Why not? He's kidnapped two other Keepers. Don't you even care?'

'A Keeper cannot use what they observe to forcefully manipulate another Keeper. If that were not the case, then I could have simply stopped Portals from travelling through the door to the past. But even that would have brought about its own set of complications. Such a young Keeper. So much like a child. He will become a burden if he does not grow up.'

'The Keeper of Portals is a child?' said Martin, still watching the ribbon.

The Keeper nodded. 'Indeed, and proving to be a difficult one. Though not as bad as Time.' The Keeper of Causality said this with a slight smile, as if reminiscing about previous encounters with the Keeper of Time. 'When one observes such a thing as time, then inevitably paradoxes have the potential to form in one's wake. He may appear wise, but one's knowledge does not preclude carelessness. He was captured, after all.'

The Keeper of Causality rose, and the crowd changed to move around her. Martin followed and it didn't take long before they were walking away from the town and back to the cliffs. Even as she spoke, the Keeper continued to spin the ribbon on her finger.

'You have frightened Questions beyond the fear he was already burdened with. You revealed to him something which has led to the creation of this mistake. But in this mistake, Martin, you were never born.'

Martin was shocked to hear his name. For some reason he was surprised she actually knew who he was. He didn't say anything and the Keeper continued to speak.

'You were never born, Martin, which means you were never able to travel through the door and reveal a terrifying future to him, a future that does not need him and now, a future that has not come into existence. The effect is here and yet there was never a cause. That is why this is a mistake. This entire future is a paradox, Martin. A paradox *you* created.'

'But I'm not a Keeper. If I created this paradox, then why didn't you just stop me?'

'If I had stopped you, other paradoxes would have come into play and established fact would cease to be. I have been placed in a difficult position. There is no set series of events which we are preordained to follow. Most of what occurs does so at my whim, but even I am not perfect. Once I allow an event to happen, I cannot revert that decision. Instead, I have to ensure that it occurs exactly as I originally allowed.'

They were standing by the cliffs now, staring out to sea.

'Is that why you let me go to the past in the first place?' asked Martin.

'Exactly. The events which resulted in you first stepping through the door had already influenced you before your hand touched the handle. There was nothing I could have done to stop you. I exist to maintain and to prevent, but my control is not omnipotent. However, you have experienced my influence over you and appreciate its power.'

Martin nodded.

'When I believe you pose a threat to causality, I will stop you, Martin. However, I feel you perhaps tire of the physical approach.' The Keeper smiled before continuing. 'This place exists, Martin. It is one of two possible outcomes from a single event. It is an event I am unable to control, and hence the paradox was created. Though this world is dying. It has existed for 396 years all so I can show you, so that you can understand. Once you leave here, it will cease to be, along with all the lives that dwell within it.'

The Keeper of Causality turned to face Martin.

'You will go back to the time of the master. When you are there, you will have to make a decision, one that I will be unable to influence. One outcome shall create this, while the other will bring about the world as it should be.'

'So you're showing me this to stop it from ever happening?' said Martin.

The Keeper shook her head, her long hair dancing behind her. 'Both outcomes have already occurred, both of them caused by you. I do not show you this place to stop it from ever existing. That is not within your power. It is a mistake, and like all mistakes, the universe will soon erase it. I show you this, as I have shown an infinite number of Martins before you, all who are part of this cycle, to make you aware of where your choice will take you. Some leave here and start a journey that returns them to the true world line, while others leave here only to create this mistake.'

'But I don't get it. How is this all on me? Why am I so important?'

'The events that led to this place, and the world you know, happened almost 400 years ago. It is history you are part of. However, it is history that you have not yet experienced.' The Keeper of Causality looked down at the crashing waves. 'You will fight against this history, Martin, because you will fight against your un-birth. Though ultimately, you will be fighting for your life twice, as it is your death that created this.'

Martin watched the sea crash against the cliffs beneath him, trying to take in what the Keeper had just said. When he turned back he saw that she had gone. The oppressive grey sky was now blue, the buildings were no more and the fields and trees had returned. The house, too, was back.

There was something on the floor. Martin bent down and picked up the red ribbon. Holding the silk between his fingers, he realised exactly what it was the Keeper of Causality was silently trying to tell him.

Martin shoved the ribbon in his pocket and ran to the house. Finally, he knew how the Keeper of Portals and Isabel would be saved.

CHAPTER
SIXTEEN

Martin placed the aeroplane on the grass. It was blue and had a wingspan just less than his outstretched arms. Martin's dad had made it as a child and had always talked of making a new one with Martin. That had never happened.

Next to the plane were several lengths of silk ribbon, all different colours and about three metres long. Martin tied them to the tail fin and started the plane's engine. It roared to life in his hand, billowing black clouds from its exhaust.

Martin stood at the edge of the cliff, his toes just hanging over. Many metres below him was the sea, and just above that, Isabel and the Keeper of Portals. Holding the plane over his head, Martin pulled his arm back and threw it as hard as he could.

The plane sailed through the air, the colourful ribbons fluttering behind it like the tail of a kite. It began to fly away from the cliffs and out to sea. Martin picked up the remote control and started to bring the plane down in large corkscrews until it was level with Isabel and the Keeper of Portals.

Martin flew the plane too close and the ribbon ripped past the Keeper of Portals and sliced through some of his feathers like razor wire due to the relative difference in time. That was when Martin noticed Isabel's hair, which had remained frozen around her, was beginning to move.

As Martin watched, always with one eye trained on the plane, he could see Isabel slowly turn herself. Their time was speeding up. Then Martin saw something else. Isabel was looking right at him. She knew he was there. Martin could only hope she understood what he was trying to do.

Martin flew the plane in a large circle below Isabel and the Keeper until the end of the ribbon nearly touched the front of the plane. Whether the Keeper of Causality was consciously presenting him with a solution as she spun the ribbon attached to her finger, Martin did not know. Either way, it was better than anything he'd come up with.

At the bottom of the cliffs the waves crashed against the rocks, causing a spray of water to fire up towards the plane. Luckily it was far enough away to avoid a complete soaking, but enough water still reached it to worry Martin. If the waves didn't break the delicate wing material then the water could easily clog up the engine or short the tiny motors that controlled the elevators and rudder at the plane's rear.

The circle the plane flew in contracted as Martin moved the rudder as far to the right as possible. The end of the ribbon touched the front of the plane and instantly began to tangle in the propeller. This was both the plan's strength and weakness. With the ribbon trapped in the propeller, the gateway wouldn't just open again when the first gust of wind came along. This meant there was no fear of it collapsing as Isabel and the Keeper were falling through it. However, with the ribbon wrapped around the propeller blades, it would not be possible for the plane to keep flying.

The plane crashed and fell to the sea and falling above it were Isabel and the Keeper of Portals. Martin focused on the circle of rope he'd laid out next to him and created a portal to the ribbon gateway.

Isabel and the Keeper, now travelling at normal speed, flew through the rope and up into the air. The plane was sinking fast, causing gallons of water to gush out from the rope circle and over the cliffs, soaking Martin's legs and spraying up to reach Isabel and the Keeper.

Martin broke the connection. The plane was lost now. Something his father had made as a teenager, a piece of his history that Martin had always treasured, was sinking to the bottom of the sea. Martin tried not to dwell on this. After all, the plane had been used to save two lives. But even knowing that, he couldn't stop feeling like his insides were being twisted.

Isabel stood, Keeper in her arms, completely drenched. She stared at Martin, unsure exactly what had happened, but aware that she had been saved. Then her face radiated the most beautiful smile Martin had ever seen. Very carefully she set the Keeper down on the wet grass and ran to Martin before throwing her arms around him.

'I did not doubt that you would find a way to save me, not once.'

Using six dead branches tied together to make two tripods, Martin hung the loop of rope off the ground. The image of his bedroom appeared on the other side and he bent down to pick up the Keeper before carrying him back to the house.

'He will recover?' asked Isabel.

Martin laid the Keeper on his bed and closed the connection. The Keeper of Portals didn't move. He was breathing, but it was very shallow. Many of his feathers had been ripped from his back, others were frayed or sheared at the tips. At least he had stopped bleeding.

Martin took a step back.

'I don't know.'

'But he is a Keeper. They are magic. Surely he won't die?'

Martin nodded. 'They can die. Only the Fundamental Keepers are immortal. All the others, they're just like you and me.'

Isabel approached the bed and stroked the Keeper's arm. 'What happens if he dies?'

'I think he'll be reborn. I still haven't quite got my head around these Keepers, but I'm starting to understand.'

Isabel left the bed and returned to Martin.

'When something is created,' said Martin, 'a Keeper is born. At the start of the universe, things like time and a load of other physics stuff just appeared in a poof.'

'A poof?' said Isabel.

'Yeah, I don't know the technical term, so… a poof. Anyway, when all those physics things like time and gravity and entropy appeared, Keepers also appeared to keep them in check. These are the Fundamental Keepers, right? They were there at the start of the universe and they'll be there at the end. But all the other Keepers, they came much later. So, when doors and gateways were first created, the Keeper of Portals appeared.'

'And if he dies?'

'I guess a new one will be born, because all the doors and stuff will still be here.'

'So he shall be reborn?' said Isabel.

'A new Keeper of Portals will be born, not another him. They're like kings. As soon as the old one goes a new one instantly appears. But that doesn't mean we should leave him to die.'

'Of course we should not! Why would you suggest such a thing?'

'Because I don't know what to do,' said Martin. 'Up 'til now it's been pretty easy: make a door here, jump through a window there. Even when I was really stuck, it was the Keeper of Causality that figured it out for me.'

'Keeper of Causality? Who is he?'

'Actually, that one's a she. I kind of met her in a paradox that was about to be erased. It's hard to explain. It's been a pretty crazy two weeks.'

'Two weeks?' said Isabel.

'Huh?'

'It took you two weeks to save us from falling into the sea?'

'Yeah,' said Martin. 'Obviously it wasn't supposed to take so long, but things kept coming up.'

'You didn't save us because you were busy?' said Isabel, a look of complete horror on her face.

'The important point is that I *did* save you.'

'Oh yes, of course, of course. And I am sure if I were in your position I too would have ensured all my work was completed before saving my friend who was FALLING OFF THE SIDE OF A CLIFF!'

'I just didn't want to rush things, all right?'

'If you had not realised, Martin, patience is not the most prudent course of action when someone falls into the sea!'

'Well you were taking so long about it so—'

'Oh! So now the blame lies with me?' said Isabel firmly.

'OK, OK, I get it!' said Martin, holding up his hands. 'I messed up. I didn't know how to save you and you nearly died. But right now that's not the problem. We need to do something about the Keeper of Portals. Plus, we have to get back to the past and I have no idea how to do that. The only *thing* that's likely to know, and actually tell us, is the guy on my bed.'

'I shall bandage him,' said Isabel decisively. 'If left in your care I fear he would bleed to death and begin to rot before you saw to him. Now find me some cloth.'

Martin walked over to his clothes drawers and started to root through his T-shirts, picking out his least favourites to be used as dressings or tourniquets.

'I also think we should not move him anymore,' said Isabel. She was leaning over the Keeper. Her long hair was gathered up in her right hand as she brought her left ear close to his chest. 'His breaths are much shallower and further apart than they were before. If we keep moving him then he will only get worse, especially if we re-open the wounds and he loses more blood.'

'You're pretty good at this,' said Martin as he dumped a stack of T-shirts on his chest of drawers.

'I do look after people for a living so this shouldn't be a surprise.'

'I know. It's just, you're pretty much my age and yet you know how to do all this stuff.'

'Like what?'

'Well, skinning animals for a start.'

'Do the girls in your time not skin their own meat?' asked Isabel with an impish smile.

'Are you kidding? Most of the girls in my time don't even know their food used to be an animal.'

Isabel smiled. 'Well then,' she said, and left it at that.

'Martin, are you in there? Is that Isabel with you?' called Jo.

Martin was next to his drawers, on the other side of the room to Isabel and the Keeper. His bedroom door was ajar and when he tried to make a connection to it to stop his mum from coming in he was refused.

Martin sprinted for Isabel. He banged into his desk as he went past. His piggy bank, a pig in a black and white striped prisoner suit, shot into the air and started to spin. His arm was outstretched, so too was Isabel's. His mum couldn't be allowed to see the Keeper. He would never be able to explain why there was a dying seven foot tall creature on his bed, or why he had a feather growing out of his head and Isabel had a crystal in the middle of her forehead. His mum had been through enough. If he could keep her believing that their life was normal, even in a world where doors led to strange places, then he would be happy.

Martin grabbed Isabel's hand. With her other hand, Isabel held onto the Keeper of Portals.

Turning around, Martin could see his mum had stepped partway into the room, looking quizzically at the row of wardrobes that hid the door to Isabel's time. Martin's mum, just like the piggy bank that hung in the air, was completely frozen. Martin, Isabel and the Keeper of Portals were now in their own time bubble, experiencing the world at a much faster rate than everyone else.

Martin looked to his hand in Isabel's, then to the Keeper, before finally turning to Isabel herself.

'What do we do now?'

Isabel sighed. 'As tyme hem hurt, a tyme doth hem cure,' she said before smiling.

Suddenly Martin realised something about Isabel was wrong. There was a crack running straight through the middle of her crystal.

CHAPTER
SEVENTEEN

Martin felt the grip on his hand tighten as Isabel screwed up her face. The piggy bank lurched, falling five centimetres before freezing again. Martin's mum was that little bit further into his room, though luckily still not looking their way.

After a moment, the expression on Isabel's face softened, along with her grip.

'That was harder than I expected,' said Isabel.

'Your crystal, it's cracked,' said Martin.

Isabel nodded. Still holding Martin's hand, she reached up and rubbed the middle of her forehead.

'I am not surprised, for I am certain I should be dead. I can hardly complain about a cracked crystal.'

'So it wasn't you who stopped your fall?'

'No. I believed myself done for, but then I was safe. I cannot explain it. My time slowed, but it was not of my doing. I also knew that my fall had stopped. It was not merely my own time which had slowed, but the time of that which tried to reach me.'

'Like a time force field?'

Isabel looked confused and shook her head.

'No, it was like a barrier.'

Martin smiled. Of course, Isabel didn't watch science fiction.

'So it was the crystal that did it?'

'I believe so.'

Martin moved over to Isabel and inspected the crack. It was perfectly straight and cut the stone cleanly in half.

Isabel exhaled and Martin could feel her breath dance over his neck. He was very close to her and quickly withdrew and addressed the window.

'It's probably some sort of safety mechanism, kicks in when you're about to die, like an airbag in a car. It's stopped you from dying once, so I doubt it'll work again.'

'You are using future words again, Martin,' Isabel admonished. 'However, I think you are correct. I would not expect my fall to be arrested if I were to find myself over the edge of a cliff a second time. Also, I believe that my… abilities have been weakened.'

'Does that mean my mum will come in? Can't you hold this?'

'This much I can manage. It was getting to this point which I found difficult and I very nearly failed. I presume it is the same for you. After all, it takes effort to open a stiff door but very little to leave it open, though a gust of wind will shut that door without your intervention. I may be able to get to this stage, but I will not be able to hold it indefinitely.'

'So what does that mean for us?'

'I do not believe I will be able to quicken my time by the same degree, so my movements will not be as fast as they once were, though that is only relative. I shall still be swift. The greatest change is, if we were to become stranded in the past, I would not be able to slow our time for long enough, or as often enough, for us to return to a time many years in the future.'

'So, that means…'

'If we needed to go into the future, we would have to do so the same way everybody else does: by growing older and ultimately, dying.'

Martin had been bandaging the Keeper for over an hour. With only one hand to spare, he'd been forced to use his teeth to tear the fabric into usable strips and the dressings he tied were slapdash. As he worked he looked down at his other hand and Isabel's hand in it.

'If I let go, what would happen?'

'I am unsure,' said Isabel. 'Though I doubt it would be pleasant.'

Martin tried to think. If anything went wrong with a gateway he created, then there was the danger of being cut in half. What Isabel had done was accelerate their time so every second of the real world lasted thousands of seconds for them. To let go would mean going from one speed to another in an instant, like slowing down a car by driving it into a wall. Martin gripped Isabel's hand tighter.

'Yeah,' said Martin, 'we probably don't want to find out.'

'Bored already?' asked Isabel.

'No. I was just curious, that's all.'

The truth was, sat on his bed holding Isabel's hand was more exciting than any kiss he'd ever experienced. He felt like he was ten years old and they were on a class trip together, at the back of the group so no one could see what they were doing.

'We can't move him, can we?' said Martin.

'No, we should not,' said Isabel.

Martin nodded and started to mop up the Keeper's dried blood and brush his feathers straight.

Martin told Isabel of what had happened to the world bereft of the Keeper of Portals, of doors that opened into other houses, other countries and even death. He explained that without the Keeper that lay near-death beside them, the world was falling into chaos. Isabel's reaction was to nod and watch the Keeper for any sign of movement. She had a way about her that Martin hadn't seen in many people. Things just didn't faze her, like her world picture was a jigsaw made from pieces of putty. When a new fact about the world presented itself, she just mashed it in. After that, everything would flow to create a different picture that incorporated the new jigsaw piece, the new fact. So many people Martin had met carried unfinished jigsaws around with them, looking for specific pieces to fit the remaining holes. If a piece didn't fit, it was cast aside, even if it was valid. Other people had completed jigsaws with them and didn't even look for new pieces, ignoring any that came along because *their puzzle was finished.* That was the amazing thing about Isabel: her puzzle was never finished.

'My parents worked in a grand house,' said Isabel.

Isabel was still watching the Keeper, as if speaking to

him the way one does a coma patient. Martin didn't say anything. He didn't even move.

'My mother was a maid and my father... Well, I am not entirely sure what his role in the house was. When there was something to be done, something that involved getting dirty or moving something heavy, he was the one that did it.'

Isabel stopped and started to screw up her nose like a rabbit. With one hand on the Keeper of Portals' chest and the other holding Martin, she didn't have any free to attend to her itch.

Without a word, Martin raised his hand and scratched the end of Isabel's nose. For a moment their eyes met. Isabel stopped looking at the Keeper and turned fully to Martin.

'There was a fire in one of the buildings. I was never told what they were doing in there or how the fire started. All I knew was they did not escape.

'We were not permitted to live in the main house. Our house was next to it, near one of the farms. It was small, like the houses in the village.

'I was only three when my parents died. I have no memories of them, only memories of the things people told me about them. Sometimes I think they are my memories, and I become happy, but then I realise I am only remembering other people's memories. Nothing I have of them is truly my own.

'The master of the house took me in and there I was raised. I had been in the house many times before. I used to... ' Isabel paused. 'I *was told* I used to follow my mother

209

around as soon as I could walk, so I never felt undeserving to be there. It also helped that there was another child in the house. The master and his wife had a daughter called Anne. She was the same age as me, and since the day I moved in, they raised us as sisters.'

Isabel looked out the window; the view was like a painting.

'Noble blood has never run through my body. My family were poor, but since the day my parents died, it was as if I became a new person. A person with a future, with wealth and with status. In a way, it was a blessing for me that my parents died.' Isabel spoke with no hint of sarcasm. 'If my parents had not been caught in the fire then we would have continued to live, as a family, in that little house. One day, when I was older, I would work for the master and then find myself a husband from the village. That never happened. My parents died, and because of that I was taught how to read, how to play the flute, and even how to press flowers.'

Martin couldn't help the corners of his lips turn up slightly when Isabel mentioned the flowers, but as hers did the same, he didn't feel too guilty.

'My parents' death gave me a privileged existence as well as a sister. Because I was young when I came to the house; I forgot I knew anything different. I believed that such a life was my right. No one told me otherwise. Of course, I knew that Anne was not my sister, and nor were the master and his wife my parents. I was told I was a cousin. Family. Why they told me this, I will never know. Perhaps it was shame on their part, to have a girl from a background like mine living with them. If everyone believed that I was family, then no one would be embarrassed.

'They gave me jobs when I turned ten. I was told they were to make me a lady. Every lady must learn how to sew, to clean, to cook. A number of these Anne had to do also, but she never did them with me and never for as long. The change from family to servant was so gradual I did not realise it was happening until the process was complete. It was like standing in a room where someone comes in every day and takes something from it. The things they take are small, and the room is so full you never notice when something goes missing. Then suddenly you realise that the room is empty. That was how it felt. All the privileges I had received, the tutorage, the love, were all withdrawn over a period of years until I was thirteen and living by myself in the house that had once belonged to my parents.'

There were bizarre parallels to Isabel's life that Martin could see in his own. A parent, or both, had died, and that had left them living in a massive manor house that seemed to be gradually disappearing. But while Isabel's house receded from her in the privileges she received, Martin's house was physically falling apart as it slowly crept towards the hungry sea.

'Anne, the girl whom I grew up with and loved as my sister, told me the truth. She did so as if she took pleasure in revealing to me my past. She was the one who told me my parents had died in a fire. I did not believe her, but it was the truth. I later heard it from the others who worked in the house. They too relished telling me. They had been forced to treat me as if I were gentry for so long they took no issue in righting that particular wrong.

'I accepted my transition. There was nothing else for me to do. The truth was I did not belong in that house and the life I had grown accustomed to was a privilege I should never have received. The work was not difficult and I even found myself enjoying it. I had to endure a lot, from both the others who worked in the house and the family, but none were worse than Anne. She tormented me. She would make a mess only so that I should have to clean it. She would criticise everything I did, safe in the knowledge that there was nothing I could do about it. I had never known her to be like that when I was younger, but that was when she thought we were equal. There is a difference between the way a person treats someone they consider an equal and one they see as beneath them. At least, there is in my time.'

Martin nodded. A lot had changed since Isabel's time, but not everything.

'Then I decided I could tolerate Anne no longer, so I hit her.'

'You hit her?' said Martin.

'Yes,' said Isabel. 'I did. And it was not a girl-hit either, my fist was closed. I caught her in the cheek and she collapsed and her face hit the floor. A tooth of hers was dislodged and remained embedded in the wood for her to discover when she finally awoke.'

'What happened? Did the master find out?'

'Of course! Anne told him as soon as she was able to speak again. And one of her teeth was missing, a front one at that. A gap in one's smile cannot simply be ignored. For all the money her family had and the privileged life she was destined to lead, Anne was not a pretty girl.' Isabel smiled, 'I suppose I only made certain of that.'

'So they kicked you out?'

Isabel nodded. 'Throwing me from the house was only the beginning. My former master, the man I'd grown up thinking was my uncle, made sure I would not be able to gain employment elsewhere. No one in the town would take me in, so I tried other towns, but even they knew not to hire me. I changed my name and altered the way I looked, but it made no difference. A proclamation from that man travelled further that I ever could hope to reach.

'So I begged, stole and slept where I could. For a while I managed to survive like that, but it was becoming dangerous. Word of me would reach each new town before I did, so they were prepared. There were a few times I was caught, a few times I nearly died. Then I gave up.'

Isabel sighed. 'I thought to myself, what is the point? I live today so that I can live tomorrow. But that day will just be the same: steal, run, hide, freeze, starve. There was nothing enjoyable about my life, so I gave up on it.

'The master, *my* master, found me when I was near death. He asked no questions. All he did was look at me. For a minute he stood there, his eyes roaming over my body like they were trying to possess it. Then he said to me, "You wish to die," and extended his hand. I took it. With my new master I had food, warmth and a job. He did beat me, yes, but I was so used to being ignored that I took comfort in it. Even when he was mad at me, or hurting me, I'd think back to when he

213

took me in, this miserable excuse for a life. I thought that was kindness. I thought he was sainted. But now I realise kindness does not exist within him. He brought me in because he knew I would always be grateful. I would owe my life to him, and because of that, I would remain loyal.'

Martin caught Isabel's eyes as she looked up from the Keeper. He expected to see tears, but there were none. She hadn't told Martin that story because she wanted his pity, though part of him hoped she wanted him to understand. Isabel had been telling the story to herself. She'd needed to detach herself from the feelings towards the master she once had. Only by allowing herself to accept the truth could she move on and realise that the man she had always thought a saint was in fact her enemy.

Isabel moved first, her hand twisting in Martin's grip. For a minute he was frightened she was trying to let go, then he realised what she was doing as he felt her fingers interlace with his. He couldn't help smiling. The feeling of being ten hadn't left him yet.

Martin needed the toilet. When he first realised, he was merely troubled. He was frozen in a time bubble with Isabel, so there was no way he could go here. He also couldn't leave the time bubble, because then his mum would see the Keeper of Portals. He tried to think of a solution, but nothing came to him.

After two hours, the troubling feeling had transformed into full blown panic.

For the last half hour Martin and Isabel had sat in silence, each immersed in their own personal worlds. Now

Isabel looked concerned, as if in pain. Martin wondered she was losing control of their time. She kept looking the Keeper, then looking out the window. The room hadn't changed at all. Martin's mum was still only halfway past the doorframe and the piggy bank remained suspended in the air by invisible strings.

'Isabel?'

She turned to him, her mouth screwed up and her brow furrowed.

'Are you OK? You look worried. Can't you hold it anymore?'

Isabel shot him a look. 'Hold it?'

'Our time. You look like you're struggling.'

Isabel tried to smile, but it was pained. 'I am perfectly fine.'

Then Martin realised something. The way Isabel's eyes were darting around and her constant fidgeting were what gave it away. This wasn't a time issue at all, it was something much more basic.

'I... umm... I'm not quite sure how to say this,' said Martin, 'but do you need the toilet?'

Isabel's eyes opened wide and she nodded repeatedly.

'Yeah, me too,' said Martin.

''Tis the only thing I have been able to think about for the last hour,' said Isabel.

'Again, me too.'

'Do you have a solution?'

'I don't suppose you can make my bladder travel at normal speed while the rest of me goes quickly?'

Isabel smiled. 'Interesting thought, but no.'

From the bed, the Keeper of Portals stirred. He'd been unconscious since leaving the master's study. This was the first sign of wakefulness he'd shown.

His large feline eyes opened slowly and flicked from Isabel to Martin. A hint of a smile appeared.

Suddenly, Martin no longer needed the toilet. Completely unaware that Isabel was next to him, he started to check with his free hand, worried he'd wet himself, but everything seemed dry.

With no free hand, Isabel was shuffling herself around like she'd lost something.

'I no longer need to relieve myself,' she said.

'Me neither,' said Martin. 'I thought I'd wet myself, but it's like it's just gone.'

In a low voice that merely tickled the air, the Keeper spoke.

'You'll be surprised what can be used as a portal.'

Isabel's eyes went wide and so did Martin's.

'I don't know if I should feel relieved or violated,' said Isabel.

'Well if it helps, I'm doing a pretty good job feeling both right now.'

'Open your mouths,' said the Keeper.

Martin and Isabel did as they were instructed and found their mouth full of hot food. In fact, their mouths were so full they had difficulty eating it. Martin was able to hold a hand up to his mouth to keep shoving the food back in, but Isabel had no free hands so food fell from her over-stuffed face and down her underskirt. When she was finished, she gave Martin a dirty look.

'I could have let the food fall out of my mouth or I could have let go of your hand only to watch your time slow down so fast it would tear you apart, which would *you* rather I chose?'

Martin just smiled. The funny thing was, he actually liked that Isabel ate with food falling out of her mouth, not that he'd want her to always eat that way, of course.

When they had finished licking their lips and pondering where the contents of their bladders had been sent, they looked down, ready to talk to the Keeper of Portals, only to find that he was once more asleep.

The Keeper's healing process was a slow one. Martin and Isabel had to wait for three days until the Keeper was fully conscious. Occasionally he would wake to feed them and rid them of that which they needed rid of, never once mentioning where it went or where the food came from. Martin spoke of his time, of what school was like, the technology they had and the accomplishments that'd been made. Isabel was shocked to hear that humans had been to the moon and especially shocked by the way Martin spoke of it as "something that happened nearly fifty years ago". Isabel too talked of her time, but she had much less to tell. Her world was very small compared to Martin's. Whereas Martin could find out facts and information about anything in the world in only a few moments, Isabel didn't know trivial things such as the capital city of Japan, a country she'd never even heard of. Clearly an upbringing as a lady of status paled in comparison to an afternoon on Google.

They had to sleep, and to make sure they always remained in contact Martin had tied their hands together, as well as Isabel's other hand to the Keeper, with the remaining scraps of his T-shirts. He had also insisted that they move around often; otherwise their blood may clot, like on a plane. Isabel initially balked at the notion that someone could die just by sitting down for a long time, but agreed to move despite that after claiming she was "feeling rather stiff".

After three and a half days, in which time the piggy bank had fallen no more than a centimetre, the Keeper of Portals awoke.

CHAPTER
EIGHTEEN

In a single, swift motion, the Keeper of Portals went from lying down on the cusp of wakefulness to sitting bolt upright. His intense feline eyes looked first to Martin then Isabel before performing a quick scan of the room.

'I feel much better now,' he said with a smile.

'We thought you were going to die,' said Martin.

The Keeper nodded. 'I nearly did. At least, I think I nearly did. You don't tend to take in your surroundings too much when you're dying. Everything becomes all blurry and it feels like people are stuffing cotton wool under your eyelids.' The Keeper's eyes hovered over Isabel before flicking to Martin. 'Isn't she the one who tried to make me dead?'

Isabel turned away.

'It was her, but also not her. She was being controlled.'

'I see… Interesting feather you have.' The Keeper turned to Isabel. 'And crystal.' He looked around the room once more, the piggy bank floated in mid-air and Martin's mum was still on pause.

'We had to slow down time,' said Isabel, finding her voice. 'You were wounded and needed time to heal.'

'I needed to heal after you nearly made me dead, correct?'

Martin went to protest but Isabel cut him off.

'No, I did not nearly *make you dead*, the master did, and he is one of you. So if you have some issue with nearly dying then I suggest you take it up with him. However, if you would like someone to thank for saving you and waiting with you whilst you healed, then that person would be me.'

Martin wasn't surprised that Isabel left out the part where they nearly fell into the sea. It was probably for the best.

The Keeper sat up, deciding not to respond to Isabel, and with his free hand, touched the feather on Martin's head.

'Did you pull this out yourself? I seem to be missing a few.'

'You gave it to me,' said Martin.

'I did? I don't remember doing that.'

'It was a long time ago,' said Martin. 'Nearly 400 years. That's where the door leads.' Martin pointed. 'Same house, same room, only 400 years in the past. That's why you knew me. We'd met before. You just forgot.'

The Keeper craned his neck forward. Martin had managed to wipe most of the blood from him, though he was still missing many feathers and most of those that remained were in bad shape.

'The past? I thought something felt wrong. There was another Keeper of Portals there so I wasn't needed. I think the universe tried to get rid of me. I didn't like that.'

The Keeper of Portals touched a crooked feather with his long fingers before reaching up and tapping the crystal on Isabel's forehead.

220

'Oi!' cried Isabel. She was already glaring at him for refusing to thank her; being poked in the head wasn't making things better.

'No guesses who this came from,' said the Keeper of Portals. 'But still,' he said, retracting his finger and turning to Martin, 'I have no memory of ever giving you a feather. And I told you before, I was certain I hadn't *met* you; I just *knew* you.'

Once Martin and the Keeper had untied the strips of T-shirt that bound them to Isabel, events unfurled like a tightly bound spring. The piggy bank started to fall and the door swung open. Before they realised what had happened, the Keeper of Portals completely disappeared, worming his way through some impossibly obscure gateway neither Martin nor Isabel could see. Jo's foot finally reached the floor and she turned around, not finding Martin where she'd expected to see him. The piggy bank smashed, causing everyone to jump. Jo froze once more, staring at Martin and Isabel who were sitting on Martin's bed, still holding hands.

Martin had already moved so that his head was pushed against the wall to hide the feather while Isabel had attempted to mask the crystal with her hair.

Jo stood in silence for over a minute, staring at her fifteen year old son caught on a bed holding the hand of a teenage girl wearing an underskirt that belonged in the Victorian age.

She sniffed the air.

Raising her hand and pointing, Jo turned away so as to hide her look of disgust.

'There's a working shower at the end of the landing.' Thick clouds of steam greeted Martin as he opened the door to the bathroom and threw in a pile of clothes.

'Wear these,' he shouted before closing the door.

The sound of the shower stopped and Martin could hear Isabel climb out.

'What are these?' shouted Isabel.

'Clothes,' said Martin. 'You can't wear dresses everywhere.'

'You can *not* expect me to wear these peculiar looking breeches.'

Martin sighed. 'They're trousers.'

'I do not care what you call them, I shan't wear them. You may have forgotten, but I am actually a lady. These are men's clothes.'

'Not in my time they're not.'

This wasn't exactly true. The trousers were Martin's, but they were too small for him. The exercise top was his mum's.

'Well, we shall be going back to *my* time and I do not intend to parade about dressed like this.'

Martin should have known this was going to be difficult.

'Well it's either that or nothing. That flimsy dress of yours was covered in blood so I binned it.'

There was a disapproving grunt from the other side of the door.

'We're going back to stop the master,' said Martin. 'Don't you think practical clothes would be useful? Or do you plan to just sit in a pretty dress and watch?'

222

'I most certainly won't!' said Isabel. This was followed by the frantic putting on of clothes.

'And tie your hair up,' shouted Martin. 'You don't want it getting pulled out.'

After a few moments, Isabel opened the bathroom door. She was dressed in dark green combat trousers and a tight fitting black vest top. Her hair had been gathered back and was tied in a high ponytail. She did not look happy.

'These clothes are ridiculous. I look a fool.'

'Actually,' said Martin, 'you look like a teenage Lara Croft.'

'And I suppose you are about to tell me that is a compliment.'

'I know you won't believe me, but it really is.'

Isabel was standing in front of the door at the end of Martin's room, one hand pressed against it.

'I could open it just like the Keeper of Portals did.'

Martin walked over to her. He knew exactly what she was thinking. The Keeper of Portals had consumed a crystal which had surely come from the Keeper of Time, using all of its energy to open a door in time that had been shut for the last 400 years. Isabel could do the same. She could open the door and they could step into the master's study in 1623. But there was a problem with that. If Isabel opened the door then her crystal would break just like the Keeper of Portals' had. Isabel would lose her ability to change time and they wouldn't be able to dodge the hordes of villagers or the master's attacks without that.

Something told Martin that if they were to stand a chance against the Keeper of Questions, they'd need the crystal on Isabel's head to stay exactly where it was, even if it had been weakened after saving Isabel's life. He thought of the Keeper of Causality and the choice she had said he must make. Was this it? Isabel opens the door, loses her crystal and the master wins, or they find another way to the past, Isabel keeps the crystal and the master is defeated. Was it that simple?

Martin explained this to Isabel and she walked away from the door. As she passed Martin's bookcase, she picked something up. It was white and shaped like a bird bath but with three porcelain curls on top.

'Martin, why do you have a salt dish in your bedroom?'

'Is that what it is?'

'You have never seen a salt dish before?' asked Isabel.

'Well, no. We keep our salt in a shaker.'

Isabel put the dish back. ''Tis almost as strange as the butter churner I saw in your bathroom. Who would churn butter in the bathroom?'

'You knew what that was too?'

'Of course! I do use one.'

Martin thought for a second and grabbed Isabel's hand. 'Come with me.' They left his bedroom and stepped straight into the kitchen.

Martin pointed to a flat brass spoon that was covered with holes. 'What's that?'

'A skimmer, for lifting the cream off milk.'

Martin then pointed to a silver bowl with two flat patterned silver handles at opposite sides. 'And what's that?'

'A pottinger, for soups and broths.'

Martin picked up a wooden box with a sloping lid that was hung from the ceiling. Isabel responded without being asked.

'A salt box, for keeping your salt,' she finished condescendingly.

Martin pointed to more utensils and Isabel reeled off more names: oven peel, bellows, flesh hooks, skillets.

Finally Martin stopped. He seemed quite satisfied with himself. Isabel just looked confused.

'Are you going to tell me the purpose of that naming game or were you simply bored?'

Martin shook his head. He was smiling now. 'I can't believe I didn't see it.'

'See what?'

'All this! You knew what it was.'

'Of course I did. They are kitchen utensils and I do use the kitchen.'

'Yes, but they weren't here before. We used to have a microwave and a blender, but they've gone. Now we've got a wood burning stove and bellows. My mum's car is a horse, my laptop is just some old paper and a quill and my trainers are leather sandals.'

'And your point?'

'You know what all that stuff is. Sure, I knew what some bits were, but the rest just looked like junk. But that doesn't matter because *you* knew!'

It was Isabel's turn to smile. She too had worked it out. 'Which meant they came from *my time.*'

'Exactly! With the door to your house open, time must

have got confused. I kept waiting, you see, for the Keeper of Time to appear, my Keeper of Time, from now. Then I realised there wasn't one. How could there be more than one Keeper of Time? He has to oversee all of Time, so he can't be in it, not like that. That's why things were being swapped. Why there are pylons in your time and salt dishes in mine.'

'But no one else can see that they've been swapped, can they?'

Martin pointed to the feather growing out of the crown of his head. 'I guess it's because of this.'

Isabel nodded and leaned against the beaten oak table.

'So because there was a door between our two times, items from my time were swapped with items from your time?'

'Swapped,' said Martin, 'or jumped. If the Keeper of Portals has to fix connections that jump to the wrong doorway, then the Keeper of Time must have to fix stuff, or ideas, that jump to the wrong time. Maybe that doesn't happen very often, but because of the door it's been happening loads, only he's not here to fix it.'

'How does this help? Just because you know where these items have come from does not mean we know how to go back to my time. The door is still closed.'

Martin walked over to the table and picked up a pewter plate. 'The door was closed the day after you and the Keeper fell from the cliffs. This plate appeared a week ago.' Martin put the plate down and walked over to the fire. 'The bellows, five days ago, the skimmer, four days ago. And that thing that looks like a bird bath you said was a salt dish, that's only been there two days.'

'You mean?'

Martin nodded. 'There's another door.'

Martin had no name for the space he visualised each time he made a connection. Standing up, the ends of the cables were just above his head and each one was a bright colour: red, green, yellow or blue. Martin grabbed a blue cable and knew what it was without thinking. The third bedroom to the right after the small staircase on the first floor. He was looking for something he didn't know. Martin tried to walk to the cables that receded into the distance, but he couldn't move. If he really tried, he could maybe move one foot and grab a few more cables that way, but that was his limit. Looking up, the thick rubber encased tubes extended up to a ceiling he couldn't see. Light wasn't coming from any obvious source; it was just there. Between the cables, Martin spotted something he'd not noticed before. It was a cable, golden and much thinner than the others. Martin reached up as high as he could, but it was just beyond his fingertips. He tried to jump, but his feet wouldn't leave the floor. The cables moved and the gold one slithered away.

Martin flung handfuls of the large cables to the side, causing them to sway and interfere with each other. He kept catching glimpses of the golden cable, but then it would disappear again. He was certain the golden cable was the door, but if he couldn't reach it, then he wouldn't be able to connect to it. Martin left his space.

Isabel was lying on her front on Martin's bed trying to read a book. She looked up when Martin opened his eyes.

'I can barely read this. You have peculiar spellings for words I should know.' Isabel closed the book. 'So, did you find anything?'

Martin stood. 'Yeah, I saw it... sort of.'

'Sort of?'

'It's definitely in the house, I just can't get to it. It's out of my reach, but not in a way I can do anything about.'

Isabel rolled off the bed and onto her feet. 'While you were having a little think, I had an idea.'

'Oh.'

'Well, 'tis a door we are after, and we all know you are *Mr Door*, but it is also a door to a different time, so I thought perhaps there is something I can do.'

'Like what?'

'I am uncertain,' said Isabel. 'But when I was lying there, I concentrated, like you were doing, and I could feel something peculiar that I could not place, like a tiny gust of wind coming through a crack in the wall. I did not know where it was; I just knew it was there.'

'This wall had quite a lot of cracks in it a couple of weeks ago. There could still be some left.'

'No, no,' said Isabel, 'not a real crack. For 'tis only there when I think about it.'

Martin took Isabel's hands. 'OK, I'll focus on my cable and you focus on your... gust.'

'What is a cable?'

'It doesn't matter.'

Martin closed his eyes again. Once more he was in

his nameless place. The thin, golden cable was above him, dancing amongst its thicker brothers. Martin jumped. His feet left the ground and his hand grabbed onto the cable. He tried to connect another cable to it, but none would fit. However, that didn't matter, because just by holding the cable he knew where the door was.

Martin and Isabel opened their eyes at the same time. 'The loft!'

Martin's open bedroom door looked directly up at the roof joists. He went in first, carrying the torch, and then helped Isabel, who wasn't as used to going through a door and finding gravity 90 degrees in a different direction.

Exposed beams a metre apart were all they had to stand on. They were both wearing shoes, Isabel borrowing some of Jo's and wearing an extra pair of socks.

Everywhere the torch beam landed there was something from another time: countless portraits, large clocks, vases, beds, and a huge number of mirrors were piled in a disorderly mess around the loft. Despite the roof being as high as every other room in the house, the loft was full to bursting. If anything else appeared, then there was a chance the beams would break and the whole lot would go crashing down into the rooms below.

They climbed over piles and piles of 17th century paraphernalia. Sometimes there was so much stuff they could feel the top of the roof scrape their backs as they moved along on their fronts.

The door was in front of them. They couldn't see it yet, but every now and again as they forced their way along they would touch hands and try to zero in on its position.

The mounds of junk ended in a large semi-circle at the far wall. Martin and Isabel were careful as they made their way down the slope, feeling things shift and break beneath them. Unlike 21st century items, which were often made from plastic with rounded edges, everything from Isabel's time was either splintered wood, broken glass or solid cast iron. At least, that was how it felt to Martin as his hands and shins were cut again and again.

'Is that it?' said Isabel.

Cracks like the branches of a tree radiated from the door in the centre of the wall. It was made from a mix of silver and gold with an ornate frame of brass leaves. While the beauty and intricacy of the door could not be denied, there was something very wrong with it.

The door was only four inches tall.

Martin lay on his front. Using a pin he found on the floor, he managed to fiddle the tiny handle of the door and push it open. Pressing his eye up against it, he could see another loft. He tried to shine the torch through. Just like the loft they were in, the loft on the other side of the door was piled with stuff, but this was stuff from Martin's time: computers, televisions, furniture. He even spotted a moped.

As Martin sat up, brushing the dust from his face, he was quite glad the Keeper of Causality had decided not to return him to the past by simply pushing him through the door.

'That's definitely the place,' said Martin.

'And you can get through?'

'Not exactly…'

Martin bent down before the elaborately decorated door. Nothing was ever simple.

CHAPTER
NINETEEN

Dust fell from the horse's mane and carpeted the floor. 'This is amazing!' cried Isabel.

Isabel was riding the rocking horse too violently and her hands slipped from the worn reins. She flew through the air, but just before she hit the floor face first, her body twisted at super-fast speed and she landed on her feet.

'Why didn't you show me this room before? These are much more interesting than your moving pictures.'

Isabel jumped on the iron framed bed and dust burst from it like a mushroom cloud before settling on her like snow. Martin got up and opened the window, taking a few breaths of fresh air. He'd managed to come up with a solution to the problem pretty fast, though it did help he'd seen it done before. The only issue was Isabel was far too excited to actually assist him.

'This stuff's old,' said Martin, leaving the sanity of the outside world as he left the window. 'It's probably been here a hundred years.'

'Old? This stuff? But it is incredible.' Isabel was holding a stuffed bear in front of her face and moving it from side to side. The bear looked rock solid and was probably full of dust mites and disease.

'Well, I suppose stuff that's a hundred years old for me is still future stuff for you. I'm kind of hurt you find an old teddy more interesting than my laptop, though.'

Isabel put the bear down, and just as Martin thought she was going to come over and help him, she dived off the far side of the bed.

'I found something!' Isabel shouted.

Martin walked over, half expecting to find her cuddling the rotting corpse of a sheep, when from behind the bed a horrifying toy doll was thrust into the air.

'Oh god, it's hideous!' cried Martin.

Isabel climbed out from behind the bed, sending more dust into the air as she stomped across the mattress and jumped down in front of Martin.

''Tis beautiful! What is it?'

'A doll.'

'A doll… What does it do?'

'Do?' said Martin. 'It doesn't *do* anything. It's a toy for girls. They play with them. Did you not have dolls?'

Isabel shook her head. 'I've never seen anything this pretty.'

The doll was about the size of a new born baby and its limbs hung down heavily as if it'd just died and been scooped off the floor. Wearing a lace dress that had turned so yellow it looked like a dehydrated dog had peed on it and sporting a misshapen half head of ridiculous curls, the doll was anything but pretty. And of course, that wasn't mentioning the fact that its skin was peeling off and it was missing an eye.

'Why are you looking at me like that? You said it was a toy for girls.'

'Yeah,' said Martin with a half crooked smile, 'I meant a toy for *little* girls.'

'And?'

'And sixteen year old girls in my time don't go around playing with dolls.'

Isabel cocked her head to the side, still looking at the doll.

'I could tell you what sixteen year old girls from my time, who are proficient in skinning animals, do to boys that hurt their feelings, but I do not think you would be able to sleep again if I did.'

Isabel placed the doll back on the bed and sat next to it. Martin sat down too, but away from the doll.

Isabel sighed. 'I don't understand why we have to go back.'

'Because we already have.'

'Are you trying to not make sense?'

'I don't need to try. Ever since I met the Keeper of Portals nothing has made sense, or at least, very little.'

'So if I am to understand correctly, we need to return to my time because that is already the past in this time?'

Martin nodded. Isabel continued to amaze him.

'And do you know what we are to do when we get there?'

'Defeat the master I guess, or at least help someone else defeat him. Though I'd be annoyed if it wasn't us. I mean it should be, shouldn't it?'

'I suppose that he has wronged us, but we are not the only ones. Surely the villagers hold a grudge against him as I am sure do many of the Keepers. It would be selfish to think of it as our battle alone.'

'You're right, but the Keeper of Causality told me that I had to go back to the master's time and make a choice. I don't know what that choice is, just that something's going to happen and the one Keeper that's supposed to control events like this can't do it because it's beyond her power. I guess that means it's something pretty important.'

'It appears so,' said Isabel, 'but you know that if we return to my time, I won't be able to bring us back.'

Martin looked up at Isabel's cracked crystal. 'I know.'

'And we shall still go?'

'Yes.'

For a moment Isabel didn't say anything. She seemed pleased with something, but tried not to let it show on her face. Eventually she asked, 'And we shall get to the past from this room?'

Martin nodded. Clearly Isabel was ready to get moving, though her hands still played with the lace of the doll's dress.

'The door in the attic, it's just like the one in my bedroom. I can't connect to it because it's a door in time and I think it's really small so the master doesn't notice it, but it's still a door. We just need to walk through it to get back to the master's house. Except…'

'Except we are too big,' finished Isabel.

'Exactly.'

Martin jumped off the bed and walked over to the door. He opened it, passed through, and then he was gone.

The dust was nearly as high as Martin's knees and he kicked it to the side as he walked. He was in the hall: a grandfather clock stood on the wall in front of him and two windows covered with lace drapes were on his left side. Of course, there was nothing on his right. He walked towards the door next to the clock. There was a dead fly in the corner of the room and Martin had to cover his mouth to stop himself from throwing up. He'd always thought he had a strong stomach for gore, but a dead bluebottle the size of a dog was more than even he could take.

Entering the living room, Martin found a high-backed chair, brushed off the obligatory layer of dust and sat down. He was staring directly at Isabel, waiting for her to notice him. There was a table in front of him, so he put his feet up. Still nothing. He coughed and Isabel's ears twitched slightly, but she still didn't move. Her hand continued to play with the doll's dress. She was starting to look annoyed; maybe she thought he'd just left without an explanation.

Martin was impatient. Isabel clearly had no idea he was still in the room with her. He got up and walked back into the dining room. With both hands he grabbed the grandfather clock and hurled it to the ground. Unfortunately, unlike a real grandfather clock, it didn't make a massive clang as it crashed to the floor, and just bounced, but it was enough, and immediately Isabel was off the bed and running over.

'You're in the tiny house!'

The house was the first thing in the room Isabel had spotted, and quite rightly. It completely dominated one wall and, unlike horrifying dolls or diseased bears, even Martin was impressed, even if it did double-up as an insect cemetery.

'The Keeper of Portals showed me. He said he could change his size to fit the door.'

'Can I come too?' said Isabel.

'Sorry, it's a Portals thing.'

Isabel folded her arms and didn't say anything else.

As Martin moved about, sitting on the intricately carved furniture or tossing a tiny green apple, he kept casting sidelong glances at Isabel. He had never seen her face this close before, never seen anyone's face this close. It eclipsed everything, she was so near, following him like a predator. Any other girl would have been self-conscious, but Isabel didn't seem to care. Up close she was still beautiful, though not perfect. No one ever is. She didn't have any spots exactly, but Martin could make out a few blackheads on her nose and her full lips were cracked. In one place she'd bitten them too much and they'd gone bright red.

She may not have been perfect, but Martin couldn't think of anyone else who'd do so well under scrutiny. And the funny thing was Martin found he didn't even care about those little imperfections. They meant nothing, and even if they were worse, and she had more spots or a hair on her chin, he knew he wouldn't care in the slightest because, to him, they wouldn't make Isabel any less beautiful.

Isabel clutched Martin to her chest as she walked up the stairs. It was the only way for Martin to remain small. If he'd just walked out of the dolls' house and back into the bedroom he would have come out full size, not his current height of three inches that he needed to get through the tiny door to the master's house.

The problem with Martin being so small was that he couldn't open doors, so Isabel had to carry him through the house. When they finally found the attic hatch at the top of a very tall ceiling, Isabel had been forced to drag furniture from the neighbouring rooms and pile it up to make a ladder.

Isabel slid down a heap of 17th century furniture, involuntarily squeezing her hand as she did. Her rough skin closed around Martin and he thought for a minute he was going to be crushed. It was strange to be carried like this by another person, trusting them so completely. Though it wasn't that Martin was scared Isabel would do anything intentionally, he was more worried she'd forget he was there and accidentally drop him or the dust would irritate her nose and she'd sneeze into her hands.

Isabel knelt down in front of the tiny door. She placed Martin on the floor, but used her hands to make an archway over his head to stop him from suddenly growing.

Martin took a step forward. The door's silver and gold surface shone brilliantly despite there being such little light. Reaching out a hand, Martin touched the brass leaves that decorated the frame before going for the door. He turned the handle and pushed the door open.

The door on the other side was also tiny, and as Martin stepped through, he felt himself start to grow. At first it was only his leg, but as he went further into the other loft, the rest of him started to follow, ballooning out before returning to the correct shape.

The only thing that remained small was Martin's right hand. His entire right arm just shrank from its normal size to something the width of a toothpick. His hand was still in his loft and he could feel Isabel's finger touching it. To do what Martin had in mind, he'd need both their powers.

Martin crouched down on the floor with his tiny right hand gripping the top of the doorframe. Then he stood, bringing his right arm up as he did.

The brickwork shattered like a shockwave had passed through it, breaking apart the already crack-riddled wall and shooting out across the loft. Martin was lifting the door, stretching it as if the frame were made of toffee. It continued to rise, up to his knee, then his thigh, destroying the wall as it went. He could see Isabel's legs on the other side of the door, dressed in the green combat trousers. With one last push he heaved the door up as high as it would go. More brick shattered on both sides of the door and Martin saw Isabel jump back.

The door was fighting him, but he was now holding the top of the frame above his head. His hand was full size again and Isabel held it tightly with her own.

The door was the right height, but only as wide as Martin's hand. He jammed a foot in the bottom and slid it out, causing more destruction and forcing the doorframe to stretch into a triangular shape.

As the door had grown, so too had the bronze leaves, but instead of growing evenly, they were twisted and deformed like the frame. Some of them had even fallen off and looked like coins rolled through a penny press.

Isabel stepped through, careful not to let go of Martin but having to almost push past him because he was right in front of the door. When they were both in the master's loft, they let go of the frame and jumped back. The door snapped into nothingness. The only thing left was a hole in the wall that now led to a different part of the loft and not to Martin's house. Even the leaves had vanished.

Martin picked up a VR gaming headset from a pile of electrical gadgets directly in front of him.

'Shame the door's gone. I could've had this.'

'The trick is to steal small things,' said Isabel, holding up a set of car keys, a charm bracelet and a USB thumb drive before shoving them in her pockets.

Martin pulled out an enormous orange bean bag, causing a pile of furniture with a sofa balanced on the top to collapse. Isabel had to jump out of the way to stop the sofa from landing on her, but luckily when Isabel did anything, she always had plenty of time.

Martin flopped onto the bean bag and Isabel did the same, half sitting on him.

'Sorry, I didn't think it would fall.'

''Tis all right,' said Isabel.

'Do you think he's in the house, the Keeper of Questions, I mean?'

'The master?' said Isabel, musing. 'I know not. Perhaps. The door is still here, so he may continue to use it.'

'We were in my house for two weeks. If this door's been there all this time, then we only left here two weeks ago.'

'Are we in the cave?'

Martin nodded. 'We must be, though we probably shouldn't visit ourselves. I don't fancy getting pushed into the sea.'

Isabel smiled, but it soon faded. 'Last time we were here, we ran. He had control of all those people and there was nothing we could do but escape. If we have been gone for two weeks, then he has had two weeks to become even stronger. Martin, if he was too powerful before, how will we stop him now?'

Martin knew they couldn't run this time. They were in the 17th century and that was where they would stay.

As Martin sat and thought, he felt something burrow its way into his conscious. It wasn't being picked up by his senses, it was coming from somewhere else, directly entering his brain without permission. He focused on it, unsure if it was wise to do so or not.

A voice he recognised spoke to him, repeating itself like a mantra over and over again. The more Martin focused on it, the louder the voice became and the more the message took hold.

'I am the answer. I am the light. I am the way. I know all. I see all. I help all. I heal all.'

Over and over again those phrases repeated in Martin's head.

'The master! The master!' cried Isabel. 'He is in my head!'

Isabel's voice was enough to bring Martin back and he forced the voice in his head into submission. It wasn't gone completely, just quieter. Yet even in hushed tones, there was something frighteningly tempting about the master's words.

CHAPTER
TWENTY

Martin and Isabel split up. Martin searched the top three floors of the house, opening doors into every room, cupboard, wardrobe and pantry while Isabel took the ground floor and the gardens.

Martin was sat by the front door when he saw Isabel racing over. Even with a crack in her crystal, she was still pretty damn fast.

Isabel stopped and shook her head. She was surprisingly free of sweat.

'Deserted.'

Martin stood up. 'Yeah, the place is empty. He must have taken everyone with him.'

'Do you know to where?' asked Isabel.

'Not a clue, which does kind of mess up the whole defeating him plan.'

Martin had expected the Keeper of Questions to be in the house, that he wasn't did make things a little harder. This wasn't the 21st century, he couldn't just Google the Keeper's new address or track his location via his smartphone's GPS. This was the 17th century: when you wanted to find someone you had to go on a quest, Martin presumed, and that could take years.

'We will have to find him,' said Isabel, 'but before that, there is something I require.'

Isabel entered the house. Martin followed her up the central staircase and then along the first floor corridor. He watched Isabel sway as she walked. Had she always done that? Before she had been hidden by many layers of skirts. It was strange, thought Martin: by wearing men's clothes, Isabel actually appeared more feminine.

'I was thinking as I searched for the Keeper,' said Isabel.

'What were you thinking about?'

'Life. And the future.'

'And?'

'And I do not know,' said Isabel. She sounded defeated, as if she'd been battling thoughts in her head and lost. 'I feel like I've been plucked from my life and thrown into a brand new one that I can never understand. I do not know what lies ahead of me because I cannot understand that which is around me. I feel that nothing makes sense and I fear it never will. The only plan I ever made for the future was to become insane and live on the streets, but now even that is wishful thinking.'

Isabel was still in the lead and continued along the landing towards the rooms that overlooked the sea. The corridor turned sharply to the left and in front of them was another flight of stairs, though these ones were dull as if built only for unimportant people. Martin followed Isabel up.

'You could live with me.'

'Pardon?' Isabel stopped walking and turned around.

'After all this is over, I mean. Well, assuming it's ever

243

over, and we're actually able to get back to my time.'

'Live with you?' Isabel looked confused but at the same time relieved.

'Why not? We've got enough space. And my mum won't mind, I don't think. She'd like a girl in the house. I don't know how we'd explain you and I guess you'd need a passport and stuff, but I'm sure we can figure that out later.'

'You ask if I want to live with you, but how do you mean? As a sister?'

Martin started to walk again even though he had no idea where he was going. He didn't want to keep staring at Isabel. She soon caught up and took the lead.

'Not as a sister exactly,' said Martin.

Isabel raced ahead of Martin and pushed open a door at the very end of the landing, meeting his eyes for a moment.

'You are very bold, Martin,' she said, smiling impishly. 'Of course, you assume it is possible for us to return to your time. You already know that I cannot do it.'

'We live in a world of Keepers,' said Martin. 'As long as they're around I get the impression everything's possible. Well, most things. It's not possible for us to get out of this. Plus, they'll kind of owe us. I'm sure they'll do whatever we want them to.'

'A fair point.' Isabel beamed. 'I look forward to living with you, *not*-brother.'

Martin sighed.

Isabel led Martin through a large empty room. The same room that had collapsed into the sea when Isabel and the Keeper had fallen. The walls were a bright pink and deep blue curtains hung by the sides of the massive windows. The wooden floor beneath them was completely unmarked as if the room hadn't been used since it was built. It was strange to think that in nearly four hundred years the whole lot would fall into the sea, Isabel and the Keeper of Portals along with it. Martin could almost feel it give way beneath his feet, but that was just his mind playing tricks.

At the end of the room were a number of smaller rooms. In one of these there was a large fireplace. Isabel squatted down in front of it, one hand on the hearth. She turned to Martin. 'I can still hear him. His voice does not cease.'

Martin nodded. He knew exactly what she meant. The Keeper of Questions had been in his head the entire time, repeating his mantra over and over. 'We just have to ignore it,' he said.

'I know, but hearing his voice, 'tis like a memory. Like he is welcoming me home. He is not a Keeper, not in my head. He is the master. *My* master.'

To Martin it sounded like Isabel was speaking of an ex-boyfriend, though he knew that wasn't the case. Isabel had only worked for the master and, on top of that, he'd beaten her at will. But still, Martin couldn't shake the feeling that Isabel saw the Keeper of Questions as something else. Martin spoke of having to destroy him, but he also realised that the creature he'd have to destroy was probably Isabel's very first crush. A small part of Martin relished the idea of defeating the master for that very reason.

'I'm sorry,' said Isabel. 'I do not know why I said that. It is not that I wanted you to think… I just, I want you to know that I do not wish for him to be in my head.'

Isabel allowed a sad smile to flicker across her face before crawling into the fireplace.

'Your room is up a chimney?'

'Yes,' said Isabel. 'Do you have an issue with that?'

'No. But you've got a massive house full of rooms; surely the master didn't use all of them.'

Isabel ducked back out. Her head was cocked to the side and her ponytail hung over her right shoulder.

'When I lived in my old master's house I was tricked into believing I was part of the family. I lived with them, ate with them and socialised with them. Then I learnt I had been living a lie. I was upset and angry, but more than that, I felt a fool. I believed I was one of them and gallivanted around, bossing the maids to do my bidding, as if I had that right from birth. I never want to feel like that again, that I am somewhere I do not belong. I found this place to make sure I do not forget.'

Isabel climbed up the inside of the chimney. Martin followed, finding that Isabel had removed bricks to use as foot and hand holds. The only problem was, as soon as he was a metre up, there was absolutely no light and while Isabel knew the exact placement of every missing brick, Martin had no idea where they were so took five minutes longer to get to the top. Of course he could have just dropped back down and created a gateway to Isabel's room, but he didn't want to admit defeat.

Isabel's room was small and consisted of little more

than a pile of rugs and blankets she used as a bed and a few small chests for clothes and other items she'd managed to drag up the chimney. She stood facing what was supposed to be a window but was in fact a hole in the wall created by removing even more bricks. Past Isabel's head, Martin could see the sea.

Isabel sighed and looked around the room like she knew she would soon be leaving it and was both sad and thankful.

'I need to change my undergarments,' Isabel quickly declared, banishing her contemplative mood.

'What?'

'These undergarments you lent me are too tight. They constantly press against me; 'tis indecent.'

'This isn't just some excuse to put on another dress, is it?'

'No. Whilst I do not like that I am dressed as a man, I do concede that my clothes are a little… impractical. However, I presume you have no issue with the type of undergarment I wear.'

'No, that's fine. Wear what you want *there*,' said Martin.

Isabel stood for a moment, regarding Martin curiously.

'And do you plan on watching me undress?'

Martin's face instantly burned red and he turned away. He kept his mouth shut; anything he said now would only be the unintelligible ramblings of an embarrassed teenage boy.

'I told you this would happen,' said Isabel in a sing-song voice.

Martin could hear her removing clothes behind him

and tried to focus on something else, but not even the Keeper of Questions' mantra was able to smash through the mental picture his mind painted.

'All the privacy you have granted has made me complacent. Now I have come to expect it. Perhaps if you were not so chivalrous, you may have been allowed a peek, *not*-brother.'

Martin's face burned even brighter.

After a moment of rustling, Isabel declared that she had finished. Martin turned around. She looked exactly as she had before, and Martin would have been convinced she hadn't even changed if he hadn't spotted the outline of her underwear beneath her trousers, just above her knees.

'I just need to find one more thing, then we can leave,' said Isabel, clapping her hands together. She got on her knees and started to riffle through the rugs and blankets she slept on before going through the boxes, throwing the contents onto the floor.

'Where is it? Where is it?'

'What is it?' asked Martin. 'I'll help you look.'

'Oh 'tis just a thing. A precious thing. I cannot leave without it.'

Isabel had a hand in a crack between the floor and the wall. 'Found it!'

Isabel pulled her hand out. She was holding a large pendant on a long silver chain, though it could have been white gold for all Martin knew. Isabel held it above her face, inspecting it like she'd not seen it for years.

'Was it your mum's?'

Isabel sent him a look. 'No. I stole it.'

'You stole it?'

'Yes, from an old lady who used to turn her nose up every time she saw me. Each day I told myself I would steal the pendant she always wore, then one day I did.' Isabel smiled, swinging the pendant like a hypnotist. 'I planned to swap it for food, but I never managed.'

'Does it really mean that much to you?'

Isabel walked over and held the pendant up to Martin's eye. 'You see this jewel here?' she said.

'Yeah.'

'It is worth a lot of money. I would never get enough food for it, and even if I did, 'twould spoil before I had time to eat it all.'

Isabel slipped the chain around her neck and tucked the pendant into her black vest top. It poked out from the material around her stomach like an alien trying to escape.

'Now I am ready to say goodbye.'

'Goodbye?'

'In your house,' said Isabel with a smile, 'my room has already fallen into the sea.'

As they left, Martin saw Isabel pick up a pressed flower from the floor. She rubbed it with her thumb before slipping it into her pocket. Isabel didn't say anything as she followed him into the chimney and Martin didn't ask.

Unlike in Martin's time, there were no portraits hung around the grand staircase in the centre of the house. No one of any importance, at least not so important as to be worth the time and effort to paint, had lived there yet.

'Is our plan to simply wander the country until we find the master?'

'Pretty much,' said Martin. 'The best we can hope for is one of his brainwashed slaves captures us. At least that way we'll get delivered to him. Save us the effort.'

Martin was about to put his foot down on the stair below when he noticed something there and quickly pulled back.

The Keeper of Pleasantries looked up, his long neck extending and his feline face breaking into a broad smile.

'Martin, it is most certainly a pleasure to make your acquaintance again, although a little unexpected.'

'What?' Martin stopped and crouched down to the Keeper's level. 'Where did you even come from? You weren't there a second ago.'

'Alas, I had wanted to wait for you, but you see, your disappearance put the master in such a foul mood that I felt it wouldn't be prudent to remain in his presence. And whilst I may only be a Minor Keeper, I do have duties of my own to attend to. I had been locked up for quite a while and have thus had rather a busy time of it since you freed me.'

Isabel too crouched down on the stair next to Martin. She reached out a hand and stroked the Keeper as if he were a real cat. He didn't seem to mind and actually leaned into her.

'But how did you get there?' said Martin. 'Can you teleport?'

The Keeper of Pleasantries moved away from Isabel, despite the obvious pleasure he was receiving from her, and walked closer to Martin. His form appeared to be a cross between a cat and a giraffe and he was nearly as tall as Martin's waist, even though that was mostly legs and neck.

'I must confess that I asked for assistance. I knew I would need to see you again, but also knew that I could not stay here and simply wait, so I asked Coincidence.'

'Coincidence?'

'Yes, I asked the Keeper of Coincidence to arrange a coincidental meeting between us when you returned to the house, as I was sure you would. Whilst meeting on the stairs this way does appear to be a coincidence, especially as I am sure I have the information you were only moments ago seeking an answer for, I do wish it hadn't involved me nearly being stood upon.' The Keeper of Pleasantries started to descend the stairs. 'Now if we are lucky, then by coincidence, we may find refreshments in the first sitting room we enter.'

Martin was sat in a high-backed armchair. Isabel was to his right, lying on a chaise longue and the Keeper of Pleasantries was in front of both of them, perched on a pouffe. To the side there was a table upon which sat wine, a still-warm loaf of bread and an assortment of unfamiliar cheeses. Martin had to pry the wine from Isabel's hands, claiming they needed to be sober if they planned to face the master any time soon. To his surprise, Isabel said she drank wine all the time as she was not fond of small ale. Apparently no one drank water in 1623; it wasn't safe.

'As you can see, Questions has left.' The Keeper of Pleasantries said this as he stretched his boneless limbs and

251

tucked them beneath him. 'The house served its purpose: its relative isolation and local labourers were what Questions desired at the time. However, now he has grown beyond what the house can provide.'

'What about the door?' said Martin. 'Doesn't he need it?'

The Keeper of Pleasantries shook his head.

'What of the Keepers of Time and Portals? Do they remain here?' asked Isabel.

'He continues to hold them hostage. All Keepers are aware of the situation, but we cannot interfere. If Time and Portals were to be freed, even then they could not go against him.'

'Why not?' asked Isabel.

'A Keeper cannot use what they observe to forcefully manipulate another Keeper. It is not that such a thing is simply not permitted, it is not possible.'

'But the master's doing it. He is controlling two Keepers by locking them up. How can he do it when no other Keepers can?' said Isabel.

The Keeper of Pleasantries stretched his neck along the pouffe until it was fully extended before turning his kind eyes to Isabel. 'Insanity,' the Keeper said. 'Questions has allowed himself to become damaged. His fear has twisted him into something he was never meant to become. But more than that, he has sacrificed himself to control the Keepers.' The Keeper of Pleasantries smiled. 'But Questions is not as powerful as he would like to think, and while there are elements of Time and Portals he can control, there are also elements that he cannot.' The Keeper of Pleasantries gestured to Martin and Isabel.

'What are we supposed to do?' said Isabel. She sat up straight and brushed crumbs from her trousers. 'Conversing like this is all well and, pleasant, I suppose, but it is not getting us anywhere. We need to stop the master and we need to do so soon.'

The Keeper of Pleasantries appeared taken aback, his head curling around his body like a snake. He was not one used to rushing things.

'I'm sorry,' said Martin. 'It's not like we mean to be rude, but Isabel's right. This is important. The master's in our heads now. The longer we wait the stronger he's going to get, right?'

'He will get stronger,' said the Keeper after a pause. 'He will get stronger because more people will listen. More will question the actions of those under his control which will feed him further. His influence will grow, reaching into the minds of those who seek the simple answers to complex questions. His answers will tempt you and, if you are not careful, they will also control you.'

'So what shall we do?' asked Isabel, clearly getting irritated by all the sitting around and chatting. 'If he is going to become stronger, then how are we to resist him?'

'You must hold onto a truth,' said the Keeper of Pleasantries, 'a truth that you know, a truth that cannot be broken. He will try to change the answers you have found, supplanting his own in their stead. That is why you must keep a single truth within yourselves, one that he can never touch no matter how hard he tries.'

Isabel looked at Martin, her eyes moving up and down him before she smiled and turned away. Martin's own eyes were closed as he tried to focus on the one truth he could hold on to, a rock in his mind that could never be shifted. Many floated around in his head. At first he could only come up with simple ones like his favourite food or favourite book. But they weren't strong enough.

A truth came to him, one that wouldn't change depending on his feelings, but along with the truth came the pain caused by the memories. He had been wrong not to see his dad in hospital. That was a truth that Martin knew with certainty and no matter what the Keeper of Questions may put in his head, he would never be able to free Martin of the mistake he had made and the truth that mistake had given him.

Martin opened his eyes to find Isabel staring at him impatiently. Clearly he had spent longer than her in finding his truth. Without pausing, Martin stood up.

'OK, I've got my truth,' he said. 'Now where is he?'

The Keeper of Pleasantries helped himself to more cheese, but stopped when he saw the look Martin was giving him.

'He is in London.'

'How do you know that?' said Martin.

The Keeper placed the cheese in his mouth and slowly chewed. 'I asked Hearsay. She knows what most Keepers are doing and where they are doing it. Unfortunately, as she is the Keeper of Hearsay and not the Keeper of Truth, there is always the concern that her information is unsubstantiated.' The Keeper of Pleasantries crossed one leg over the other and rested his head on them. 'But in this instance, I believe her. She is always so keen to talk, but I had to practically rip the information from her. She wouldn't have been so unwilling to part with what she knew if she did not believe it to be true, and also dangerous.'

Isabel got up. She appeared excited and started to touch her hair, making sure it was in place.

'I have never been to London before.'

Martin was about to say that he'd been loads of times with his parents, but then he realised the London he knew was not the London of 1623. How many buildings there today remained in his time?

Isabel was still attending to herself when they got up to leave. The Keeper of Pleasantries remained on the pouffe, cleaning up the last of the cheese crumbs from the plate. He called out to Martin who waited by the door.

'Word of you has spread, Martin.'

Martin turned. 'Of me?'

'Yes, and what you did for the Keeper of Buttons.'

Martin held onto the doorframe and bowed his head.

'I didn't do anything,' said Martin. 'I failed him.'

'Of course you did, but by failing you opposed a Fundamental Keeper to save a Minor Keeper, not to mention those of us you freed from Questions. When the time comes, Martin, do not be afraid to ask for help. For whilst our sizes may be small, our numbers are great, and you, Martin, will be known by us all.'

CHAPTER
TWENTY ONE

Martin and Isabel tracked through field after field towards the nearest village. The wind turbine spun loudly as they passed it, reflecting the red glow from the late evening sun. The only other noises they heard were the rustling of wind through distant trees and across the fields of wheat and rye.

'The labourers should still be out. It isn't fully dark,' said Isabel

'Maybe they took a half day and went back to their families,' said Martin.

'A half day?' Isabel shook her head. 'No one works a *half day*. You start work when the Sun comes around and you stop when it sets.'

'Where do you think they are then?'

'I do not know. They should be here.'

Dew was starting to settle on the long blades of grass they walked through, soaking their trousers. They marched on purposefully until they met the proper path to the village. Searching the house's land trying to find some method of getting to London had thrown them off track. Martin had suggested they simply run to London using Isabel's augmented time and arrive there in only a matter of seconds, but Isabel had pointed out London was a good seventy miles away, and not only did she not wish to run that far, she was unsure her current control of time would allow it.

The village was deserted, everyone having already left with the Keeper of Questions. As Martin and Isabel walked along the central dirt street, the village not fortunate enough to have been built on a Roman road, Martin noticed items from the future scattered around the tiny cottages. Several proudly sported satellite dishes while another had a large double glazed window instead of a small hole covered by a wooden shutter. Up ahead, an intersecting road was lined with streetlights, painting the thatched roofs yellow. One cottage even had a collection of garden gnomes by the front door. Now that there were no longer any doors to the future, no more items would be swapped between this time and Martin's, but they'd remain here until the Keeper of Time was freed and able to return everything to its rightful time.

'If we find some horses we could ride them to London,' said Isabel.

'Do you think there'll be any left?' asked Martin. 'Won't they have taken them?'

'Probably,' said Isabel with a sigh, 'but the man who never looks, never finds. Of course, we can walk, but it is woods for most of the journey and they are dangerous places. I would certainly not wish to start tonight.'

Martin thought about spending another night in one of the cottages with Isabel. For some reason, he got the impression she wouldn't be too quick to share a bed with him this time. He wasn't sure what was happening to her, but it seemed she was developing some form of modesty. Better late than never.

Though the village was small, they split up. Martin was just about to walk through his first door when Isabel appeared by his side like an apparition.

'I have found a thing.'

'What is it?'

'I am unsure,' said Isabel. Her brow was heavily furrowed and she was biting the skin on her lip with gusto. 'I believe it may be a carriage of some description.'

Isabel grabbed Martin's hand and dragged him behind a couple of cottages and through a herd of confused sheep. She stopped and pointed at what sat alone in the middle of a small field.

'Now that right there is definitely a thing,' said Martin.

'You know what it is?'

'One hell of a coincidence, that's what.'

'For why?'

'Because we wanted horses and we got this.' Martin banged on the blue panel of the Bowler Wildcat, heavy-duty off-road vehicle.

He opened a door for Isabel and stood to the side as she got in. 'Your carriage, milady.'

Isabel still looked confused as Martin got in the driver's side and settled himself behind the wheel.

'And what of the horses? Do not expect to simply sit and wait for them to arrive. They are not so well trained.'

Martin was looking around in the glove compartment,

under the sun visor and down the side of the seats, desperately searching for something. Whether this was truly a gift masterminded by the Keeper of Coincidence or not, it would be useless if there weren't any keys.

'It's already got horses,' said Martin as he bent down to search the floor.

'Where?' said Isabel. 'Is that what you look for?' She started to search the inside of the car too, though what she was expecting to find was anyone's guess. A mini horse?

'They're not in here,' said Martin, 'they're under the bonnet.'

'A hat?'

Martin rolled his eyes. 'The front bit. And there's not just a few horses either, there're hundreds of them!'

'This is a future thing, isn't it? There are no horses in here at all.'

Martin smiled. He was about to reply when he suddenly sat up and turned to Isabel. 'Your pockets, what's in them?'

'Interesting future things.'

'Show me.'

Isabel dug her hands into her pocket and pulled out the items from Martin's time she'd stolen from the master's loft. Among the Bluetooth earbuds and cheap jewellery lay a set of car keys. Martin picked them up and slid them into the ignition. This was definitely the work of a crafty Keeper!

Martin started the car and it roared to life. The high-powered halogen headlights lit up the village like the blast from a nuclear weapon in freeze frame.

''Tis shaking!' said Isabel.

'That's the engine. Cars like this are designed for power, not comfort. Things can get a little... bumpy.'

Martin placed his feet on the pedals and grabbed hold of the steering wheel. It was at this point his confidence deserted him. He had never driven a car before.

After much grinding of gears they were beating along the path at a respectable thirty miles per hour in third gear. Isabel spent the entire time as far forward as her seatbelt would allow, marvelling as things suddenly came into view of the blue tinted headlights. At one point, she was so engrossed in the passing night-time scenery that Martin thought she'd been hypnotised by it and beeped the horn. The horn was astonishingly loud, causing Isabel to punch Martin and Martin to swerve violently, almost crashing into a tree.

Soon the path ended and they were greeted by a sparse copse. Martin stopped the car and left the engine running. He got out to have a quick pee and see if they'd missed a turning. They hadn't, the path just finished. When he got back to the car, he found Isabel sitting quite happily in the driver's seat.

'I think it is my turn to ride,' said Isabel.

'It's a car. You don't ride it, you drive it.'

Isabel shrugged. 'It is still my turn.'

Martin tried to give Isabel tips on how to drive a car, but considering he'd never driven one until about forty minutes ago he wasn't the most qualified instructor. But the basics were there: foot on the accelerator to make it go and foot on the brake to make it stop.

'OK, put your foot on the left pedal and push it down.'

Isabel felt around with her feet before pushing the clutch down. Martin took the gear lever and slid it into first.

'OK, now slowly lift your foot off the pedal.'

Isabel did, the clutch found the bite point and the car started to trundle forward.

'Now,' said Martin, 'you need to use the pedal on your right. Just remember, this is faster than a horse, so don't be scared. Just take it easy.'

Isabel nodded and slammed her foot down as hard as she could on the accelerator.

The wheels spun for a moment, sending dirt and gravel flying in waves behind the car. Martin was thrown back into his seat as the beast lurched forward in a single gut-retching movement. The spindly trees were approaching fast. Martin scrabbled for his seatbelt, desperately trying to plug it in as he screamed at Isabel to hold onto the steering wheel.

Isabel simply nodded and leisurely took the steering wheel before whipping the car around the trees and crashing through the copse. They were already going 50 mph and the engine was screeching desperately for a gear change.

Martin grabbed the gear stick and told Isabel to push down on the clutch again. She didn't take her foot off the accelerator and the engine whined like a banshee as Martin jumped straight from first gear to fourth.

He'd almost put it in neutral and pulled on the handbrake, when he realised that Isabel was actually an amazing driver. She dodged the larger trees while ploughing down the smaller ones and swerved in wide arcs through the mud to avoid large boulders and rocks. She even managed to turn on the full beams as she pressed and flicked every button and switch she could find.

The car left the air for several seconds as they jumped a bank and landed in a stream sending out showers of water higher than the car. Inside they were thrown about, but the wheels soon found traction and the car roared up the other bank and demolished a cluster of arm-thin silver birch before charging ahead into the copse and towards London at speeds you'd expect to see on a motorway.

With both hands on the steering wheel, Isabel threw the car around an upturned tree.

'I think I shall enjoy living in the future!'

After storming through streams, racing up hills and flattening a large number of innocent trees, the all-terrain car was a wreck when Martin and Isabel reached the south bank of the river Thames. Both of the wing mirrors had been torn off along with one of the left side body panels. The driver's side window was completely smashed in after Isabel failed to spot a large branch and there was a scraping noise like a child's scream coming from the rear right-side wheel. All of that wasn't including the car's mud coverage, which was total.

Driving along Old Kent Road, they could see London coming into view in the early morning sun. They had travelled for most of the night, making many wrong turns and occasionally getting stuck in mud, but eventually they had found their destination. After her burst of maniacal driving, Isabel had declared that she would let Martin drive if she was allowed to sleep.

Martin stopped the car and stepped out. The London before him was so unlike the one he was used to, with Hamleys, the London Eye and the Shard, that it was hard for him to believe it was even the same place. Apart from the Thames, nothing looked the same.

Here on the south bank there was very little of the city, with most of it north of the river. Old St Paul's Cathedral, which would be gutted by the fire in 1666 and rebuilt in 1708, stood out amongst the red-roofed houses, shops and church spires. There was only a single bridge spanning the river, but even that was strange, crammed with buildings five or more floors high.

Isabel slammed the car door and ran to Martin.

'I cannot believe I am in London. Look at it! Have you ever seen anywhere so incredible?'

Isabel marvelled at her surroundings like she'd arrived in paradise. Martin thought of when he'd get to show her 21st century London. Compared to that, this London was a dump. In fact, compared to pretty much anywhere, this London was a dump. Martin had finally worked out what the pungent smell was. The place was covered in crap, both animal and, by the looks of it, human. Despite the foul stench, and disturbing squishiness underfoot, Isabel still appeared enraptured as she ran over to inspect the bars and hotels that lined the street. She seemed to have forgotten completely about the car, so Martin left it and followed obediently.

They walked along Borough Street and through Southwark, passing a prison, a hospital and several churches. To their left, if they had bothered to look, was the Globe Theatre, the original one, not the modern copy that stood in Martin's time, and in front of them, next to the river, was St Saviour's Cathedral, a square tower extending from the centre of its nave, and just to the right of that, at the end of the road, London Bridge.

'It's deserted,' said Martin, 'just like the village.'

'The master is here. I still hear him in my head.'

'So can everyone else, I bet. He must have the entire city under his spell.'

'What do you think he does with them?' asked Isabel.

'I don't know, but if they're anything like the villagers then we're in trouble.'

'So you too think he will use them as a weapon against us?'

'Yeah, not that he'll need them all. Even with the gifts from Time and Portals, he'd only need the people from one street to stop us.'

'You sell us short. At least two streets, Martin!' said Isabel. 'Though it is strange. If the people of London are to be his army, then why are they not here? Perhaps the master is unaware of our arrival.'

Martin was about to reply when he saw something. Sitting by the side of the road, dressed in what appeared to be filthy rags, was a little girl. She looked no more than five years old and was missing her right hand. Martin instantly recognised her.

'It's the girl from before,' said Martin.

'The girl from before when?' asked Isabel.

'From the master's house. She was outside when you chucked me out of the kitchen. She hugged me.'

Isabel raised an eyebrow.

'I didn't ask her to!' Martin said defensively. 'She just ran up to me. I thought she lived in the house.'

'She does not,' said Isabel. 'I have never seen her before.'

The little girl was splashing in puddles and laughing wildly as they approached her.

'Do you think the master cannot reach her mind because she is a child?' asked Isabel.

'I don't know. Maybe. But it's not like she's the only kid in London.'

Even when they stood before her, feet in the puddle, the little girl still didn't acknowledge their presence. She continued to splash in the disease-ridden water and was holding something in her hand that she pushed along the ground. Martin bent down to see what it was but jumped back when he realised it was a dead rat. The word *plague* flashed up in bright red letters across his mind. That had been carried by rats, or more accurately, the fleas that lived on the rats. It was something they hadn't realised until hundreds of years afterwards, which meant that Isabel had no idea of the danger.

The little girl put the dead rat down and Martin took the opportunity to kick the thing as far away as he could. The girl looked up at him like he'd just stolen her ice cream. For a moment Martin thought she was about to cry, but then she seemed to recognise him before her eyes became unfocused again and she started to splash her feet in the puddle and laugh to herself.

Isabel squatted down in front of the girl. 'What is your name?' she asked.

The girl tried to look at Isabel but it was as if she were staring at something miles away.

'My name is Isabel, pray tell me yours?'

The girl continued to splash.

'Where are all the people?' pressed Isabel. 'Where are your parents?'

The girl still refused to speak, splashing her hand in the water before wiping it over her face. Isabel stood up.

'It is no use. I believe the girl to be retarded. She will be unable to help us.'

'You can't say that!' said Martin.

'I can't say what?'

'Retarded! You can't just call her that.'

'Why not? She clearly is.' Isabel poked the girl a few times in the head. Apart from occasionally screwing up her face and looking a little confused, the girl didn't seem to care and continued to play in the puddle.

'See, the girl isn't in control of her mental faculties; she is a dimwit, a dullard and not worth our time. We should leave her. Without anyone to care for her she will die soon regardless.'

All words and thought appeared to desert Martin as he stared at Isabel open-mouthed. He realised there was a lot he'd need to teach her before he actually let her out of the house to meet the people of the 21st century.

'Do you know where the people are?' Martin asked the

266

little girl. 'We need to find someone. It's very important.'

The girl stood up. Martin thought she was going to lead them somewhere, but it seemed that she was just bored and wandered off with no real destination in mind.

'Leave her, Martin.'

Martin refused to give up. This girl may be the only other person in the city. Did she even hear the Keeper in her head, continuously repeating his mantra as Martin and Isabel heard it, and if so, could she understand it, or was it simply a background noise that could easily be ignored?

'Argh!' Martin cried out in frustration. 'Come on, you must know something! There's a whole city here and no one in it. Do you even realise they're gone? That you were all alone until we came? Do you even have a single thought in your head?'

The little girl stopped walking and turned to Martin. Her dirty blonde curls fell over her shoulders and her cherubic face smiled. She was finally seeing Martin and as Martin looked back he saw something new in her eyes. Recognition.

'The people!' shouted Martin, waving his arms around at the buildings and streets. 'The people. Where are all the people?'

The girl closed her eyes and it almost appeared like she was thinking. She looked up to the sky before pointing at a cloud. Martin was about to turn away in despair when the girl's arm dropped and she was pointing somewhere else, west of the city. She turned to Martin and the hint of a smile crossed her face before she dropped to the floor to play with her feet.

Isabel walked over to Martin. 'Maybe the girl is not as dim-witted as I first believed.'

'How come?'

'Do you not know where she pointed?' asked Isabel.

Martin shook his head. 'It's kind of hard to know where everything is without all the landmarks I'm used to, and even then it helps if I've got my phone.'

'I have never even been to London and yet it appears I know it better than you. Clearly in the future you are too busy watching your little moving pictures to know where it is you are.'

Martin shrugged his shoulders. She had him there.

'She pointed westwards after where the river bends. Past Whitehall Palace.'

'Clues aren't going to help,' said Martin. 'Just tell me.'

Isabel smiled with obvious relish.

'She was pointing to Westminster.'

'Of course!' said Martin. 'The Houses of Parliament!'

'The what?'

Martin took the little girl to the top floor of an empty house on Borough High Street. He opened a few doors and stole some blankets and food for her too. Isabel was right: left alone the girl would die. Even in a house with food and warmth, she wouldn't last long. If by some miracle, the Keeper of Questions could be stopped, then people's minds would be returned to them and she would be found. But if the population of London held the same views as Isabel, then she'd probably find herself back on the streets with no one to look out for her.

Martin made a mental note of where the house was. If he ever did get out of this, he'd probably end up taking the girl with him too.

Isabel was already waiting by the car as Martin said goodbye. The girl didn't appear to listen to him and was clutching a loaf of bread that Martin had stolen for her. She continued to gaze around the room as if following a trapped fly no one else could see. Martin waited for any sign that she even registered his presence, but saw none. At least she wouldn't know he was leaving her.

Martin left the bedroom on the fifth floor of the house and stepped out the door of a shop in front of the beaten-up car.

Isabel was already inside and the engine was rolling. She made it rev high in neutral while waving Martin over and simultaneously banging on the horn like a frustrated taxi driver. Not only had Isabel learnt how to drive a car, she'd learnt how to drive a car like a jerk.

CHAPTER
TWENTY TWO

The stone entrance to London Bridge passed above them as they left the south bank. The heads mounted on pikes were starting to rot, but the smell would only be noticeable up close: the stench from the Thames overpowered everything else. Even breathing through the mouth it could still be tasted, settling on the tongue like putrid snowflakes.

Buildings that looked ready to fall into the river flew by on either side as Isabel floored the Wildcat over the Thames to the north side of the city. She swerved west where Fish Street met Canwicke Street, thundering across the uneven and filth-covered road as houses that leaned forward drunkenly whizzed by in a blur.

St Paul's Cathedral passed by on their right as they continued along Fleet Street and onto the Strand. The road followed the river, and as it turned so did they, heading south and past the impressive Whitehall Palace and on to Westminster.

Isabel slammed on the brakes and the car skidded to a stop. To their right was the Palace of Westminster and directly in front of them were Westminster Abbey and Hall. Martin had expected to see the Houses of Parliament with Elizabeth Tower rising from it, but it wasn't there. It mustn't have been built yet. Martin had always thought that was the building Guy Fawkes had tried to blow up, but if it wasn't there in 1623, then it certainly wasn't there in 1605, when the plot was foiled.

In front of them were hordes of people. Some were dressed in rags, some in practical labourers' clothes while others donned their finery. Men wore bright doublets and breeches with dazzlingly white ruffs and cuffs and the ladies, gaudy dresses with enormous bustles.

The crowd turned when they heard the car. None of them showed any surprise at seeing something from the future and instead started to move forward, acquiring items that could be used as weapons as they went.

'Shame we can't just run them down,' said Martin.

'Actually,' Isabel revved the engine so its roar could be heard over all of silent London, 'I am confident we can.'

'OK… I mean we *shouldn't* run them down.'

Isabel sighed. 'I suppose you are right.' She turned to Martin. 'Get out.'

'Why?'

'Have faith,' said Isabel with a smile, 'and get out!'

Martin opened the door and jumped out. Immediately the car accelerated forward. It was heading straight for the moving cluster of people, but veered to the side at the last second and smashed into a shop front, tearing straight through the timber building. The crowd started to approach as flames began to lick the walls.

Martin felt someone grab his hand before he realised Isabel was standing next to him. Her trousers were on fire but she quickly beat out the flames.

'It appears I am not as swift as I once was.'

Martin glanced at her cracked crystal and then at the fire. 'You sped up your time and jumped out the car at the last second?'

Isabel pointed to the massive burnt hole in her trouser leg. 'The *very* last second.' She looked concerned for a moment. 'You don't think I shall set the entire city alight?'

'Don't worry,' said Martin, now running with Isabel as the crowd were momentarily transfixed by the burning shop. 'That won't happen until 1666.'

Martin and Isabel ran past the abbey to Westminster Hall. Two towers with battlements at the tops stood either side of the hall's main entrance, an arch the height of several people. Above that, a window made from many panes of glass housed in a stone frame rose up the height of two floors before the roof pointed upwards with a small tower at its apex. Martin suddenly realised he'd seen this before when he'd been to London. The hall still existed in his time, only the rest of the Houses of Parliament hid it from the river.

'He must be in there,' said Martin, nodding towards the hall. 'In my time it's the Houses of Parliament, where they basically run the country. I guess it's the same now.'

''Tis the greatest court in the land,' said Isabel, 'but I do not understand why the master would come here.'

Isabel was right. Westminster Hall wasn't exactly central. In fact, they'd passed straight through the walled city of London to get there from the south bank.

'It's a place of power,' said Martin, 'where questions

are asked and answers debated. Sounds about right for the Keeper of Questions.'

Martin spotted something moving in his periphery. Most of the crowd were still gathered around the burning shop and surrounding buildings, though some were starting to pull away. What he'd seen was over the other side, away from the river. He turned and watched the little figure skip along the road, jumping into puddles as she went, dirty blonde hair flying behind her.

Martin walked over to the figure, leaving Isabel to marvel at Westminster Hall. At first he thought it must be another child, but as he got closer he saw she was missing her right hand and knew with certainty that it was the girl he'd locked in a room on the far side of the city. But what was she doing here? Even if she'd managed to get out of the room, Martin and Isabel had come by car, and that had been anything but slow. It would take at least an hour to walk that distance.

Martin left the girl and returned to Isabel. They could worry about lost children some other time. Right now they had a Keeper to stop. He was about to run over to Isabel, who was still mesmerised by the hall, when he stopped. Someone was behind her. Martin went to shout, but by the time he opened his mouth, the man had already cracked Isabel over the back of the head with a lead bar. Isabel fell to the floor. It didn't matter how well she could control time, there was nothing she could do against a surprise attack.

The man bent down and picked Isabel up, hauling her limp body over his shoulder. Martin could hear people charging towards him and saw a group of at least fifty heading his way. Added to that, the proximity to the master was making the mantras unbearable. The words didn't just become louder; hearing them actually hurt.

The crowd was gaining speed, but their clothes were clearly not designed for running, so they weren't making fast progress. In fact, they almost appeared comical except for the blank expressions on their faces. Martin looked for the little girl, fearing she would be taken too. He spotted her further down the street, struggling in the arms of a large man and clearly in distress.

Through the throngs of the finely dressed gentry class, the workmen, store owners and labourers burst, unencumbered by impractical clothes. Martin started to run. Without Isabel's augmented time he felt slow, but compared to the people chasing him, who all seemed shorter than the people in his time, he was fast.

Martin dived into a door and ran out another just in front of the man carrying Isabel. Martin raised his fists. It was the only thing he could think to do. The man was still coming towards him, completely unfazed by Martin's stance. As he passed, Martin swung, catching the man's jaw. A blow appeared to come from nowhere and knocked Martin to the floor. The man bent down, ready to pick Martin up too, but Martin kicked backwards and fell into the open door, only to fall back into the street about five metres away, just behind the man carrying the little girl.

Martin stood and rubbed his head. It throbbed. He wiped his hand across his forehead and cleared away the dribble of blood that was threatening to fall into his eye.

The man was almost upon him, still walking purposefully with Isabel dangling over his right shoulder. Martin squared up again, cursing his own stupidity. In a time where men were on average a few inches shorter, Martin was trying to fight someone who'd be considered a giant even in his time. Looking down at the floor, Martin saw a long wooden leg, probably from a table that was used as an outside stall. He picked it up.

They were just people, thought Martin, normal people who were going about their lives until the Keeper of Questions appeared. None of this was their fault. This giant of a man didn't want to take Isabel away and kill her – Martin's grip tightened – but that didn't mean he wouldn't, and there was no way Martin would let that happen. Martin needed Isabel. He wouldn't be able to stop the Keeper of Questions without her, but more than that, he needed her because Isabel was special. Those little things normal people did that could drive Martin crazy, Isabel didn't do. And Isabel had suffered, just like Martin had. That was something which had brought them together in a way neither of them had felt before, and there was no way this man or any other was going to tear them apart.

Martin cried out as he swung the wooden leg as hard as he could, cracking the man on the back of the skull. The leg instantly snapped in half, sending splinters of rotten wood flying into the air. The man stood frozen in shock. The pain was yet to fully register as he just stared at Martin; not a man controlled from within, just a normal man who, despite his size and intimidating appearance, looked upset and confused. His spare hand reached up to touch the back of his head before he realised he was carrying a young girl. Then the Keeper took control once more and the man became a slave. He lifted his arm up, ready to strike. Martin was almost too stunned to move. The guilt at having attacked an innocent man with such force made him feel hot and his clothes started to stick to him. Before the blow came, he jumped backwards into the doorway, the room beyond flashing to a bedroom before flicking back to a shop.

Martin was in a bedroom on the fifth floor of a townhouse. He was a little way in front of the man carrying the girl, and behind that man was the one carrying Isabel. The resolve to save her, to save both of them, hadn't dimmed within Martin. He didn't just need to save them, he *had* to.

Every situation he'd come across, every obstacle he'd overcome, he'd done so using the ability of the Keeper of Portals. So why had he thought that saving the little girl and Isabel was any different? Hanging out of the open bedroom window, Martin saw an opportunity. He both looked and felt for all the doorways he would need. Everything seemed to line up. There was only one chance to make this work and it was almost upon him.

Letting go of the wooden roof beam, Martin fell from the fifth floor straight towards the road below. There was an open barrel directly beneath him, probably once used to hold beer. The barrel was large enough for Martin to fit through, but judging exactly where he would fall from such a great height wasn't easy, and even if he just clipped the edge, he'd probably cut himself badly. His plan was simple: fall into the barrel and come out of a second floor window on the other side of the road. By the time he reached the barrel, he'd be going so fast he'd fly out of the window, across the road and through a door on the other side. But even though he'd be moving fast, that didn't mean he wouldn't be falling too. If he came out at street level he'd end up scraping along the floor before he got to the other side of the road.

The hard part was timing it so that he flew past at the same time the men reached the door; then all he'd have to do was snatch one of the girls, put her in a room to keep her safe, then repeat for the other one. The man holding the little girl was in front, so she would be the first to be saved. He hated feeling like he was using her as practice, but it was true. He couldn't mess up when it came to saving Isabel.

Martin hadn't positioned himself quite right and the hem of his trousers caught the lip of the barrel, causing them to rip. By this point he was already flying horizontally out the window and across the road, and while his positioning may not have been perfect, his timing was impeccable.

Martin stretched out his hands, looking for a moment like a dive-bombing superman. He grabbed the girl by her shoulders but she began to flail and twist and Martin struggled to hold onto her. The door in front of them burst open at Martin's command, but the wriggling girl threw him off course and they crashed straight into the wall. Falling to the floor in a heap, Martin looked down to see the girl still in his arms. She seemed unhurt.

Behind the man who'd been carrying the child, Martin saw Isabel and her abductor, and behind them, a hoard of people. They'd found him. Martin tried to stagger towards Isabel, but a pain shot through his leg as soon as he stood up. He stopped and psyched himself up for the rescue, but then he saw the man holding Isabel charging towards him like a rampaging bull. As he watched, Martin saw Isabel's eyes open and hope fill her face. There was nothing Martin could do, no way he could possibly save her now the enormous man had noticed him. Martin had failed Isabel. He turned, the small girl still in his arms, and hobbled as fast as he could to the open door. He allowed himself one last backwards glance before he escaped. His eyes locked with Isabel's. In her stare he saw hurt and betrayal before the overtaking bodies blocked her from sight. Martin disappeared into the house, connecting to another building as far away as he could manage. He wanted to explain to Isabel, wanted her to understand that it was too much for him: he just wasn't good enough to save them both.

Martin sat the girl down on the bed in the corner of the room. She looked how she had when they'd first met, infinitely curious and pleasantly content: as if her capture had never happened. Martin sat down next to the girl, finally understanding what Isabel's look had meant. She wasn't upset that he hadn't saved her, she was upset Martin had saved the little girl *instead* of her. The little girl that Isabel had called retarded and claimed would be dead before too long. Martin had chosen to save her life instead of Isabel's.

CHAPTER
TWENTY THREE

Shards of evening sunlight cut through the interior of Westminster Hall from the high windows. Two rows of stalls lined the walls: the topmost level with the chandeliers that hung from the ceiling on long chains and the bottom row directly beneath, elevated off the floor. The arched entranceway Martin had come through carried on into the hall, making it look like a miniature castle.

The rows of stalls were empty. The only occupied seat resided at the far end, placed in the centre and resembling a throne. The figure who sat upon it was hunched over and appeared to be deep in thought. Orange light streamed in from behind, giving them a golden aura.

Martin walked forward. He was waiting for something to happen, but everything remained still. He thought of the little girl, far away from here now. They had jumped through many doors to get to a house on the furthest side of London.

The Keeper of Questions sat in his human form, dressed in black with his grey hair tied in a ponytail so as not to hide his handsome face. Not that Martin could see it. The Keeper was leaning over. His hands were by his head and his fingers were rubbing his temples.

The sound of Martin's footsteps echoed around the cavernous hall, announcing his approach with every step. This was a suicide mission, Martin knew that. Isabel was gone, and there was no way he could do this by himself. He couldn't even run. If he tried, the Keeper of Causality would just force him back. He had to finish what he'd started. The only problem was that finish wouldn't be the one he wanted. He'd already made the mistake he'd come back in time to prevent. Because of that, Isabel was gone. Now there was no choice but to try and fight the Keeper of Questions, only to lose.

Martin scanned the sides of the hall as he approached the Keeper. No one new appeared, Keeper or human, to help him. Remembering what the Keeper of Pleasantries had told him, Martin kept the truth he knew in his head, holding onto it like a dear friend who'd been swept into a fierce river.

The master's mantra continued to torment Martin to the point where he found it difficult to walk. Defiantly, maybe even foolishly, Martin forced it down. If he gave in now, he would become a slave to the Keeper of Questions. The Keeper wouldn't want him dead if he no longer opposed him. Still, even knowing the only thing that would come of this was failure, he couldn't bring himself to surrender so willingly. Thoughts of Isabel were too strong. They didn't get this far together just for him to give up.

The Keeper of Questions sighed and a hint of annoyance flashed across his face. Martin stopped. He was in the middle of the hall now, equidistant from defeat and the false hope that he'd be allowed to escape.

The Keeper didn't stand and Martin didn't move. They regarded each other in silence. It was Questions who spoke first.

'I can hear them.'

Martin didn't respond for almost half a minute. 'Hear who?'

'Not who,' said Questions. 'What. Those Questions you ask in your head. Can I kill him? Is Isabel already dead? Will he let me go? Your fear, your doubt, it all leaks out of your head and into mine.'

The Keeper of Questions stood and slowly walked forward.

'Can he really hear my questions? Does that mean he can control me? Is he controlling me now and I don't even realise?'

Questions stopped, still some distance from Martin. Martin remained where he was, unwilling or unable to move. His doubts were being replayed back to him, making them seem even more real than when they were only in his head.

'Can I control you?' the Keeper of Questions asked himself. 'Of course, if I could control you then I'd simply make you run into that window behind me and slice your body until you bled to death at my feet. Let us try that.'

The Keeper of Questions' grey eyes burst open until they were perfectly round beneath his finely shaped eyebrows.

Martin felt himself lurch forward before he realised his feet hadn't moved. He nearly fell on the floor and had to steady himself with his arms. When he looked up again he saw the Keeper smiling.

281

'I cannot control you. How can you not know this? Do you think I would have let you come this close to me through choice? Why would I do that? Because I think you're special? Because you managing to escape from me once warrants some kind of personal revenge on my part?' The Keeper suddenly became grave and regarded Martin with utter contempt. 'I suffer no such sentiments. I will dispose of you as soon as is possible. However, as it appears your mind actively thwarts me, I will have to resort to more primitive methods.'

Hordes of people streamed into the hall. There were more than Martin had seen outside, and certainly many more than the master had control of at his house. Everyone appeared to be dressed the same; there was no finery, only the clothes of people who worked hard for a living. Martin recognised a face, charging towards him swinging what looked like a cauldron above her head. It was the woman Isabel had stolen a pear from. These were people from the villages, the ones who had been with the master the longest. They were the most loyal and the most faithful. The ones who felt the true strength of Question's control.

Martin tried to find something he could jump through, but he was in the middle of a massive hall and there didn't appear to be any usable entrances anywhere. Just like when he'd saved the Keeper of Portals and Isabel with the ribbon tied to the end of a remote controlled plane, Martin needed to get creative.

He whipped off the fabric belt he wore and threw it on the floor before jumping into the gateway it made. With no obvious door to come out of, and not wanting to run away, Martin came through an archway created by the thick wooden roof joists. He landed on the top stall at the right of the hall.

Below him the villagers ran around waving their various weapons high in the air, trying to find Martin. Then in unison they looked up and charged at the far wall, grabbing and clawing at the pillars that supported the lower stalls and pulling their way up. The Keeper of Questions moved through the chaos like a shark through a school of wary fish.

The Keeper of Questions stood below Martin as the villagers started to crawl over each other, working together to make human ladders.

'Yes,' said Questions, 'it is pointless, because of course, you can simply climb through another one of those holes in the roof joists and come out somewhere else. But you see, I have to do something. I cannot simply sit here and wait until you have the good grace to either capitulate or die, can I?'

As dirty hands grabbed the front of the stall, Martin did exactly what the Keeper had suggested, the very course of action he was questioning in his head.

Martin appeared from a hole in the roof joists on the opposite side of the hall, dropping down into the upper stall again. He watched as the villagers grabbed where he had just been. Was running away really the only thing he could do?

As the human ladders started to dismantle themselves and the villagers charged towards him once more, Martin watched the Keeper of Questions. He didn't look to be controlling them. There were no barked orders or waving of arms. No, his control was rooted much deeper. The villagers, the people that would if they caught him, be the ones that killed him, were not Martin's enemy. If Questions was stopped, then they would stop too. He had to remove the head so the body would fall. All he had to do was think of a way how.

Martin cried out and fell to his knees. It felt like razor sharp claws had reached into his head and were shredding his brain. The Keeper of Questions wasn't just forcing the mantra into his head anymore, he was trying to answer every question Martin's brain asked, removing his free will completely.

Martin reached up, grabbing the front of the stall and using it to stand. His breath came out heavy and his mouth hung wide open. Below, the villagers were climbing higher, the tips of their weapons nearly level with Martin. The Keeper was down there too, still on the other side of the hall. So that had been his plan: to attack Martin in one big push, enough that he wouldn't be able to run and maybe even lose consciousness. Questions didn't appear annoyed that it hadn't worked the first time. That only proved he was testing Martin. The worst was still to come.

Martin climbed onto the stall's front barrier. Someone made a desperate swipe for his feet as he jumped and grabbed onto a wooden beam. He hadn't realised how sweaty his hands were and nearly slipped off before making a desperate lunge and grabbing hold properly. He swung his leg over and managed to pull himself up and stand on the beam. He was just below the ceiling and the Keeper of Questions, who stood in the middle of the swarm, was directly beneath him. The crowd shouted up to him, taunting and threatening Martin. But he knew these were not their words. Questions was still in control.

Martin leaned back, holding onto the sides of the beams before swinging himself through the hole created by the roof joists he used to form a portal.

He came out of an archway over the large stone entrance and walked forward until he was right at the very edge, overlooking the hall.

He had to focus. Had to think. He needed to shut the Keeper of Questions out of his head for good. This wasn't something he could do silently. The Keeper had to know.

'My questions are not for you!' Martin shouted. The Keeper of Questions looked up. 'I will not let you listen to them. I will not let you answer them. I will not let you fill my head with your lies and become your puppet! You have no place inside my head, Questions. You have no place inside anyone's head!'

Martin stood there, still breathing heavily, but this time because of achievement instead of fear. He was waiting for some kind of reaction from the Keeper below him, but he just stared back, angrier than Martin had ever seen him.

Martin heard the mantra in his head begin to fade. Speaking those words aloud, no, shouting them at the top of his voice, had made them more real, just like the doubts that were voiced back to him by the Keeper. Before, he thought he believed it; now he knew he believed it.

285

Something touched Martin's hand. The little girl stood beside him smiling. In a light voice below a whisper she said, 'Thank you.'

The little girl let go of Martin's hand and screwed up her eyes and fist as tightly as she could. That was when Martin realised the rags the girl was wearing, which before had been covered in mud and most likely worse, were now spotlessly clean, even if they were still tatty.

Suddenly, something started to change below him. The crowd of villagers continued to call out to Martin, attacking with their words as they struggled to get close enough to use their weapons, but there were new voices now. Amongst the combined anger of the crowd, Martin could hear confused whimperings. Then he could see them: villagers standing in the middle of the hall brandishing a knife or metal pan asking people what was going on.

The crowd started to split. At first it was just a few, but soon more and more appeared to come to their senses. After realising they didn't know where they were, they became scared. Some started to scream, some ran, and it didn't take long before fights broke out. The tower of people who were trying to reach Martin collapsed in a heap of broken bones and open fractures as those on the bottom appeared to wake up and panic, causing the entire thing to topple.

The Keeper of Questions glared at Martin, but then he looked up at the little girl. Recognition swept over his face and his anger grew anew. The little girl looked different: no longer around five, she appeared seven or even eight. Her golden blonde hair was longer and she now wore a simple white dress.

Suddenly, something flew through the air and crashed into the solid stone window frame behind Martin and the girl. They both turned around to see the broken body of a now dead villager.

Looking down, they saw the Keeper of Questions in his full Keeper form. He was massive, at least twice the height of a person and, with his many sets of dark grey wings extended, he was as large as a billboard. He picked up another panicking villager and hurled her at Martin. The villager spun in the air, limbs flailing in every direction. Her head struck the archway beneath Martin's feet, snapping her neck and killing her instantly before her lifeless body followed and crashed onto the floor in front of the little girl.

The little girl collapsed. She was crying and shaking her head from side to side.

'They weren't supposed to die. They weren't supposed to die.'

Pushed right up against the window above the raised entranceway, the little girl bent over and wept, hiding herself from the horrors below as more villagers came flying towards her.

All of the villagers were in control of their own minds once more. Most had run away screaming; even those that had decided to fight had left, realising that anywhere was better than here. Some lay dead, either from falling from the top of the human ladder or after being hurled by the

Keeper of Questions. Others were merely injured and tried to escape by limping or dragging themselves along the floor.

It wasn't long before the hall was empty and the Keeper of Questions stood alone. The only other bodies apart from his, Martin's and the little girl's, were devoid of life.

Martin stood on the stone entranceway he'd first walked through. The Keeper cocked his head, extending his three sets of dark grey wings behind him. He opened his mouth and his black tentacled tongue fell out and rolled down his body. Tar-like ink fell from the tongue in large globules and splashed onto the floor.

The Keeper of Questions was deforming. In places he was bloated and one of his back wings appeared to twitch spasmodically. He had absorbed too many Minor Keepers and stolen too much energy through the door in his study. He was like an intricate balloon animal that had been overinflated. He'd pushed himself and his body too far to become what he was, and if he wasn't careful, he was going to burst.

Martin knew that whichever Keeper the little girl was and whatever power over people she held, it wouldn't be enough to free everyone from Questions' control. She may have severed the link to everyone in the hall, and even then, maybe only temporarily, but beyond that, Martin doubted she'd done anything else. That meant more people would arrive.

Martin started to walk backwards and forwards across the entranceway. Below him the Keeper didn't move; he was probably too busy summoning people to him, but this time it wouldn't be a few villages' worth of people, he would bring an army.

Martin had to remove the head to kill the body. And right now, the Keeper of Questions had no one else to protect him. If heads were going to roll, it would have to be soon.

Martin looked for something he could use and spotted it hanging in front of him. It wouldn't be the first time he had used one of these to thwart the master. The only problem was the Keeper was in the wrong place. But that wouldn't be a problem, Martin just needed to move him. His belt was still on the floor and attached to itself to form a loop. A portal. Martin turned to the little girl. She was still sitting against the wall and crying.

'I'll be right back,' he said.

The girl didn't smile, didn't nod and simply continued to sob.

Martin grabbed hold of a roof joist and swung himself up and through, leaping right out of Westminster Hall. But Martin wasn't running away; he would return. And when he came back, he would end the Keeper of Questions for good.

Martin burst out of a doorway in Westminster Palace. He had no time to take in his surroundings and ran to the first painting he could find. It was huge, depicting a court scene and taking up an entire wall. He ripped the canvas right out of the frame, grabbing as much of it as he could and screwing it up into a ball. Then, without another glance, he ran straight back through the door and out of the palace.

The wreckage of the Wildcat continued to burn, half protruding from the shop front. The building itself had almost completely gone. Martin held the balled-up canvas in the flames until it caught, then he ran through the nearest open door, ready to take on the Keeper of Questions.

Martin burst through the window above the hall's entrance, burning fireball of art in hand. He threw the canvas as hard as he could through the hole in the roof joists directly in front of him.

As Martin's feet touched the top of the stone entranceway, the fireball shot out of the portal he'd created to his belt and straight into the Keeper of Questions, who lurched violently backwards.

The Keeper's birdlike face twisted into a smile.

Martin concentrated. The Keeper of Questions was exactly where he needed him.

'It appears that I can no longer hear your questions; however, let me answer the one I am sure you are asking yourself, regarding whether you can stop me, a Major Keeper, by merely setting me on fire.' Already the flames were starting to die down as if deciding to give up the fight. 'As you can see…'

Martin focused on the chain holding the circular chandelier directly above the Keeper of Questions. He concentrated on a single link in that chain and created a gateway to the entrance of the hall. The connection between the links either side was lost, breaking the chain in two. The chandelier started to fall.

As soon as the chandelier passed over the Keeper's head, Martin made another gateway to the entrance of the hall. The gateway only lasted for a split second, but that was all he needed to separate the Keeper of Questions' head from his body.

The severed head landed on the floor with a heavy thunk. For a short time the body remained standing, the Keeper's tentacled tongue extending out of his neck and flailing around in panic, flinging the thick ink in every direction. Soon that too stopped and the body collapsed to the floor.

As Martin watched the giant avian form of the Keeper topple, he felt an elation he'd never known before. He'd actually done it. He'd been certain that without Isabel there was no chance of him even getting close to the Keeper, let alone being able to kill him.

Martin was about to create a portal in the window and leap down to the decapitated body when he saw two figures appear from the back of the hall.

Once they'd moved closer, he realised they were the near-skeletal forms of the Keeper of Portals and the Keeper of Time. Had they been waiting in the side-lines, ready to congratulate Martin on defeating a Keeper when they were powerless to even raise a finger?

Martin was about to call out to them when he noticed the way they walked was jerky like reanimated corpses. When they were only a few paces from the body of the Keeper of Questions, they collapsed onto the floor.

A creature the size of a large cat was buried waist deep into the backs of their skulls. Martin watched as the creatures removed their arms from the Keepers' heads and used them to extract themselves.

Covered in red and white ooze, the two tiny creatures staggered forward, leaving Portals and Time unconscious on the floor. Squinting, Martin realised they were miniature versions of the Keeper of Questions. One went to Questions' body, burying itself into his neck while the other ran to his head and scuttled up his trachea.

Martin waited for something to happen. Then he saw it. The severed head of the Keeper of Questions moved. At first Martin wasn't sure what that meant and hoped it was some errant electrical impulse making it look like the Keeper was still alive, but then Martin realised that couldn't be it because the Keeper's eyes were searching the room until they locked firmly onto Martin. Then there was a pause.

Then the head of the Keeper of Questions smiled.

CHAPTER TWENTY FOUR

The Keeper of Questions' tongue extended from his grotesque body and slapped the floor of Westminster Hall like a whip.

One of the tentacles smacked down right next to the Keeper's massive avian head. The tentacle twisted and worked its way through the trachea of the decapitated head until it poked out the razor-sharp, teeth-filled beak.

Soon the other tentacles joined the first, slithering along the floor before working themselves through the Keeper's head and out of his mouth. The tentacles then rose and the Keeper of Questions' head slowly slid down onto his neck. The tongue retracted and the head was firmly attached before the Keeper turned to face Martin.

For a moment he just stood there, exactly as he had done before, as if trying to find a way into Martin's mind.

The Keeper started to shift his bloated body forward.

'A Keeper cannot use what they observe to forcefully manipulate another Keeper. This is not a rule that has been imposed, it is a fundamental fact. Time exists outside of Portals. Causality exists outside of Question. All are unique. Isolated.'

Martin was still on the stone entranceway. Behind him

the little girl was silent. She was smaller now. Whatever she had done to make herself appear older had faded and she once more resembled a five year old girl dressed in filthy rags. The only difference was this time she wasn't playing. In fact, she didn't move at all.

All those feelings of elation had left Martin in an instant, not even leaving behind the aftertaste of victory. The Keeper of Questions stood below him, even larger than before. Martin's brilliant plan to cut his head off hadn't worked, and it wouldn't work again, the Keeper was too large now, the chandelier wouldn't fit.

The Keeper took a step forward and as he did, shrank to his human form like an explosion in reverse. His steps became light. Unlike his Keeper form, this one suffered no deformities or unnatural protrusions.

'Of course,' continued the Keeper, 'I discovered a way to control the Keepers of Time and Portals. It was imperfect, which I admit, and I have recently come to realise that the control I held over them was far from total. However, it was enough. Those two creatures you saw were part of me. But as I am the real Keeper of Questions, they could not be the Keeper of Questions, and are, in fact, not Keepers at all. This was how I was able to control Time and Portals, by controlling those parts of myself. This also meant that, should anything untoward happen to me, the mantle of Keeperhood would be passed onto my miniature copies. And they, of course, returned to me.'

The Keeper of Questions now stood directly below Martin.

'Will you continue to hide up there? Is that your plan?

Of course, you must realise that I am amassing an army of people as we speak. In fact, I have already done so. They are here, waiting outside the hall. When I wish for them to enter, they shall. Of course, you can use that *gift* of yours to run away, as it appears you so often do, but I don't believe you wish to do that. From the small amount I gleaned from your mind, there were very few questions regarding the best way to escape. Of course, there were some. You are not that brave.'

The master about-turned and walked to the back of the hall, passing the motionless bodies of the Keeper of Portals and the Keeper of Time.

'I have a suggestion for you, Martin. There is something I would like you to see very much and so I would appreciate it if you could come down from there.'

Martin felt safe where he was, not only because of the height, but the ample holes formed by wooden beams that could be used as portals. On the hall's floor there was very little, except for his belt.

Martin thought for a moment. He had no reason to trust the Keeper, even though he did seem less threatening in his human form. Like he could be reasoned with. But at this stage there really was nowhere else for Martin to go.

Martin dived through the window behind him and shot out through his belt loop. He came out the way he'd gone in, head first. As soon as his feet were through, he closed the portal and let gravity take hold beneath him. He landed gently and quickly bent down to pick up the belt.

The master stood alone at the far end of the hall. Aside from the few dead bodies of villagers and two unconscious

295

Keepers, it felt like nothing had changed since Martin had first entered.

'Go on, then!' shouted Martin. 'What do you want? Clearly I can't stop you. There's no point me even trying, is there? The Keeper of Causality said I could. I just had to make the right choice, but I guess I messed that one up because you just won't bloody die.'

The Keeper of Questions smiled. 'You're right, I won't. However, I am not the only one.'

Isabel appeared from the back of the hall. She was alive. Martin was certain she'd been killed, or at the very least imprisoned. She was no use to the Keeper so why bring her here? Was Questions truly that bored? Did he really feel the need to take them both on at the same time to get any kind of satisfaction from the fight? Well, if that was what he desired, then Martin was more than happy to oblige. That Isabel would too, went without saying.

Martin moved forward, preparing himself to break into a run. All those feelings that had grown inside him since he'd first met Isabel had to be pushed aside the moment he'd stepped into the hall. Now they came flooding back.

Martin stopped dead. At first he thought she was shy, or maybe even embarrassed. Why else wouldn't Isabel be running towards Martin as he ran to her? Then he saw where she was going. And where she had stopped.

Isabel was standing next to the master, on his right hand side. She appeared demure, head slightly bowed and hands clasped neatly in front of her. She didn't move from that position. The master continued to smile.

Martin walked backwards, getting as far away from

Isabel and the master as he could. Neither of them moved. The master appeared unfazed by the cowardly retreat.

For a moment Martin allowed himself to think it, the most disgusting thought that had entered his head since he had first stepped through the door in his bedroom and into the past. *Had Isabel been working for the Keeper of Questions all this time?*

As soon as the thought popped into Martin's head, he hated it. But more than that, he hated himself. It wasn't possible; after all the doubts he'd had at the beginning and all the time he'd spent with her, there was no way she could have betrayed him like this. But as she stood there, next to the Keeper of Questions in the master's guise, the remnants of that thought remained, like a footprint in sand that was too far from the lapping sea.

'What have you done to her?' shouted Martin.

The Keeper placed an arm around Isabel's shoulder, pulling her nearer.

'The girl is where she belongs; there is no need for you to concern yourself. All I have done is restore the natural order of things. Though I do not approve of her current attire.' The Keeper took Isabel's chin between forefinger and thumb and turned her face towards himself while looking at Martin. 'Perhaps I should punish her?'

The master raised his hand high and smacked Isabel across her face so hard she fell to the floor. Without a sound she picked herself up and moved to stand next to the master once more. She didn't rub her cheek or acknowledge the pain in any way, just simply bowed her head like she had before.

Martin wished the Wildcat still worked so he could crush the master's body between the grill and a large stone wall.

'The girl had a wretched life before I took her in. She told you this. I have access to her mind. I know what she told you and what she chose to keep a secret from you. You've thought of them yourself, haven't you, those things she never spoke of?' The Keeper of Questions continued to smile at Martin. 'You knew the girl would have done anything I asked of her. She even received her punishments without complaining. You want to know what else I made her do. What else I did to degrade her. I do not need to be inside your head to see the way you look at her.'

The Keeper was right. Martin had thought those things. He hadn't wanted to, hadn't wanted to know the answers either in case they were ones he didn't like. So he never asked. For her part, Isabel never told.

'I was aware that she had been captured,' said the Keeper of Questions as he ran a finger down Isabel's bare arm. She was still wearing the black vest top and green combat trousers she'd put on at Martin's, only now they were torn and filthy, the burn hole on her thigh revealing a patch of near-white leg. 'I was also aware that she fought me. There was a single thought inside her head that was forcing me out. But that thought was fading. Would you like to know what that thought was?'

'Tell me,' said Martin.

'This pleases me,' said the Keeper of Questions. 'This will be the last time someone is able to answer a question without me dictating the response for them. I am heartened when I hear the answer I want in such a situation. Still, this changes nothing.'

The master walked away from Isabel and bent down to pick something off the floor. It was a pike, the kind heads were displayed on at the Southwark entrance to London Bridge. The master returned to Isabel and handed the pike to her. She took it without a word.

'He will always find a way to save me,' spoke the Keeper of Questions.

Martin had ripped Isabel from her existence of suffering and while there had been danger and the very real fear of death, he had been with her for all of it. For Isabel, that must have been worth more than she was ever able to say. But Martin had let her down. He had saved the little girl, the bizarre Keeper, over Isabel, leaving her to be carried away by those under the control of the Keeper of Questions. That one truth she held in her head to ward off the Keeper's mental advances, that Martin would find a way to save her, had been a lie. He had abandoned her and then he had become angry at her. He'd thought she'd deceived him this whole time, been a puppet of the Keeper of Questions and only pretended to be his friend. But she hadn't. She'd been his friend, a real friend, and, more than that, she'd believed in him enough to stake her life on it. No, Isabel wasn't a traitor, she was just a fool, because she'd picked the wrong person to believe in.

Martin awoke from his thoughts. Isabel was moving. She wasn't as fast as she had been, not with her crystal cracked like it was, but she was still quick. Isabel was now fast enough to see, but not slow enough to avoid.

Isabel ran with the pike thrust out in front of her. Martin needed an escape. He extended his search as far as he could. Then he felt it, something he could create a portal with. It would stop Isabel, of that Martin was certain, but the problem was it would do more than just that.

The long silver pendant. All Martin had to do was use it to create a gateway to somewhere else, and just like with the master, Isabel's head would come off, rolling on the floor as her momentum carried her body forward until it tripped over itself and collapsed in a heap. It was the only way to save himself. It wasn't just a selfish need not to die that made Martin consider it; it was more important than that. If Martin survived, then there was still the chance that he could actually defeat the Keeper of Questions. If he died now, then that could never happen.

Watching, he saw the indifference in Isabel's eyes as she ran towards him. Martin thought of all the lives he would save and the future he would create by killing Isabel. This was the choice, another one Martin had been faced with. He had to do the right thing, disregarding his own feelings for the good of everyone. Martin closed his eyes and focused on the long silver pendant hung around Isabel's neck.

He couldn't do it.

Something burst out from Martin's mouth like an explosion of steam and thick cotton wool, forcing its way out so fast Martin felt like he was being blown over. In the next instant, something struck him in the chest and his legs automatically stepped backwards to stop himself falling over.

For a moment he remained there, eyes closed with something hard pushed against him. His mouth felt empty and he was waiting for the pain and the awful realisation that three foot of pike was sticking out of his back and death was only seconds away.

The feeling never came. In fact, Martin felt no pain at all.

Opening his eyes, Martin's view was obstructed by a very tall, very thin creature with a skin like white rubber. The Keeper of Portals had appeared before Martin, leaping out of his mouth only moments before Isabel killed him.

Martin felt something wet land on his shoulder. It was blood. The Keeper of Portals had done what he'd intended and shielded Martin from Isabel's onslaught. The pike had been forced straight up so that the barbed tip came out where the Keeper's head joined his neck.

Too shocked to speak, all Martin could do was gawp. The Keeper had both of his multi-fingered hands on Isabel's head. Isabel did not move. At the end of the hall the master once more appeared in his Keeper form. He beat his wings menacingly. Outside, Martin could hear people. They were coming in.

The Keeper was shaking and struggling to stay alive. 'There are more portals than those which a person can pass though. All can be used. This you will learn. Most are to stay open, to allow access to all. But there are some which need to be closed, to stop those who wish to do harm from getting in.'

The fog lifted from Isabel as the Keeper of Portals removed his fingers. Her eyes found Martin and her face melted with relief. She took stock of herself. First she noticed the Keeper of Portals in front of her, then she spotted the weapon she still held tightly in her hands, one end going in through the Keeper's abdomen and the other coming out above his neck.

'No! No! Not again. Please no. I can't have!'

Isabel let go of the pike and the Keeper fell to the floor. Isabel bent down to try and help him. Martin knew she wanted to speed their time up to allow him to heal, like they'd done before, or rather, would do in the future. But before Isabel touched the Keeper, he started to glow a brilliant white.

'Martin, what is happening to him?'

Martin was too busy looking at the approaching people to take notice of the Keeper. They just kept on coming, converging on Martin and Isabel. Once they reached them the entire hall would be packed solid with bodies. Then Martin felt something else. He was different. What this difference was he couldn't explain until it suddenly hit him and he knew. He knew that and so much more.

As Portals continued to glow and slowly disappear, Martin grabbed Isabel's hand and leapt into the crowd. He could see them all. Every portal, doorway, passage and entrance. All of them. There was one directly in front of him, two people were close together, one was pushing the other, hand on his shoulder. The floor, their bodies and the arm across the top. It would be their entrance. Martin used it, pulling Isabel through before anyone realised what they were doing.

Then they were above the door, coming out through one of the windows. The girl was sitting on the edge of the stone entranceway, enthralled by the goings on below, but still looking like a filthy five year old.

Martin grabbed Isabel's shoulders and pulled her into a hug. At first she seemed confused, but she quickly hugged him back, grabbing hold of his T-shirt with her fists and pulling him as close to her as she could. It was a moment before she let go. Already several human staircases were being formed on the hall floor so those below could literally run up them instead of climb.

Isabel pulled away.

'Martin, the Keeper of Portals, what happened to him? I was going to change our time, but he started to shine so brilliantly. Where is he?'

'Right here,' said Martin.

'What do you mean?'

Martin smiled. '*I* am the Keeper of Portals.'

Isabel's mouth dropped open, but before she could speak, there was the sound of something flying through the air. Both Isabel and Martin turned, ready to defend themselves. A thick piece of wooden flooring sailed towards them. The Keeper of Questions was literally ripping the hall apart and hurling it at Martin and Isabel in a furious rage. The objects were intercepted mid-flight and crashed to the ground. Martin and Isabel looked down. On the floor, there were three broken tiny-winged creatures. They had flown straight for the objects, shielding Martin and Isabel with their lives.

The fallen bodies started to glow before they were

trampled by the many feet below. Then there was a sound that Martin could only describe as a swarm of rat-sized wasps. They broke their way in through the doors and windows, filling the massive space above the hall with their varied and peculiar bodies.

Martin and Isabel watched in awe. The Minor Keepers had arrived.

CHAPTER
TWENTY FIVE

The reason the universe existed as it did rested on a single fact. It was lazy. Why create something complicated when something simple would suffice? Even the existence of Keepers, which may appear an overcomplicated solution, was the simplest method of dealing with the problem the universe had. So when the Keeper of Portals was killed, the universe did not create a new Keeper of Portals. In the same way that two parts of the Keeper of Questions had become the new Keeper of Questions, the feather that grew from the crown on Martin's head marked him as the next Keeper of Portals. And so the Keeper of Portals, who had held the position since the universe first deemed that portals required a Keeper, died, and the mantle was passed to Martin.

The change came as no shock to Martin, because along with it came the associated knowledge of being a Major Keeper. Of course, Martin did not know everything as much of what the previous Keeper of Portals could do was learnt from having that position for so long.

Alongside the knowledge of what he was, came the feeling of being connected to everything that could be used as a doorway or entrance. Before becoming the Keeper he'd had to focus on them, retreating into his mind to visualise the room full of hanging cables. As he'd grown used to his ability, that process had quickened until it was nearly instantaneous. Nearly, but not quite. Things were different now: every portal was there. He could reach them without the focus and there was no confusion over which one was which. He knew every portal like they were his children.

Isabel grabbed Martin's hand and dragged him backwards.

''Tis them, isn't it? The Minor Keepers?'

Thousands of them filled the air, flying around the Keeper of Questions like a demonic halo. The largest were as big as Labradors and the smallest couldn't be seen without a microscope. But despite that, Martin knew them all. Each and every one of the 75,567 Minor Keepers Martin could identify like he could the portals. Looking up he saw them zip past in a blur of angry wings and fierce determination. The Keeper of Paint, the Keeper of Caution, the Keeper of Chickens, the Keeper of Misery, the Keeper of Dust. He could have named them all if he wished.

The Keeper of Questions threw a long shard of wood through the air. A dog-sized Keeper swerved to intercept it. The shard of wood pierced its body and the creature fell to the ground in a glowing ball of light. As Martin and Isabel watched, the body of the Keeper vanished and a new one appeared from nowhere, starting off as only a faint glow before becoming a brilliant ball of light. That ball of light then dimmed to take on the shape of the dog-sized Keeper that looked more like a miniature bear. Without further

306

preamble, the Minor Keeper took to the air once more and continued to circle the Keeper of Questions.

'It hurts.'

Standing with them on the entranceway were the Keeper of Pleasantries and the Keeper of Ennui.

'Every time. When die. It hurts,' said the Keeper of Ennui, his mouth floating around his furry slug-like body.

The Keeper of Pleasantries unrolled his long neck from around his torso.

'These were as many as I could find. We are all thankful to you, but not all will fight for you. As the Keeper of Ennui says, it hurts to die. Of course, as long as that which we observe continues to exist, we shall be born anew. However, that does not detract from the pain. If we are required to do so, we will make the process of ending this form of existence as quick as possible. But unfortunately, such a desirable outcome is not always granted.'

The Keeper of Pleasantries looked down into the hall. People were running up the human stairs towards Martin, Isabel and the three Keepers, but each time they got to the top, a swarm of Minor Keepers would fly into them, pushing them back onto the throng of people below. The problem was, many of the people held weapons, and they used them to attack the clouds of Keepers. The Keepers were losing limbs but not dying. They lay all over the hall, writhing in agony. Martin saw another Keeper, visiting the dying Keepers in turn. He was the Keeper of Mercy. Martin hated to see what that Keeper was forced to do over and over again, but it had to be done.

'Thank you,' said Martin, turning to Ennui and Pleasantries, 'for helping us.'

The Keeper of Pleasantries nodded. 'We wouldn't be here if we didn't think we could help,' he said with a smile.

'All we need now,' said Martin, 'is a way to stop him.'

The Keeper of Questions plucked people from the floor and threw them at Martin and Isabel. Most of the time a cloud of Minor Keepers would intercept, but sometimes they weren't enough and the person would burst through to appear next to the two teenagers. When that happened, Isabel would charge them with her altered time and shove them back down to the hall floor. Despite the drop, there were enough people below to break the fall.

Martin grabbed Isabel's hand and pulled her through a window behind him. They appeared in Westminster Palace, where Martin had ripped down the painting.

'We shan't run again, Martin!'

Martin shook his head. Something felt strange. Then he realised that just like the previous Keeper of Portals, he had long blue feathers growing all the way down his back.

'We're not running,' said Martin. 'You're right, we've done too much of that. *I've* done too much of that. We need to fight, but to do that we need a plan.'

Martin gave himself a moment to look around the interior of the palace room. It was grand enough to make even the master's house appear plain.

'The Keeper of Questions. I know he's there. But I can't get to him. I can't make any connections. It's the same with the Minor Keepers. I just can't connect to them.'

'What do you mean?' asked Isabel. 'Cannot connect?'

'I'm the Keeper of Portals. I have access to every doorway and entrance on the planet. All of them. I can walk into one door and come out any other door in the world without even thinking.'

'And?' said Isabel.

'Well, it's sort of the same with people. We have portals too.'

'Pardon?' said Isabel, but already she was starting to look uncomfortable.

'Your mouth, your ears, your nostrils. I'm connected to them all. I can use them just like the front door of a house.'

Isabel's eyes went wild. Her face started to twitch and her teeth were showing behind curled lips.

'My *portals*? You are *connected* to them?'

'I'm not... It's not... They're just there. I can't make them go away. I won't do anything, I promise.'

Isabel punched Martin. It felt as strong as a punch from a grown man.

'That was twice my speed. Never speak of my *portals* again.'

Martin nodded, painfully. Isabel looked slightly more relaxed, so Martin continued with his explanation.

'The Keepers, they all have... portals: mouths, ears, noses. Well some of them do; others, it's hard to say what they have. But the point is I can't connect to them. It's like they've been barred from me. I can't make a connection like that to *any* Keeper. It's just like Questions said: a Keeper cannot use what they observe to forcefully manipulate another Keeper.'

'So what does this mean?' asked Isabel.

'It means,' said Martin, 'that I may be the Keeper of Portals, but I can't use that against the Keeper of Questions.'

'Could you not create a doorway to another place, a dangerous place, and push the master through?'

Martin shook his head. 'I thought of that too, like, push him into the mouth of a volcano or some crevice at the bottom of the sea. That would kill him, but I couldn't do it. I mean, I could create the portal, but I couldn't push him through.'

'Would she stop you, that female Keeper?' asked Isabel.

'No, it's not her. Someone else would stop me, but even I don't know who. I'm only a Major Keeper, there are things even I don't know.'

Isabel walked over to one of the paintings. It depicted a mighty army going to battle. Two warring sides charged at each other on horses with swords and spears raised. 'The Minor Keepers, could they not push him through?'

'He's too big,' said Martin. 'Even if they worked together, they wouldn't be able to do it.'

'So if the master were weaker—'

'Or the door sucked!' said Martin, eyes coming alive as an idea bubbled inside his head. Isabel was still trying to speak to him, but he had to ignore her. He needed to find out if this would work. If it did, then he'd be throwing Questions into a prison he could never escape from. He concentrated and for the first time since becoming a Keeper he actually had to search out a portal. Then he got it. It was immense, more powerful than anything he could have conceived. But it was there, and that's what mattered.

Isabel was staring indignantly at him. 'Will you not listen to *my* idea?' she said.

'What? No, I've got it. I can't believe I can actually do this!' Martin took one last look around the hall, savouring the calm. 'We need to head back, the Minor Keepers won't hold him off forever.'

'I still think you should listen to my idea.'

Martin smiled and put a hand on Isabel's shoulder. 'Isabel, trust me. I know what I'm doing. I *am* the Keeper of Portals.'

'I was wondering how long it would take for that to go to your head.'

Martin walked over to a suit of armour and pulled a sword from the clutches of its right hand. It shone in a brilliant silver.

'Here, have a sword,' said Martin. 'It's a shiny one.'

'You cannot simply placate me with *shiny things*,' said Isabel as she took the sword. She started to swing it around, moving it faster and faster until it produced an incredible amount of wind. She finished up by attacking the suit of armour. Her sword moved so fast she cut it clean in half.

'Dangerous things, however,' said Isabel as she pointed the sword in the air and inspected the blade, 'those, I will accept.'

Martin nodded. It wasn't that he wanted to kill the Keeper of Questions without Isabel, but he was the Keeper of Portals now.

Isabel was among the Minor Keepers, attacking the Keeper of Questions relentlessly. With the help of Pleasantries and

Ennui, she had instructed the minors to fly low, keeping Questions' gaze on the ground so he wouldn't notice Martin above him.

Martin was balanced on the rafters, watching the fight below. Isabel was fast, but he could still make her out as a blur that darted in the cracks between the crowd. She would slash at Questions before avoiding his counterattacks to strike again, sending out a wave of blood with each slice of her sword. The Minor Keepers flew in groups, attacking like squadrons of fighter jets, flying straight into Questions and gouging at him with their fingers, claws and teeth. But despite the attacks, Questions still stood. He was too powerful for them. Even Isabel's attacks were healed by the time she struck again. He had control of so many people now. Millions upon millions of questions were being directed at him by the second, making him stronger than ever. The damage caused by the Minors and Isabel was of no significance, but then, it was never meant to be. While their attacks were weak, their numbers were many, and though Questions wouldn't fall to them, he was certainly kept busy.

Martin had moved to sit on a chandelier that hung over the centre of the hall. This was the third idea he'd come up with that involved a chandelier and he'd yet to understand exactly why. He had no real interest in them and yet here he was, drawn like a cat to a sofa, ready to use a chandelier to solve all his problems once more.

He saw Isabel. She had run to the far end of the hall and managed to climb up the archway over the entrance.

She was with the little girl, who was still cowering in shock and hiding herself in the corner. Martin now knew who that little girl was, what she observed and what Questions had taken from her. Defeating Questions would save her too.

Martin created a connection to the window, pulled Isabel up through the bottom of the chandelier and helped her sit on the rim. Then he broke the connection to the chain and they started to fall.

Isabel took Martin's hand and grabbed the chandelier. Their descent slowed like they'd been tied to a bungee cord, but instead of pinging back to the roof, it just got slower and slower.

'This is as slow as I can go now. Will it be enough?'

Martin regarded the scene below him. He watched as droves of Minor Keepers slowly crashed into Questions, as the people that filled the hall to bursting tried to arrange themselves in a shield around the mighty Keeper's body, as the Minors dived and wove between legs and arms, managing to make it through most of the time but occasionally getting knocked out of the air by a man wielding a shovel or a young woman brandishing a knife. Then he noticed something else. Minor Keepers were suddenly disappearing as if magically plucked from their flight. Even at this speed, Martin couldn't work out what was doing it.

'This'll do,' said Martin.

'You have still not told me your idea,' said Isabel. She looked annoyed and her grip felt strong, though Martin sensed it wasn't through fear.

'It's hard to explain,' said Martin. 'It's pretty crazy, but I think it'll work. Basically, I can't *push* Questions through a doorway, so I thought, what if I found a doorway that sucked.'

Isabel seemed to think for a minute before she asked, 'And what gateway have you found that can suck?'

'A black hole, and don't ask me to explain what it is, because I don't really know. Just trust me. Even though he's way bigger than the chandelier, Questions will be sucked straight through it. I don't think it'll be pleasant to watch.'

'But you will still force him through,' said Isabel. 'I thought you were unable to do that.'

Martin smiled. 'I can't *push* Questions through. That's why I've got a gateway that can suck. So even though I'm creating the portal that will destroy him, it's the portal itself that forces him through and that means I can't be stopped because the connection's already there. The problem is, I will have broken the Keeper law, or whatever it is, and I'll be punished. I'm pretty certain I won't be the Keeper of Portals anymore. But that's good because it'll break the connection and the black hole won't be able to suck anything else through, like the rest of the world.'

'Do you expect any punishment other than no longer being a Keeper?' asked Isabel.

'Well I guess the universe might just get rid of me altogether, but I don't think so. Causality said that me dying brought about the paradox, so if I defeat Questions, then I won't die. I mean, she didn't exactly say that, but I figured if I defeated him, I'd get to live. I hope. It'd be pretty crap if I died either way. Plus, this can't fail. It's a black hole! Those things can suck up entire stars!'

'*You* defeat him?' said Isabel.

The look of satisfaction slipped from Martin's face. 'What?'

'Before it was *us, we;* now it has become *you.* I had a plan, Martin. I still do. I know how we are to defeat the Keeper of Questions. That this method is the correct way is something I am certain of, but you did not even ask me what my idea was. You'd rather attempt your idea, which could kill you, than even *listen* to mine.'

'No, it's not that, I just thought it would work and...'

Isabel glared at him. He couldn't even defend his actions. She had every right to be annoyed, and yet here she was, still helping with his plan.

'You believe yourself to be better than me,' said Isabel flatly. 'You are from the future. You never had feelings for someone who abused you. You were not the one who tried to kill the Keeper of Portals not once, but twice. And now you believe that you are better than me because you are a real Keeper and I am not.'

Martin did nothing. Said nothing. He didn't even dare blink.

'You did not listen to your mother when she begged you to see your father before he died. Even though you knew she was right, you still chose to ignore her. I thought you would have learnt from that, Martin, but it appears that is something you are incapable of doing.'

Isabel's grip around Martin's hand was starting to loosen. He'd already made it clear that he was better than her, so why should she stay?

Then Martin realised it: this was the moment the Keeper

of Causality had spoken of. This was the choice he had to make. Before, all the other choices Martin made could have been influenced by her, but now that he was the Keeper of Portals, there was no way she could control his fate.

Only the tips of Isabel's fingers remained brushing Martin's hand when he reached out and grabbed her.

'You're wrong.'

'Let go of me!' shouted Isabel.

'No, I won't.' Martin gripped her wrist as hard as he could, aware that he was probably hurting her, but he wouldn't let her leave, not because it would ruin his plan, but because of what he needed to tell her.

'Isabel, I am in awe of you,' said Martin. 'All I've done since I met you is try to keep up. You're tougher than me, stronger than me and you know how to do things that make me shudder just thinking about. You saved my life when the Keeper threw a red hot poker at my head, when I made us run out of the top floor window, you got us back to my time, you pushed me back when I was about to fall into the sea even though you were going to die. I mean, I know I saved your life too, and Portals', but that took me *two weeks*. I just thought, now that I'm a Keeper I could, you know, be the one that saves us, properly, and not have it take forever. Sorry. I didn't mean to take charge. I just wanted it to be me.'

Isabel's face softened slightly. 'And?'

'And… I guess I wanted to impress you, just a little bit.'

Isabel took Martin's hand again. 'I'm sorry too. I should have given you your moment. I was being selfish. I believed that because he was my master, I should be the one to stop him. I will stay, Martin, and I will help you defeat him.'

Martin shook his head. 'We'll do your plan. If there's no chance of me dying, then it has to be the right one.'

Martin created a gateway using the chandelier as they continued to fall towards the Keeper of Questions. They jumped through and as they landed on the archway overlooking the hall, they saw Questions' tongue crack the chandelier clean in half, sending shards and splinters of wood flying through the air.

Martin's plan would have failed.

If he had not grabbed Isabel's hand at the very last second, the chandelier would have continued to fall and the Keeper of Questions would have destroyed it before Martin had made a connection to the black hole. Martin would have fallen into Questions' lap, or, more likely, his mouth. If Martin was consumed, then Questions would become the Keeper of Portals. Isabel had saved his life. Again. Martin tried not to let it get to him, or the fact that his brilliant plan would have got him killed and created the Keeper of Causality's alternate future.

Isabel was next to Martin as he watched the fight below. The Minor Keepers were still attacking Questions, keeping low, but their numbers were diminishing. Some were being killed as Questions lashed out, but more were being consumed as Questions' tongue struck the air and pulled them from the sky and into his mouth, consuming them so they could no longer be re-born.

'Your idea,' said Martin. 'What is it?'

'Physical attacks cannot stop the master. He is too powerful. Therefore, we must make him weaker.'

'How?'

'We remove his purpose.'

Martin was unsure for a moment, but then he understood what Isabel meant. A Keeper is only required for as long as that which they exist to observe remains. For example, when there are no doorways or entrances, there will be no need for a Keeper of Portals, and when there are no trees, there will be no need for a Keeper of Trees. But this Keeper was different: he didn't maintain an object that could be destroyed.

Isabel answered before Martin could ask. 'I know what you are thinking,' she said. 'How can you get rid of questions? But that is not what he is anymore.

'When the master was inside my head I had a connection with him. I could not read his thoughts, but I knew of them. I knew what he had been and what he had become, though I did not know why. He is not the Keeper of Questions, though he once was. What he is now is something else, something that is not supposed to exist. He does not need questions to exist; he needs admiration, devotion, subservience. He needs people to completely sacrifice themselves to him. To worship him almost. That's what he feeds off. Remember in his study, what happened when he experienced your time?'

Martin thought back. Just standing in front of the door had weakened the master so much he nearly died.

'Your time, Martin, where you have moving pictures and fast horseless carriages and hot water whenever you wish it, that is a poison to the master. I could feel it. The people in your time, they are not like the people in mine; that is how they managed to create such things, by solving the problems, *the questions*, for themselves.'

'But we're not all like that,' said Martin. 'People detonate bombs in shopping centres and fly planes into buildings because someone put stupid ideas in their heads. We're not that different.'

'But you are! It is not about the people who follow blindly, it is about those who refuse to. They are the ones that weaken him. Even if there are many people who will devote themselves to the Keeper of Questions, there would not be enough to quash those he cannot abide.'

There were many more people in Martin's time than Isabel's. If more of them devote themselves to the Keeper of Questions, feeding him in the hope that they're sending their devotion to a plethora of non-existent gods, then why wouldn't he be stronger? How did the actions of the minority overcome those of the majority? Thoughts ran manically through Martin's mind, trying to understand what Isabel was saying, when one tripped and fell into a science lesson. People were like air. Everyone needs oxygen to live. You increase that oxygen and you become stronger and can work for longer, but if you reduce the oxygen, then you become listless and weak. To Questions, the believers are his oxygen, but those who don't believe are carbon dioxide. If you increase the amount of carbon dioxide until it becomes poisonous, it doesn't matter how much oxygen there is, you'll still die. Martin's time may have more oxygen, but it was also rich in carbon dioxide.

'It will completely destroy the crystal,' said Isabel, pointing to her forehead.

'Can you still do it with the crack?'

Isabel nodded. 'Yes. I believe it is something the crystal can do regardless of its state, but it is something that can only be done once.'

The Minor Keepers continued their attack on the Keeper of Questions, but their numbers were even lower. Only 7,531 remained. The rest had been consumed by the grotesque warping of flesh and feathers in the centre of the hall that had once been the handsome master.

Martin needed a door large enough for the Keeper, but he was so big there was nothing left that he could fit through. Even the massive door to the hall was too small.

Then Martin looked up and saw it.

'Take my hands.'

Isabel instantly understood.

'I shall miss changing my time,' said Isabel. 'I greatly enjoyed it.'

Martin nodded. What could he say? Isabel was losing all of her power while Martin's had increased. He knew it wasn't fair.

They both closed their eyes and concentrated, Martin on the where and Isabel on the when.

The crystal on Isabel's forehead exploded in an eruption of brilliant light. Above them, the roof, which was built onto the walls of the hall as if it were the lid to a box, disappeared and was replaced by a blue sky.

The Keeper of Questions cried out and the Minor Keepers quickly withdrew. Soon all eyes were looking up, except for Martin's. He watched the Keeper of Questions dry out and shrivel until he was only a tiny fraction of his former size. Then he changed, once more appearing as the master, but the old frail version he had seen before. He was not dead, merely in shock. The world he lived in still asked questions to him; it was only the lack of devotion that could be felt through the portal to the future that sent his body reeling. If it was closed, then he would recover as he had done before. But for now, he was weakened.

Martin watched the people below. Those still standing were looking towards the ceiling at the futuristic sky. Martin followed their gaze. He expected to see his own time, filled with tower blocks and contrails. But the sky that shone brightly above him was not one he knew.

Piercing the blue sky were skyscrapers the likes of which Martin had never seen before. They resembled twisted curls of molten glass that constantly moved and reconfigured. But the strange buildings weren't the only thing that shocked him. The Earth: it didn't curl outwards, it curled inwards. Land with buildings and forests, oceans and deserts, rose up either side to meet above the open portal. At the far ends the land extended for hundreds of miles and was filled with millions of humans living on the inside of an enormous tube with one end pointed at the Sun. What Isabel had connected to wasn't a place on earth. She hadn't just opened a door to the future a few hundred years away, this future was over a thousand years away. It was a future where so much had been achieved by individuals solving problems and answering questions themselves that they would have no need for what the

321

Keeper of Questions had become. All Martin and Isabel had left to do was send him there.

Martin stepped through a window at the front of the hall and came out through the doorway directly below. He walked into the hall, a path appearing before him. No longer controlled by the Keeper of Questions, the Londoners that had been forced to fight for him didn't understand what they were seeing: both the strangely dressed boy with long electric blue feathers growing down his back or the bizarre sky above them. Many had left, either in pain, confusion or fear, giving Martin enough space to move and approach the withered body of the Keeper of Questions.

The Keeper tried to sit, but was unable to. All he could do was raise his head and even that took considerable effort.

'Portals.'

'Questions.'

There was a moment of silence as the two Major Keepers regarded each other, one in the shrivelled body of an old man, the other in the body of a fifteen-year-old boy.

'I do not seek absolution,' said Questions. 'I know that I have lost and that is something I cannot change. But before you destroy me, I will answer that one question you so seek an answer for.'

Martin didn't say anything. They both knew what that question was.

'All questions asked, I control. Some questions are simple. "What shall I eat?" "Where shall I go?" These questions I barely even hear. They are like whispers to me.

It is the questions asked with feelings that are the loudest, questions that are asked to the sky ring out above all others. As a Keeper, I only had to make sure the questions were being asked. But one day, I decided to listen to the questions.'

The Keeper of Questions was breathing deeply and his body appeared to crumble before Martin.

'I discovered how much emotion came with the questions: hopefulness, sorrow, joy, but most of all, fear. For there was one question, a question that was asked with so much fear that I could not ignore it. It was one of the first questions to be asked, and has always been the most powerful.'

The master's desert-dry eyes locked with Martin's.

'"What happens when I die?"' The Keeper's eyes, which had once seemed impossibly cruel, now appeared sad. 'You know the Keeper who masquerades as a young girl and you know what I stole from her. But even she did not possess the answer to this question.'

That was all the Keeper of Questions could take. The strength from his neck went and his head crashed to the floor.

A small part of Martin could understand the Keeper. The fear that had been asked with that question had implanted itself within the Keeper of Questions, slowly growing until it became a part of him. That had been why he had sought the power to become a Fundamental Keeper. Fundamental Keepers never die.

Martin turned around. While he understood the pain and the fear that was so deeply rooted within the Keeper's psyche, it would never be enough to justify the control he had forced upon others and the lives he had taken.

Behind him, Martin could hear the Minor Keepers gathering. They lifted the Keeper's frail body off the ground and flew him towards the futuristic sky above.

Isabel held Martin's hand. Not to alter time, just to hold it. He felt her fingers intertwined through his and he smiled.

'For Credence!' The Minor Keepers shouted, moving higher. 'For Salt! For Leaves! For Despair!' The Minor Keepers continued to cry out the names of the bravest who fell to the Keeper of Questions. When they were just short of the portal to the future, they paused.

Martin could feel it, and looking at Isabel he knew she felt it too. One more name to be called. One more Keeper to be remembered before the Keeper of Questions was destroyed.

Everyone's voice shouted in unison, their call filling the hall, reaching out to the 17th century city of London and into the future above them.

'FOR BUTTONS!'

The Keeper of Questions was thrown into the air, passing the threshold from 1623 and into the distant future. As he ascended, his body started to break up like a sheet of paper on fire until all that was left to fall to the earth was dust.

CHAPTER
TWENTY SIX

The inside of Westminster Hall was filled with brilliant flashes of light as thousands of Minor Keepers were reborn. All those that had died at the hands of the Keeper of Questions and those that had been consumed by him appeared once more into the world. Less than seven thousand remained after the battle and many of those were badly injured. A group of a few hundred had been mobilised to recover their broken bodies. Some were taken to a place where they could rest or be healed and others, who were beyond hope, were taken to the Keeper of Mercy.

Martin watched the Keeper of Scales, an orange lizard-like Keeper, being carried through the air by many much smaller Keepers towards the Keeper of Mercy. The Keeper of Scales looked at Martin with weary eyes before turning away. Martin couldn't help but feel responsible for the Keeper's impending death, and the deaths of so many others he'd witnessed that day. He wished there had been a way to stop Questions without involving the Minor Keepers, but the truth was, he and Isabel wouldn't have succeeded without them.

Martin felt Isabel grab his arm.

'Look!'

Martin turned to see the Keeper of Time walking towards them. The bustling Minor Keepers and even the remaining Londoners subconsciously cleared a path for the Fundamental Keeper. His mirrored features were in a constant state of flux as he moved. Some raced ahead and aged at an astonishing rate while others seemed never to change. Then suddenly, the features that had been ageing dramatically froze and other parts of him began to grow old and wither. Martin saw Isabel rub the smooth skin on her forehead where her crystal had once been.

Walking behind the Keeper of Time was another Keeper. She looked human and a couple of years older than Martin. She had long curly blonde hair and wore a brilliantly white lace dress.

As soon as Isabel saw the girl her face turned sour.

The blonde-haired girl ran over to Martin and started to prod and poke him.

'So you're the new Keeper of Portals? I approve! Not that there was anything wrong with the old one,' the girl grabbed Martin's cheeks and pulled his face close to hers, 'but you're young and I like young.'

The girl let go of Martin's face and linked arms with him.

'So, Portals, where are you going to take me? I fancy somewhere hot. Yes, definitely hot. Oh, and with a beach!'

'Excuse me, but *who* are *you*?'

The blonde girl looked past Martin to Isabel, who, compared to the pristine white dress and flawless blonde hair of the girl clung to Martin's arm, was covered in thick black ink, wore torn clothes and had hair that stuck out in every direction.

'Me?' said the blonde girl. 'Why, I'm the Keeper of Answers.'

'There's a Keeper of Answers?' said Isabel.

'Evidently.' Answers clapped her hands together. 'I've missed that! It's amazing: you don't realise how useful something is until it gets bitten off. Though I suppose it was my fault. I knew I should have done something about it, but he begged and begged and then one day, he just took.'

'The little girl? That was you?' said Isabel.

Answers nodded with a smile. 'That I was. And it's thanks to Portals here that Questions has been stopped and I'm back to my usual self, both hands accounted for.'

Isabel looked the Keeper of Answers' mature body up and down. 'Yes, and we are *so* grateful that happened.'

'Aren't we just!' said a cheeky Keeper of Answers before performing a dainty twirl.

Isabel growled under her breath. 'Now why is it the Keeper of Time appears to be a tall creature made from mirrors whereas you look like some highway harlot?'

If Answers was offended by Isabel's comment, she didn't show it. Instead she just laughed. 'Keepers don't look like anything!'

Martin and Isabel looked at each other with confused expressions. The Keeper of Answers laughed again.

'We're concepts, not physical beings! We don't have bodies in the same way you do. Of course Portals here is an exception being as he is actually a human, but for the rest of us it's different. The way we appear depends on how we want to be perceived. Of course, sometimes it's those who perceive us that define how we look.' Answers winked at Martin when she said this. Isabel glared at him.

'So *you* made her look like this?'

Martin didn't know how to respond. Had he decided how the Keeper of Answers would appear to him and everyone else? If he had done, it certainly hadn't been conscious. Though that may actually make it worse.

'In his defence, when he first saw me I was virtually nothing,' said Answers. 'I am a Major Keeper, but at the time I would only have been a Minor Keeper, and a worthless Minor Keeper at that. It's only natural that he perceived me as a confused little girl. It's hardly his fault that the little girl grew up to look like this.'

Isabel's glare softened.

'Though,' said Answers, fingering the hem, 'this dress *is* surprisingly short.'

Isabel's glare re-intensified.

'He is ready,' came a voice that spoke like a full orchestra playing at different tempos.

Martin, Isabel and Answers looked to where the Keeper of Time pointed. From the far end of the hall, a figure composed entirely of light approached them. With each step, the light lost its intensity and the figure it shrouded was revealed.

Human legs supported a torso that quickly gained dark grey feathers the further up it went. The two arms, though covered in feathers as well, appeared human for the most part and ended in smooth, dextrous hands. The head was owl-like with large round eyes and rings of pure gold for irises. From its back grew a single set of wings which at first had been fully extended, but as the Keeper approached, were retracted and tucked completely out of sight.

The Keeper of Questions stood before them; its eyes were filled with a mixture of inquisitiveness and fear.

'I. Hear. Questions.'

The Keeper's voice was soft and he sounded confused. He'd only just been born and was already being flooded by the millions of questions from those who had been enslaved by the previous Keeper.

Answers left Martin and sidled up next to Questions. 'Ignore them, Questions dear. They need to learn to solve their own problems.'

Questions nodded, though he still appeared confused.

'You humans are troublesome,' said the Keeper of Answers. 'The previous Questions was like this too. We're Keepers of Sentience; that's why people often perceive us as humans, or human-like at least. He was kind and gentle, but he was also curious. That was why he started to listen. He heard the questions you asked and that changed him. He wanted me to help, but I refused and that is why he stole a part of me. At the time I was too strong for him to simply consume, but what he took was enough for him to weaken me and in part become the Keeper of Answers himself. That was why I put the answer into your head, Portals. I sensed that you were different and knew that, without your help, it would not be long until Questions devoured me completely.'

Holding hands with the Keeper of Questions, the Keeper of Answers addressed Martin and Isabel.

'He was my closest companion and I loved him dearly,

but what you did had to be done. There was no salvation for what he had become. Thank you, Portals. Martin. For stopping him and allowing his rebirth. Thank you, both.'

'Thank. You,' said a rather clumsy sounding Keeper of Questions.

Hand in hand, the Keepers of Questions and Answers spread their wings, making Answers appear like an angel, and together they rose into the air.

'Somewhere hot, please!' shouted the Keeper of Answers.

Martin concentrated and the roof of Westminster Hall once more transformed into a portal. Above, the summer heat of the Caribbean filled the room. As soon as Questions and Answers flew through, the portal was closed.

A small figure flitted in and out of Martin's vision, weaving between the many Minor Keepers that filled the air. Martin held out his hand and the tiny Keeper alighted before dropping down on one knee and bowing his head.

'Keeper of Portals, I have heard of what you did for my past incarnation, and from the depths of my being you have my undying gratitude and thanks.'

The Keeper of Buttons stood up. He was only four inches tall, a mouse's head on a faery body. His wings were long strands of golden hair and Martin watched as they knitted themselves into a plait along the Keeper's back.

Having seen so many Minor Keepers die in this hall, Martin found it strange that the death of the Keeper of Buttons still affected him so much. Possibly because it had been the first, Martin had felt it so much stronger. Though perhaps it was the defiance that Buttons had shown that had resonated so strongly with Martin.

'For as long as that which I exist to observe remains, I and any future incarnations of my Keeper form shall be your servants. Of that, you have my word.'

The Keeper of Buttons bowed once more and his hair-like wings unfurled gracefully. He took to the air and joined a group of Minor Keepers carrying another severely wounded comrade to the Keeper of Mercy.

Isabel held Martin's hand. 'He was reborn.'

All Martin could do was smile and nod. He was filled with an immense sense of satisfaction, but it was still laced with sorrow and regret. Just because the Keeper had been reborn, did not mean that he had never died. The new Keeper was not the same as the old Keeper. What they observed may be the same, but they were still a brand new being with only notional memories of the Keeper that came before.

Martin squeezed Isabel's hand. 'It's time we went home.'

'How?' said Isabel. 'I do not have a crystal.'

Martin gestured to the Keeper of Time.

'We have a quicker way now.'

Martin and Isabel stood with the Keeper of Time in the master's study. All it had taken was for them to step through the entrance of Westminster Hall to return to the house. Together, Martin and Time had opened the door at the back of the study to Martin's bedroom. The time on the other side corresponded to five minutes after Martin and

Isabel had crawled through the tiny door in the loft.

'I won't be the Keeper of Portals when I go through, will I?'

The Keeper of Time slowly nodded his silver head. 'Correct. There already exists a Keeper of Portals in your time. When you step through, you will no longer be a Keeper and a new Keeper shall appear in this time.'

Martin understood. The same thing had happened to the Keeper of Portals when he first stepped through into the master's study. In that time there was already a Keeper of Portals and the universe had no need for two, so his feathers had started to fall out and he had grown weak enough to be hurt by Isabel's attacks.

Martin walked through the doorway and already feathers started to fall from his back and drop silently to the floor. He felt the connections to every doorway and entrance on the planet begin to dessert him like migrating birds looking for a better home and knew that the freedom Portal's abilities had granted him would be gone for good.

Isabel stood in the master's study. Behind her was the Keeper of Time, and behind him there was a glowing ball of light that was slowly starting to take shape.

'Are you ready?' said Martin.

Isabel beamed at him before nodding.

'As your room fell into the sea, I guess we'll have to find you a new one. But that's OK. I think we have a couple we're not using.'

Martin was giddy with excitement. What he should have felt from stopping the Keeper of Questions had been instantly supplanted by the knowledge that Isabel was actually going to live with him. As soon as victory was assured, his mind had played out various scenarios of their life, starting with telling his mum, going to school together and even going on holiday. As for the other side, what they felt for each other, Martin tried not to focus on it. He didn't want to jinx it. But secretly, deep down, he knew what he wanted to happen. He just hoped Isabel felt the same way.

'Come on, Isabel. We've got things to do! I suppose we should go and find my mum first. It'll only get awkward if we wait a few weeks to tell her.'

Isabel was right in front of the door and looked up at Martin with red-rimmed eyes.

'I cannot.'

Martin almost felt his knees give out.

'No, Isabel, you *can*. Trust me. You're going to love it here: there's so much more to do; it's so much safer and you'll even live longer. I know you're scared, but that's perfectly natural. Change is scary, God do I know that, but it can also be amazing. Just step through the door, Isabel. You won't regret it, I promise you.'

'No, Martin. I did not say I will not; I said I *cannot*.'

Martin watched as Isabel held her hand up to the door. Exactly at the point where she should cross over into Martin's room, her palm became flat as if it were pressed against a plane of glass.

'No,' said Martin. 'No, no, no, NO!'

He ran to the door, ready to grab Isabel and pull her through, but as soon as he got close, he was forced back into his room.

For a moment, Martin just stood there, knowing it would be pointless to charge the door again and again. He wasn't the Keeper of Portals anymore.

'You have to be kidding me!' shouted Martin. 'After everything we did, this is how you thank us?! We nearly died back there. We risked our lives to clean up your mess! What? Do you think this is funny? Make us do your dirty work then shaft us right at the end? 'Coz I'll tell you something, that's not funny! That's messed up. So just let her through, all right. Just let her through. You owe us that much. After everything we did, you owe us that much!'

No one responded. The room was silent. Martin could hear his blood beating in his head. In the room on the other side of the door, Isabel and the Keeper of Time watched Martin. Time with a curious gaze and Isabel with tears streaming silently down her face.

'The silent treatment again? Can't you do anything else but mess up people's lives and hide? Come on, Causality, I know you're here.'

Martin looked around the room, trying to spot any hint of movement.

'This isn't funny. Just let her through you *stupid bitch*!'

Martin's feet were lifted off the floor as he flew through the air. He crashed into the wall on the far side of his room and fell face-first on his bed. When he got up, she was there, standing just in front of the door.

Martin walked purposefully towards her. The Keeper of Causality's face was stern and her purple hair and white robes flew around her angrily, but as Martin moved closer, the anger faded and the expression on her face became one of pity.

'You know that which I observe and you know of its importance. Isabel has not been stopped from coming to your time through any form of malice or punishment. She has to remain where she is because of what she has yet to do.'

'Then I'll go to her time,' said Martin. 'We'll stay there and live in the house. It's not like the master needs it. That'll be all right, won't it? We almost did that anyway, so we can do it again.'

Isabel seemed to smile, but it was a defeated smile. Next to Martin, Causality shook her head. 'Just as what Isabel will do shall impact the future of people in your time, events that you are pivotal in will affect the lives of those who come after you.'

Martin was completely dumbfounded. So this was it? After everything they had done, the sacrifices they had made and the risks they had taken, they didn't even get the one thing they both wanted? How was that fair? And the worst part of all, the part that cut the deepest, was that Martin understood completely. The Keeper of Causality was right and he couldn't dispute that.

Isabel leaned forward and knocked on the invisible glass that separated the two times.

'Keeper of Causality, if it isn't too much trouble, I have a request.'

Causality walked up to the door and bent down to Isabel's level. Once she had heard Isabel say her piece, she stood up fully and sighed.

'If you wish. However, I fail to see what that will achieve.'

Isabel pushed a hand forward, and instead of being stopped, it passed straight on through into Martin's bedroom.

Martin ran over and took first that hand, then the other one. He pulled, but everything below Isabel's hips refused to move.

'I don't get it. Wasn't she going to let you in?'

Isabel shook her head. 'No.'

'Then what?'

Isabel smiled. 'For a boy from the future, you don't know very much.'

Isabel let go of Martin's hands and grabbed hold of his face, pulling it towards hers. She didn't hesitate for even a second before she kissed him.

Martin's hands found their way to Isabel's shoulders and he pulled her as close to him as he could. He could feel her shake in his grip as they continued to kiss.

'You've had enough, I believe. There are others present,' said the Keeper of Causality.

Martin felt hands on his chest and arms, pushing him away. He craned his neck as far forward as he could to continue kissing Isabel, but eventually they were wrenched apart.

'I was never sure,' said Martin, 'that you liked me that way. I mean I hoped, but you know, I didn't actually know.'

'I knew,' said Isabel, 'but then you are not so difficult to read.'

Martin pulled a face. The door was starting to close as the last of his feathers fell to the floor.

'I'm never going to see you again,' said Martin. 'This is it.'

Isabel shook her head. 'We live in a world of Keepers, where doors through time actually exist. We have already proven ourselves, Martin. I'm sure the Keepers will need us again. I have no doubt of that.' Isabel bowed her head before looking up. 'There are so many more things I wish to say, but they shall have to wait until the next time you so rudely interrupt my life.'

Despite their parting Martin couldn't stop himself from smiling. 'There's more I want to say too. Maybe we'll get the chance over a nice handful of rabbit guts.'

Isabel sniggered. 'Indeed we shall. Though, while I am certain I will miss you, I fear I may miss your bath even more. Perhaps I will have to devise a water heater of my own, unless, of course, you come back soon.'

'I'll try my best,' said Martin.

'I should expect so! Until then, Martin Lockford.'

'Until then, Just Isabel.'

At the back of the master's study, Martin could see the figure of the Keeper of Portals. The light had deserted it and now the Keeper stood staring at him. Martin watched as the Keeper of Time pulled a new crystal from his skin and placed it in Isabel's hand. For a moment Martin thought the crystal was a gift to allow Isabel to see Martin again, but then he realised it wasn't for Isabel to use, it was for her to hide and for Martin to find in 400 years. The Keeper of Time explained this to Isabel before approaching the Keeper of Portals, who continued to stare at Martin and the door. Together they left through the back of the room, going to wherever it is that Keepers go. In Martin's room, the Keeper of Causality had already left.

Only the pair of them remained. Martin in his bedroom and Isabel in the master's study. Neither of them spoke as the door cut them off from each other forever. They stared into each other's eyes, thinking all the things they wanted to say until the door shut completely, immediately followed by a loud click.

The door in Martin's room began to crumble, falling to the floor in a matter of seconds until only a pile of black wood dust remained.

That was when Martin realised that Isabel was truly gone. For the next hour he just stood staring at the wall. It was only him and his mum now, the two of them living in a house that was slowly falling into the sea. Martin knew that his life was still going to improve, that he would meet people and make new friends, but for now nothing else was further from his thoughts. And so Martin remained in front of the wall, staring at the space where the door had once stood. A door that had taken him to the past. A past where he had met the most amazing girl ever. And that same past, where she'd been forced to remain.

EPILOGUE

Two weeks had passed since Martin had returned to his house and the door at the end of his bedroom was destroyed. After that, he felt he could no longer stay in that room. The memories of his time with Isabel were too rich to the point where they became painful, so Martin found a room closer to his mum's.

Life had returned to normal surprisingly easily. Doors no longer led to places where they weren't supposed to and objects from the 17th century weren't usurping their modern counterparts. The swapping doors phenomenon had yet to be explained, and while many people worked feverishly trying to understand it, as it no longer posed a threat to the general population, most forgot about it and attributed reports of such bizarre occurrences to heatstroke or drunkenness.

Martin had spent the final two weeks of the summer holidays exploring the house with his mum. Though he had seen most of it before, for his mum it was brand new and Martin enjoyed sharing his knowledge with her.

It was when Martin and his mum were in one of the bedrooms on the first floor that the book had been found. The room itself was unlike many others in that most of the furniture remained.

At the back of the room was a small bookcase with only a handful of books on the shelves. Jo was convinced that somebody would pay quite a high price for such old books, and was flicking through them with care when a pressed flower fell out from between the pages and floated gently to the floor. That flower triggered something in Martin's memory, something he had completely overlooked.

Martin had found the sledgehammer in one of the many cellars but the room he was after took a lot longer to find. At first he'd smashed cellar walls at random, but they had been thick and those that did yield only revealed dirt on the other side. After that failure, Martin had gone for a systematic approach, and over the course of two days had drawn a map of every single room in the house. That was when he discovered it: a space on the first floor where there should have been a room but where no door led to.

When his mum had left to go shopping, Martin, armed with the sledgehammer and a torch, smashed a hole through the wall.

He shone the torch around the large room. It was completely empty, but he knew there would be something in there. The room turned a right angle, and no longer became lit by the light from the hole. That was where Martin found the book. He picked it up and the pressed flowers fell from the pages like cherry blossoms. Martin bent down and scooped them up, pushing them back between the pages. Then he noticed something else on the floor. Putting the book down, Martin unfolded the two items of clothing, now brittle and rotten. One pair of dark green trousers and a black vest top.

340

Martin felt like his insides were being pulled down through his body as he handled the clothes he'd last seen her wear.

Standing up, he shone the torch at the wall. He saw his name in the text that had been carved into the wood. All this time, it had been Isabel's writing.

Martin walked back to the door. He found the first entry and started to read.

It has been three months since the door closed and I am now seventeen. I continue to wait by it every day. I know such a thing is stupid, but with no master, and no one claiming ownership of the house, there is little else for me to do. I found this room by accident and felt compelled to use it as a diary that I know shall not wither with time. If I have managed to complete a single wall by the time you appear, I will be very cross. However, I feel any anger shall be fleeting, as long as you return.

Martin paused and swept the room with his torch. Every inch of wall had been covered by writing, scratched into the wood over a period of what must have been years. That was when he knew with certainty that there would be no declaration of feelings left unsaid over a handful of rabbit guts. He was never going to see Isabel again.

Martin stayed in the room all day, only leaving to tell his mum he was ill and would spend the day in bed. Isabel told Martin of her life, how she spent every day waiting before realising that the house needed to be looked after and Martin would come when he came.

At the age of 18, after living alone in the house for a year, Isabel became its legal owner through some trickery with paperwork and deeds that Martin didn't understand. It was that year that she begun to hire people to work in the house. Despite technically being the lady of the house, she did more than her fair share of the labour. She claimed it was in her blood.

By the age of nineteen, the farms in the estate were prosperous and producing enough food to sell and make a tidy profit which continued to rise year after year.

Isabel spoke of the harsh winters, of deaths, and births of those who worked for her and the happiness she felt from being able to provide jobs for people while paying and treating them fairly. But despite the happiness she spoke of, there was an undercurrent of loneliness in Isabel's writings that hurt Martin to read. Most entries would talk of the house and even stories about the people who worked for her, but other entries pleaded and begged Martin to return. Sometimes she was upset, while others she was angry with him for not appearing. Though as time passed these entries decreased, and by the time Martin was halfway around the room, they no longer occurred. Martin felt like he had been forgotten. But then he had seen Isabel two and a half weeks ago. It took Isabel over five years to stop begging for him to return.

Then the entries took on a different style. A name started to appear more regularly. Charles. It was clear that he was becoming a greater part in Isabel's life and, instead of writing about the house, she would write more about him and the time they spent together. Martin was unsure why Isabel had done this. Was it to make some point that she'd moved on? But if that were the case, then why continue to carve diary entries into a wall to be read by a fifteen-year-old boy 400 years in the future?

Isabel and Charles married when she was twenty-six.

Then Martin found Isabel's final entry.

Martin, I do not know how old you are when you read these. Are you the fifteen year old boy from the future I fell in love with or are you much older? Perhaps closer to my current age or even older still? Maybe you will never read these because the house has fallen into the sea before you discover the room. If that were to happen, it would break my heart.

This entry shall be my last. I cannot spend the rest of my life pining for my first true love like the heartbroken child I still believe myself to be. Charles has a son from another. He is three and I have decided to raise him as my own. In truth, I do not wish for children, but in raising Edward I have found a new purpose.

I want you to know, Martin, that even after ten years I still wait in front of the door in the master's study. I know you are not coming through, but then, I always knew. But knowing cannot stop a maiden's heart from wanting. In truth, I'm annoyed that I still pine for you, but after our experiences together, there is no way I could not.

My feelings for Charles are just that, feelings for him. I do not burn for him, nor do I obsess over him. I love him, of this I am sure, but it is a love of convenience, and for us that is all we need.

As you know, I have no name apart from that which I gave myself. Charles is the same, raised by people who found him. The name they gave him was not his own and so he has cast it aside in favour of the one I have suggested.

For the last year I have been known as Isabel Lockford. Call this my last folly, if you will. Charles and Edward are now Lockfords also. After I made this decision, I came to realise the implications of my actions and the reason I had to remain here. It appears I must owe the Keeper of Causality thanks, for if I had left you would never have been born and we would never have met.

I shall now leave you, Martin. You will always be in my heart, but that is where you must remain, locked inside and hidden from others.

I cry as I write this. I love you, Martin. You gave me hope and you gave me life. That is something that can never be forgotten.

Isabel Lockford 1633

Martin stood up. Part of him wanted to collapse on the floor and cry and part of him wanted to run and never

344

stop. But before he could make a decision, he spotted a figure standing in the doorway.

'Mum, I…' Martin paused. 'Portals?'

The Keeper of Portals entered the dark room, giving off his own glow.

'You found the room,' said the Keeper.

'This whole time, did you know?'

The Keeper shook his head. 'Only afterwards, when I had fixed the doors, did I realise who the girl was.'

'You were here with her, weren't you?'

'I watched her grow, though I never spoke to her. Together we would sit and stare at the door. I never revealed myself to her, but I felt like she knew of my presence.'

'What happened to her?' asked Martin.

The Keeper of Portals smiled. 'Come with me,' he said.

Martin stepped through the doorway Portals had created to the dark room and appeared in a different landing overlooking the stairs.

'I've missed doing that,' said Martin. 'At least it explains how you knew me.'

'I told you that. You were the Keeper of Portals before me. I told you many times in fact, but not once did you react, as if being the Keeper of Portals was no big deal, which I can assure you, it is.'

'No. You said you knew me somehow but you didn't know where from.'

The Keeper of Portals smiled. 'Ah, that'll be Causality.'

'Huh?'

'What I said and what you heard were clearly different things. I must have been telling you something you weren't

345

supposed to hear. I am a Keeper, so she can't stop me from speaking, but what you hear, and what you remember, *that* she can change.'

Martin started to feel uneasy. He had no idea her power was so deceptive. He wondered what else he'd misheard when the Keeper of Portals pointed to the painting in front of him with a long white finger. It was the painting of the old lady that hung over the stairs.

'The nameplate has been damaged, but I don't need to tell you what's written on it, do I?'

Martin stared at the painting. The old woman with her knowing smile looked back at him.

'Isabel Lockford.'

Finally, he knew what she knew: that all the time Martin and Isabel were in that house together, an enormous painting of her hung for them both to see.

Martin turned to the Keeper of Portals, ready to ask him another question, but he had vanished. Instead, he saw his mother approaching from the far end of the landing. She stopped when she got to Martin and leaned over the banister with him.

'Do you know who that is?' she asked.

Martin nodded.

'I researched her when I was in school,' said Jo. 'We had to pick one person from our family history who achieved something. I picked her.'

They both studied the painting.

'Why?' asked Martin.

'She was where it all started for us. Without her we wouldn't be here, but more than that, she was a fascinating woman: highly intelligent and very shrewd. You have to remember, we're talking 350 years ago here; back then, women just didn't have that much power, but Isabel Lockford wasn't a normal woman. People said she knew things that others didn't; not witchcraft or anything like that, but she had ideas about what people needed or may need in the future and she created those things. She was an amazing inventor and a brilliant business woman. But she kept herself to herself. I had to really dig to find out anything about her.'

Jo blinked several times as she stared at the image, as if realising something for the first time, but she quickly shook her head as if to dispel the thought.

Then she took another look at the painting before turning to study her son's face. Without a word, she put an arm around him and felt his head fall onto her shoulder.

They remained there, the three of them, until the hot summer sun had set and the house became dark.

Afterword

This is the section of the book where I try, and fail, to recall everyone who helped make the published version of *The Keeper of Portals* a reality.

To add a little background, I started planning this book in October 2012. I began the first draft in January 2013 and finished it in July. The three and a half years between finishing that first draft and the book being published was filled with different version, MANY edits, and a few other stories along the way. I also learnt to drive, got married, bought a house, changed my job and had two children. It's been a busy period and I'm glad to see that *The Keeper of Portals* has reached an end and not become another shelved project that never sees the light of day (so far six novels and a sitcom).

After deciding to self-publish *Portals*, I realised that I couldn't afford to produce the book the way I wanted to. My thanks go out to: Danny, Jan, Simon, Suzie, Kingsley and Anne for investing in the publication of this book and providing the story direction. I think some of you, like me, have lost count of how many times you've read it. Maybe we'll indulge in one more sneaky read now it's in book form! OK, now the hard part, thanking all the people who read the many different versions of the story and provided their feedback. If your name hasn't appeared, then I apologise – I've clearly forgotten about you.

Thanks to: Paul, Shirley, Tiger, Helen (your suggestions made it in), Mike (always good getting feedback from a fellow author), Liz (collies are much smaller than sheep!), Emily (did you even finish it?) and Rob (I hope you're getting somewhere with your story). Also, thank you to everyone who has read my unpublished, and often unpublishable, stories. Sadly, you bet on the wrong horse. Special thanks to: Grace (I think you read two!) and Allison (support from someone who's actually been published was great).

Thank you to Cressida (The Book Analyst) for the copy editing and everyone who helped me at Matador, what a nice bunch!

Big thanks to Tiberius for the cover, especially for putting up with my constant stream of changes to the design!

A final thanks to my long-suffering friend Hannah, who was the first person to read one of my stories 13 years ago. Sorry that one was so awful.

OK, one more. A final-final thank you to you for reading this book. I just looked on the internet and apparently it will take 60,000 years to read all the books ever published. As recorded human history only goes back 5500 years (thanks again internet), you can bet that 60,000 years will increase exponentially until humans die out. So thanks for taking the time to read my story in a world of endless choice. I appreciate it!